SHADY
CROSS

ALSO BY JAMES HANKINS

Brothers and Bones

Jack of Spades

Drawn

JAMES HANKINS

SHADY CROSS

THOMAS & MERCER

Published by Thomas & Mercer, Seattle

www.apub.com

Amazon, the Amazon logo, and Thomas & Mercer are trademarks of Amazon.com, Inc., or its affiliates.

ISBN-13: 9781477820988
ISBN-10: 1477820981

Cover design by David Drummond

Library of Congress Control Number: 2014946860

Printed in the United States of America

For Colleen.

ONE

"YOU JUST GOT OUT OF jail? Seriously?"

Stokes heard nothing but curiosity in the guy's voice. No judgment, no fear, just curiosity and maybe a little slur from the alcohol.

"Didn't say I was *in* jail," Stokes said. He took a sip of Budweiser and wiped his mouth with the back of his hand, the one that held the bottle. "Said I was *at* the jail. They had me in for questioning. No big deal."

The guy looked at him in drunk-eyed wonder, like he was a rare species of lizard. "Wow. In jail." He took a sip of his manhattan. "I guess you must not have done whatever they thought you did, though, or they wouldn't have let you go."

Stokes knew it didn't always work like that, but why get into it?

"Like I said, no big deal." He looked at the guy's tailored suit again, the suit that had led Stokes to the bar stool next to him in the first place. "So what's your deal?"

"Tom."

"What?"

"My name's Tom," the guy said.

Stokes nodded, waited for an answer to his question, didn't get it, so he asked again, "So what's your deal, Tom? You from Shady Cross?"

"What's Shady Cross?"

Stokes smiled amiably. "This little city you're in."

"Shady Cross?" the guy repeated as if he'd never heard of the place, like a few drinks had erased the name from his mind.

"They say it was built up a long time ago around the crossroads at the center of town," Stokes said. "Used to be shady, I guess. So anyway, what's your deal?"

"My deal? What do you mean?"

Stokes indicated the rest of the bar with a tilt of his head. It was on the seedy side, the kind of place people went to drink hard, to shoot pool, to swap bullshit stories about sexual conquests, to bitch about their blue-collar jobs or their bosses or their wives. Sometimes they went looking for a fight. Sometimes they went just to be left alone. And more often than not, whatever reason they were there, they also went wondering whether they might meet someone drunk enough, lonely enough, and tolerably attractive enough to spend a little time with after last call.

"You sort of stick out around here, Tom," Stokes said. "Nice suit, polished shoes. Your hair's all combed. So what's your deal? I told you about jail, you can tell me your story."

Tom turned his head to face Stokes. His glassy eyes caught up a fraction of a second later.

"Not much of a story. In town on business. Staying at a motel just down the road."

"The Rest Stop?"

"Yeah, that might be what it's called. You know it?"

Stokes did. He'd spent a few hours there two Saturdays ago with the waitress across the room. He nodded.

"Finished my business here this morning," the guy said, "but can't get a flight back to Pittsburgh till tomorrow. Just killing time now. Stopped in here for an early lunch, but, well, I met you instead and my lunch, uh . . ."

"Turned liquid?"

Tom looked at Stokes for a long moment, then laughed loosely. Stokes could have asked what business the guy was in. It was probably expected of him. But he didn't think Tom was tracking the conversation very closely any longer. He was tottering on his stool now, his vacant eyes staring sightlessly at the mirror behind the bar. Stokes could have looked at that mirror, too, but he didn't.

"You a cowboy?" Tom asked, chuckling like he'd made a joke.

"A what?"

"You're wearing a cowboy shirt."

Stokes looked down at his Western-style shirt, black with white stitching near the shoulders, which he wore over a black T-shirt.

"Nope," he said. "Not a cowboy. Not even close. I don't even like country music. It's just a shirt I found in a thrift store. So what do you say, Tom? One more for the road?"

The guy said nothing for a moment, the words seeming to wander aimlessly through the fog in his mind for a while before finally finding their way. He looked at Stokes.

"Another? No way, man. Thanks, but I've prob'ly had enough. Thanks again, though, for buying all these drinks for me. Nice to find someone friendly in a strange place."

Tom's eyelids were sagging over tired, empty eyes.

"Yeah," Stokes said, "you've had enough. You drive here this afternoon?"

"Drive? Yeah, I did. My rental."

"Yeah, well, you're not driving back to the motel. I'll call you a cab, OK? You can come back for the car in the morning, on your way to the airport."

3

"Cab?" He shook his head, looking like he was about to protest as he stood. Then his foot caught a leg of his stool and he just barely managed to grab the bar in time to save himself from a tumble onto the grimy, beer-stained cement floor. "Yeah, maybe a cab's good idea."

Stokes had called for a taxi ten minutes ago. He figured it would be pulling up outside just about now.

"I'll help you," he said, grabbing the guy by the arm, guiding him across the bar. Halfway to the door, he caught the eye of the waitress, Annie, the one he'd spent a few decent hours with a couple of Saturdays ago. She rolled her eyes at him before turning her attention back to her customers.

The taxi was idling in front of the bar. Stokes reached into the guy's suit jacket, into the inner breast pocket, and removed a soft leather wallet. He opened the back door of the cab, helped Tom inside, and took out one of the guy's twenties. He gave it to the cabbie and told him to take Tom back to the Rest Stop. Stokes counted the rest of the money, put forty bucks back into the wallet, and slipped $230 into his own pocket before leaning into the cab and returning the wallet to Tom's jacket.

"See you, Tom," Stokes said as he closed the door.

The taxi pulled away and Stokes walked back inside, heading to the bar without looking Annie's way.

"What was it?" Stokes asked the bartender, money in hand. "Four manhattans for my friend Tom and two Buds for me? What's that come to?"

The bartender frowned, turned his back to Stokes, and punched a few buttons on the cash register. He turned around again. "It was three Buds. Forty-four bucks."

Stokes peeled off two twenties and a ten and put the bills on the bar. "Keep it."

"What a guy, Stokes," the bartender said. "Hard to believe the cops could ever question the character of a saint like you."

"Hey, feel free to give me that tip back, Chuck."

The bartender put the money into the register, took out the change and stuck it into the tip jar beside the bottles of hard liquor.

Stokes smiled. "Maybe I'll be in again later. We could shoot some stick, if it's quiet. I could try to win that tip back, huh?"

The bartender shrugged. Stokes grabbed his leather jacket from his stool, nodded to Annie has he passed, and stepped out into the crisp fall day. In half a minute he was straddling his Yamaha SZR 660, helmet on and buckled, the motorcycle's engine ready to roar. Five minutes later, he'd left behind the county highway, with its motels and diners and gas stations and seedy bars strewn along it like litter tossed from passing cars. He was flying along a wooded back road. The early-October leaves were nearing their fall peak, the last of the green having given way to fiery reds and glowing golds, but summer wasn't so far behind that the leaves had started dropping in great number yet.

Stokes was feeling all right. His night in jail was behind him, and even though the sun wouldn't set for hours yet, he was surrounded by trees full of sunset colors whipping by in a kaleidoscopic blur as he gunned his bike, sailing through the straightaways, leaning into lazy turns. He'd head back to his trailer, relax for a few hours, and maybe after dinner—

Leaning to his left, Stokes took the next curve way too tight, well over the centerline. He was halfway around the bend when a dark car appeared, was suddenly right on him, and there he was, leaning into the turn, leaning toward the car, *speeding* toward it, horribly exposed, nothing but soft flesh covering brittle bone, and he knew it was over, *oh shit*, it was over for him . . .

He was barely aware of the car lurching toward the far shoulder of the road as he jerked the handlebars of his motorcycle to the right, trying to wrestle the bike back into his own lane, away from the car. He watched the vehicle's glittering headlight assembly sail toward his face, then zip just under his ear, his helmet nearly brushing the front quarter panel. He felt the huge metallic bulk of the car, throbbing with deadly power, blast past him, just inches away from him. And then, incredibly, he was beyond it, beyond the car, with nothing in front of him but road and trees, his bike cutting sharply across his lane, his front wheel turning now, seemingly on its own, beyond his power to control it, and in a deafening, bone-shaking, world-tilting moment, his bike slammed into a guardrail and he was flying, twisting, spinning through the air. Everything went unnaturally silent for the briefest of moments, and then he heard a violent, metallic crash from somewhere, just before he slammed to earth and his breath and consciousness exploded out of him.

The guy was dead. No doubt about it. Somehow Stokes wasn't, but the driver of the car sure as hell was.

Stokes had come to rest near the bottom of a gentle incline sloping away from the road, on a thin blanket of dead leaves over a mattress of soft, moist ground. He'd lain for a moment, staring up at the trees all around him, at first wondering where he was and how he'd gotten there, but remembering soon enough, then wondering how the hell he'd flown fifteen feet into the woods and rolled down the hill without hitting a single tree. And, apparently, without breaking any bones.

He left his helmet by his mangled bike and climbed the little slope back up to the road. He stepped from the woods and looked for the car that had come so close to sending him elsewhere, either hell or purgatory or somewhere like that—certainly not heaven, if such a place existed. The car was nowhere in sight. For a moment

Stokes thought it might have simply swerved around him and kept going wherever the hell it had been going when their paths had crossed . . . and then he saw them. Across the road, ten yards farther along, parallel grooves running through the gravel on the side of the road, grooves leading off the shoulder and down the hill on the other side, into the trees.

Stokes looked in both directions. Not a car in sight. He walked over to the tracks in the gravel. No skid marks on the road that he could see. The driver hadn't even had time to hit his brakes, at least not before he hit the gravel on the shoulder. Stokes squinted into the woods, where the still-thick canopy of leaves dropped dense shadows to the forest floor. He looked down at the tire tracks in the gravel, where they led onto the soft earth by the road. He followed them with his eyes, down the gentle slope, through the first trees. And there it was. Maybe thirty feet in. A black car accordioned against a thick tree. Stokes looked down again at the tire marks in the gravel, then slid the sole of his boot over the marks, obliterating them. After one more look for cars on the road, he stepped into the woods.

And now there he was, staring into the car, staring through a spiderwebbed window at the bloody face of a body slumped over the steering wheel. Either this car didn't have an air bag or it had been defective and hadn't deployed. Or maybe the dead guy had unwisely deactivated it. The poor bastard's eyes were open. Open and staring and totally lifeless.

Stokes took a step back. The woods were silent but for the ticking of the cooling engine. Most people would have called 911 by then, he knew. Then again, most people wouldn't have spent the last night being interrogated by the cops about a burglary. Nor would they have been arguably at fault for this accident—and therefore this man's death. And the fact that Stokes had recently had a couple of beers would surely complicate matters. No, Stokes wasn't going to be calling the cops. Instead, he decided to hide his twisted wreck of a motorcycle as best he could, then leave as fast as possible. Maybe he'd come back after things died down around here and dispose of the bike properly, if no one had found it by then. Or maybe he wouldn't—fortunately, it wasn't registered in his name.

He was just about to implement his plan, such as it was, when something caught his eye through the window of the rear door. He leaned closer to the glass, careful not to touch the car, and peered inside. He blinked. He blinked again. He reached up under his shirt, gripped the door handle through the fabric, and tried the door. It swung open.

On the floor of the car, behind the passenger's seat, was a backpack. But that wasn't really what had snagged his attention. Rather, it was the bundles of money spilling out of the bag that had caught his notice.

Thousands of dollars.

Stokes swiped a hand across his forehead. It came away wet with sweat despite the cool autumn air in the shadowy woods.

That was a hell of a lot of money lying there. And that was merely what had spilled from the bag. If there was more inside, which there looked to be, it would be more than Stokes had made in years, maybe a decade—certainly far more than he had made honestly. And it was just lying there.

He saw two options: leave the money, knowing it would probably wind up under somebody else's mattress—maybe whoever found the car, maybe the first cop on the scene—or take the money. The dead guy sure didn't need it. Stokes sure did. The decision wasn't a tough one for him.

TWO

2:42 P.M.

IT TOOK STOKES LESS THAN a half hour to walk back to the two-lane county road on the edge of town, backpack slung over one shoulder, its flap fastened securely. He'd rather have ridden his bike, but the motorcycle hadn't fared nearly as well as he had in the accident. After leaving the car in the woods, Stokes had half pushed, half dragged his Yamaha as far into the trees on the other side of the road from the wrecked car as he could. He left it in a deep depression, along with his helmet, covered them both with leaves and fallen branches, and scuffed away the drag marks as best he could. Shame about the bike. It had been with him eight years. But he could buy himself a hell of a new one now.

He crossed the road and headed into Tootie's Diner. Even though Tootie's was just a short walk from Chuck's bar, where he'd wasted countless nights and a lot of money—some of it even his own—he'd never been inside the diner. When he came here to the outskirts of Shady Cross it was to drink, not eat.

A bell jingled softly as the door knocked it swinging. Stokes kept his head down and moved toward a booth in the back. As he passed through the joint, he heard conversation and clinking silverware and smelled coffee and apple pie and, most of all, meat loaf, which must have been Tootie's special of the day. He squeezed into a booth in the rear of the place, head still down, his back to the room. A moment later, a fat-ankled waitress slid a menu under his nose while he examined the gray Formica tabletop. She might have been Tootie herself for all Stokes knew, if Tootie was still alive, or ever existed, and was even a woman and not a man, and still worked here, assuming she ever did. When the waitress was gone, Stokes took the backpack from his shoulder and placed it beside him on the cracked red vinyl seat of the booth. He turned his head casually. An elderly couple sat at one of the tables—looked like the meat loaf for both of them. A mother and father and small boy ate at a booth near the door. A heavyset woman in a faded denim jacket, her hair gathered into a loose bun on top of her head, sat two booths away with her back to Stokes. Trucker, Stokes figured, remembering the rig he'd seen on the shoulder of the road out front. The only other patrons were two old men sitting on stools at the counter, arguing in their dusty, old-man voices about something Stokes couldn't hear. Other than the patrons, Stokes saw his waitress, who was just as chunky above the ankles, another middle-aged waitress serving the men at the counter, and a thick-armed fry cook sweating over the grill. No one paid Stokes the slightest attention until his waitress noticed him looking her way and came over.

"Coffee to start?" she asked, empty coffee cup and steaming Pyrex pot already in her hands.

"Coffee only, I think," Stokes replied. He thought he saw a slight frown in her mud-colored eyes, annoyance at his taking up a booth and her time with the promise of only a microscopic tip for her troubles. Realizing that this made it more likely she'd remember his being there, he quickly added, "That meat loaf smells OK. Maybe I'll have that, too."

The waitress's face brightened a bit as she poured his coffee. "Early bird special it is then," she said as she scooped up the menu and waddled away. Stokes glanced at the backpack beside him. Dark green on the outside, money green inside. He placed a hand on it, felt its solidness, its *realness*. He had to think things through. Someone might find the dead guy's car soon. Probably not, seeing as it would only get darker out now, the autumn sun sinking earlier every day than the day before, and the car was pretty far into the woods, and Stokes had wiped away the traces of it going off through the gravel on the shoulders of the road. Still, he'd wanted to get out of those woods and away from the entire area as quickly as he could. So instead of emptying the backpack onto the leaves and counting the money right there like he wanted to do, he'd hoofed it back to the road and into the diner, now just another guy waiting on the meat loaf special. Fortunately, he already had enough money in his pocket for his meal. The last thing he wanted to do was open the bag in here, give the waitress with the fat ankles or someone on the way to the restroom a peek inside.

He sipped his black coffee and wondered how much money was in the backpack. A lot, that much he knew. Certainly enough to pay off his $100,000 debt to that son of a bitch Frank Nickerson . . . if he wanted to. But was there enough to do more? Enough to change his life?

He heard the waitress approaching before he saw her, and a plate slid in front of him. Meat loaf and mashed potatoes smothered in thick brown gravy and a multicolored pile of chopped vegetables to the side.

"Anything else?" the waitress asked.

Stokes shook his head and was alone again, alone with his meat loaf and his thoughts. And his money. When this day started, he'd been just about out of options. He'd woken up in a cell and spent the morning being grilled about a burglary by a cop with Egg McMuffin stuck in his teeth until they'd had to let him go. But before they did, they made it clear they'd get him eventually. Sergeant Lance

Millett, a guy Stokes had gone to high school with, had questioned Stokes in the past—just a couple of weeks ago, actually—in relation to a different break-in. They'd had nothing on him but the fact that he'd been seen in the area and had a questionable personal history, so they had to kick him loose. Then they hauled him in again last night on suspicion of another break-in. Millett and the other cops were a little more peeved this time. They told him the homeowner had surprised the burglar, who had clocked the guy with a blunt object before fleeing the scene. Apparently, the homeowner's skull was cracked and he wasn't doing too well that morning. Well, Stokes had no intention of letting them pin the B&E on him, or the assault and battery, which would escalate to something far more serious than assault and battery if the guy ended up dying. No, he wasn't going down for that. Shady Cross wasn't the biggest city in Indiana, but there were plenty of other guys around who could have pulled that job, plenty of other guys who could take the fall for it as easily as Stokes could. Fortunately, he had money now, which meant he had options.

The question was, should he pay off Nickerson before leaving town? If he did, his backpack would be a hundred thousand bucks lighter, but Stokes wouldn't have to worry about the loan shark sending his lunatic sons after him to retrieve his money and make an example of him. That would hurt, maybe permanently. On the other hand, with the kind of money he had now, he could probably keep all the dough for himself and disappear somewhere farther than Nickerson would bother to look. After all, a hundred grand might have felt like a million bucks to Stokes but it probably wasn't really that much to Nickerson. Hell, if Stokes disappeared well enough, Nickerson wouldn't even lose face. If anyone even knew about the debt, they'd just assume Nickerson had *made* him disappear, never to be seen by anyone, anywhere, ever again.

With his mind pretty much made up, Stokes dug into the meat loaf and was surprised to find that it tasted pretty damn good. He was about halfway through it when a phone rang.

At first, he thought it might have been a pay phone around the corner, near the restrooms. It rang a second time. Stokes frowned. The phone wasn't around the corner. It was in the backpack next to him. It rang again. Must have belonged to the dead driver. The guy sure kept the ringer loud enough. The phone rang a fourth time, and Stokes started to feel uncomfortable. *Hang up already.* It rang yet again and Stokes wondered when voice mail would pick up. After a few more rings, he knew no voice mail was going to stop the ringing, which he realized was now the only sound in the room. Conversation had stopped. Silverware no longer clinked against plates. Stokes knew if he glanced over his shoulder he'd see everyone in the diner staring back at him, staring at the guy in the corner letting his phone ring twenty times without answering it, not even to say "I'm in a restaurant, I'll have to call you back." Being stared at was definitely not what he wanted just then. He heard footsteps coming his way. The waitress probably. With his back still to the room, he held up one hand in apology, mumbled, "Sorry, folks," and reached quickly for the backpack. The footsteps faltered, but the damn ringing kept up as he patted the bag's outer pockets, felt a bulge in one, and fumbled with the zipper until he got it open. As he pulled a black cell phone from the pocket, it rang loudly in his hand. He looked at it, feeling a whole lot of eyes on his back, and flipped it open, killing it in midring. He was about to snap it closed again when he heard a small voice on the other end of the line. The voice made him pause. He looked at the open phone in his hand. He couldn't hear the words, but he heard the voice. Slowly, he raised the phone toward his ear, the words becoming clearer the closer it got.

"Daddy," the little voice said, "are you there? Can you hear me? They told me you're coming to get me soon. That if you give them money, they'll let you take me home."

Stokes blinked.

The little girl's voice spoke again. "Daddy?"

THREE

"DADDY? HELLO? ARE YOU COMING to get me?"

Stokes sat with the cell phone pressed to his ear, listening to a little girl addressing her dead father, a father whose death was mostly Stokes's fault. Well, maybe more than *mostly*.

"Are you there, Daddy?"

Stokes blew out a breath. Maybe it was a grunt. Whatever it was, the little girl heard him.

"Daddy! There you are! Are you coming to get me soon? I really want to go home now. I don't want them to hurt me again. Please come get me."

Stokes stared down at the meat loaf in front of him, which no longer looked the least bit appetizing. He didn't say a word. There was a brief fumbling on the other end of the line, and a new voice spoke. A man's voice.

"Your three o'clock call, as promised. As you can hear, she's OK."

Stokes glanced involuntarily at his watch. Three o'clock.

The man continued. "I sure as hell hope you'll have the money, though, like you said you would, or she may not be OK for long." A pause. "You there, Paul?"

Stokes said nothing.

"Paul, you there? Answer me."

Stokes sat silent.

"Answer me or I'll hurt your daughter. And you know I will."

"I'm here," Stokes said quietly, not wanting to hear the kid get hurt, and also not wanting to say too much, or say it too loudly, since he wasn't Paul.

"Good. You'll have the money, right?"

Two syllables. That's all he'd spoken. He'd sneaked them by the guy, who hadn't been able to tell that Stokes wasn't the girl's father.

"Paul? Get a grip, OK? You only gotta hold it together for a few more hours. Now, I asked you a question. You gonna have the money?"

"Yeah." A single syllable that time.

"Good. Be a shame if you didn't. Talk to you in an hour."

The phone went dead. Stokes closed it and slipped it into the inner pocket of his scarred leather jacket. He shut his eyes.

"Well, will you look at that?"

He snapped his eyes open. The waitress stood next to his booth. "What?"

He dropped his eyes quickly to the backpack, afraid that some of the money was somehow peeking out.

"You've left some of Donnie's meat loaf," she said. "You're the first person I can remember didn't eat it all and lick the plate clean. Don't let Donnie see that."

Donnie must have been the short-order cook. Screw Donnie. Screw his meat loaf.

"More coffee?" she asked with a smile.

"My check," Stokes said.

"Pie?"

"My check."

The waitress's smile disappeared. She fingered through the receipts in the pocket of her little red-and-white plaid apron and pulled out a check. She placed it facedown on the edge of the table and huffed away.

Without looking at the check, Stokes pulled from his pocket one of the twenties he'd taken from Whatever-his-name-was at the bar a couple of hours ago and dropped it on top of the check. He stood, slid the backpack onto one shoulder, and headed for the door. Then he remembered that his motorcycle was a twisted wreck lying deep in the woods two miles away.

Back near the restrooms, Stokes dropped a couple of coins into the pay phone and dialed the number of the cab company he'd called not long ago for Whatever-the-hell-his-name-was—Tom, maybe. Stokes could have used the dead guy's cell phone to make the call but he didn't feel like opening it again.

It was a short walk from the diner back to the bar, where he'd told the cab company he'd be waiting. It would have been easier to wait at the diner, but he wanted to get the hell away from there. People looked at him funny on his way out, possibly because word had gotten around that he hadn't finished Donnie's meat loaf, but more likely because of the phone incident. Anyway, he figured he'd think better walking than waiting around Tootie's.

He strode through the diner's gravel parking lot, then along the shoulder of the road toward Chuck's bar, thinking as he went. Things had changed. His list of options had grown from two to three. The first option, the safest one, was to pay off Nickerson and keep whatever money was left over. The second, and riskiest, was to skip town with all the cash and hope Nickerson or the two thugs he had for sons wouldn't find him. Then there was the option number three, the new one: he could use the money for what the dead father had intended to use it for—to ransom the little girl—which would leave Stokes with nothing but his goddamn $100,000 debt to Frank Nickerson. He hated option three.

He arrived at the bar and took a seat on an old wooden barrel in front of the building. Neon from the window behind him glowed cold blue. He held the backpack in his lap, his arms wrapped around it. With the slightest squeeze he could feel its firmness. It was *full* of cash . . . cash he'd love to keep.

He'd had a big hand in killing the girl's dad, though. He had to admit that.

A taxi pulled into the lot. Stokes dropped his eyes to the backpack in his arms. The money in it could buy freedom for him, or for a little girl, but not for both.

He thought about the girl's voice, asking to go home, pleading with her father to take her home, a father she had no idea was never going home again.

The cabbie tapped his horn. Stokes looked up. He looked back down at the bag in his arms. He thought he could smell the money inside.

He heard the girl's voice in his head. *Daddy?*

Aw, shit.

—

Fifteen minutes later, Stokes gave the cabbie another of What's-his-name's twenties and pocketed the change, minus tip. As the cab pulled away, he hiked the backpack higher up his shoulder and headed into the Shady Cross Bus Depot. Inside, he checked the departures board, saw that the next bus out of town was leaving in just over an hour. Without much thought about where it was going, he bought a ticket from the guy at the booth, a guy he thought he might have gone to high school with twenty years ago. In fact, he thought he might have beaten the guy up once during gym class. Maybe twice. Whatever. He stuck the ticket in the back pocket of his jeans and found a seat in a deserted corner of the station, where he sat with the backpack in his lap and started thinking about what he was going to do with his money. Thirteen minutes later, the dead guy's cell phone rang in Stokes's jacket pocket, surprising him. He'd forgotten all about it. He pulled it out and looked at it. He looked at his watch. Four o'clock on the dot. He stood, walked over to a trash can, and dropped the ringing phone in. He returned to his seat and his thoughts and tried to ignore the phone, its ringing muffled by a day's worth of trash.

FOUR

THE ENGINE OF THE BUS idled soothingly. They'd be pulling away in a few minutes, leaving behind Shady Cross, Stokes's problems, and problems that belonged to other people, people he'd never even met, like the kid on the phone. Stokes sat in the last row, next to the john. The backpack was on the seat beside him, next to the window. His elbow was resting on the bag, his head was tipped back, his eyes were closed.

He felt comfortable with his decision. Nickerson wasn't going to worry about $100,000. Stokes would be out of sight, out of mind. He wasn't worth Nickerson sending anyone to look for him, least of all Nickerson's batshit-crazy sons. No, Stokes would take his money, take it far, maybe to California, and just disappear. Start a new life. Start a business, something that could make a buck or two but wouldn't be too hard. Maybe a hardware store, something like that. He didn't know much about hardware, but how tough could it be? You hang a sign over your door, companies send you hammers and screwdrivers, you hang them up or put them on shelves. Better yet, you hire someone else to do that. Yeah, that sounded OK.

He glanced at his watch: 4:09.

Nine minutes since the dead guy's phone had rung. Nine minutes since Stokes had ignored the kidnappers' call. He wondered what that meant, his ignoring the call. He wondered whether—

Forget it. Not his problem. Besides, when they realize they aren't going to get their money, they'll probably let the kid go. Leave her somewhere, make an anonymous call to the cops, telling them where to find her.

He forced his mind to move on to other things. Damn, should he have paid off Nickerson? There was a shitload of cash in the bag under his elbow. If he paid Nickerson a hundred thousand bucks, he'd probably still have plenty of money left; plus, he'd have peace of mind. He never should have borrowed from the bastard in the first place. That's what he got for trying to walk the straight and narrow. He wasn't used to doing it, so naturally he'd screwed it up, tripped along the way. He should have known he didn't have it in him. He'd tried it once years before, and he'd suffocated in that life until he couldn't take it anymore and just walked away. Since then, no real work, at least nothing steady, or even legal. There were a couple of relatively brief stints in prison, too, which didn't feel all that brief when he was in the middle of them. Then, a year ago he got the bright idea of starting his own contracting business. He knew even less about being a contractor than he did about owning a hardware store, but he figured he could cut wood and pound nails and figure out the rest. So he borrowed $75,000 and bought a retiring contractor's business from him. Got himself a bunch of fancy new tools, too, to go with the guy's old ones. He didn't like the guy's dented old truck, so he bought a shiny new one and had a sign painted on its door, professional enough to fool a few people into thinking he was the genuine article. And he'd tried to be. Things went OK for a few months. He had a few jobs, did decent work on some, got complaints on a few others, but nothing serious. Then he caused an electrical fire in someone's house and the fact that he wasn't licensed or insured became a big deal. The home owner sued him and Stokes lost in court, which wasn't much of a shock to anybody involved. He had no money to pay the damages awarded to the plaintiff, which was even less of a shock to everyone, so he was forced to sell his tools and his truck and give the money to the son of a bitch home owner.

A year later now, an exorbitant interest rate had turned the $75,000 debt into a $100,000 debt. Stokes shook his head. Stupid. He shouldn't have gone to Nickerson. But with no assets, a spotty-to-nonexistent employment history, and a prison record, he had no chance of getting a loan from a bank. Once he'd come to grips with that fact, he had two choices: get the money from Nickerson, or try to get it from Leo Grote.

Despite the name Shady Cross, which sounded like it should have been the setting of *Leave It to Beaver* or something, and which brought to mind images of neighbors sipping lemonade under big leafy trees while their kids played hopscotch on the sidewalk nearby, the place was far from idyllic. The city may have grown up around a shady crossroads in the middle of a small town, but in the hundred-fifty-odd years of its existence, Shady Cross had gotten quite a bit bigger and a lot uglier. Sure, it had its upper-middle-class and even upper-class neighborhoods where reasonably wealthy folks lived when they weren't working in the bigger—and better—cities, like Fort Wayne or South Bend or Gary, but Shady Cross also had plenty of areas at the other end of the spectrum, neighborhoods ranging from lower-class to downright dangerous, where tenements and projects housed poor people living side by side with criminals and criminals-in-training. And if you were one of those criminals, you operated with the implied or express permission of, and often paid a percentage to, one of two men: Leo Grote or Frank Nickerson.

Both guys were bad dudes—guys with reputed mob connections, guys with their fingers in everyone else's pies, employers of muscle who'd break your legs if their bosses thought you needed a lesson. They each also had legitimate business—funded with ill-gotten gains, of course, but legitimate nonetheless. And they each turned out to be surprisingly good businessmen, investing in the right enterprises—both legal and illicit—and getting richer and richer by the day.

Despite their successes with their lawful endeavors, though, neither abandoned his less-than-legal ones. So for anyone in Shady Cross shopping for a loan he had no chance of getting through legitimate channels, Grote and Nickerson were the only games in town. And dangerous games they were.

But while other people in Stokes's situation could pick their poison, Stokes had no choice. He'd worked for Grote for a while as one of the people who might be called upon to snap a bone or two for his boss, and the job had gone well enough until he'd been asked to break some old guy's knees. The guy had missed one too many payments, and Grote wanted his knees pulped. Stokes, who had done a mostly fair job following orders up to that point, had trouble with this assignment. Something about the old guy. Maybe he reminded him of one of his grandfathers, but Stokes doubted that because he couldn't really remember either of his grandfathers. Who knew what it was? Whatever, Stokes was able to smash only one of the poor bastard's knees. Took a baseball bat to it. But for some reason, he just didn't want to do the second knee. The guy screamed and cried, then he puked, then he cried some more, and Stokes had had enough. He walked out, leaving the guy a sobbing wreck with only one good knee. Stokes thought he'd gotten Grote's message across pretty damn well, but the boss wasn't happy. He expected his orders to be carried out. His employees weren't paid to think, just to do whatever the hell he said. And if Stokes was too much of a pussy to use a little muscle on some worthless old piece of shit, then Grote had no use for him. Stokes said a few things he definitely shouldn't have said, but Grote was in a magnanimous mood, because all he had his guys do was work Stokes over a little before dumping him in the alley behind one of his buildings. Could have been a lot worse. The point was, when Stokes decided to set himself up as a contractor, he couldn't go to Grote for the money. So he turned to the only remaining option: Frank Nickerson.

Nickerson's operations were on the other side of town from Grote's. What Grote didn't have his hands in, Nickerson did. While they both had boatloads of money, Nickerson probably took in 40 percent of whatever illicit gains were to be had in the city and the surrounding area, while Grote raked in 60. They'd coexisted that way for years, and both were rich, so neither bothered the other. Everyone was happy—except for anyone who wasn't Leo Grote or Frank Nickerson.

Stokes had gone to high school with Nickerson's identical twin sons. They were mean, crazy sons of bitches, but Stokes never had any problem with them. So when Nickerson asked his boys whether Stokes would be good for the money, they said they thought he might be. So Stokes got his loan. But when he practically burned down that goddamn house, he lost everything in the lawsuit and ended up in debt for what eventually became $100,000 with nothing to show for it. And unfortunately, he was now just two weeks away from the due date of a $10,000 payment that he didn't have . . . until now. But he wasn't going to pay it. He wasn't going to be around to pay it. He was going to be far from Shady Cross by then. Maybe New York. Or Boston. And the first leg of his journey was going to begin in just a few minutes. He looked at his watch: 4:17. Three minutes until the bus was scheduled to depart. Seventeen minutes since the dead guy's phone had rung. Since the little girl had called for her father and gotten no answer. Since Stokes had tossed the phone into the trash. He wondered what would happen to her.

He closed his eyes and rested his head on the seat back. Not his problem. He tried not to think for a while. When he looked at his watch again, it was 4:22. They were two minutes late leaving, and the damn driver wasn't even on the damn bus.

Daddy?

The little voice in his head said it again, *Daddy*, then added, *Are you coming to get me?*

Stokes wondered if he should have at least wrestled a little more with the moral dilemma of whether to take the money and run or try to help the girl. Shit, what did it say about him that he barely considered helping the kid? To hell with it. It said that he was a guy who'd been through some shit, gotten knocked around a bit, that he'd never gotten much of a break in his life before now, that he had enough problems of his own. He opened his eyes, looking for the goddamn bus driver, and that's when he saw two of those problems of his stepping onto the bus. Stokes sighed. There, at the other end of the bus, filling the aisle, were Frank Nickerson's psycho sons.

FIVE

CARL AND CHET NICKERSON WERE as identical as twins could be—so identical that *no one* could tell them apart. Not their friends. Not the girlfriends they went through over the years, it was said. Not even their father, or their mother before she passed away. They liked it that way. They got their hair cut together, identically. They went shopping together, buying all the same clothes. If one of them was out alone and saw something he liked—a shirt, a jacket—he bought the identical item for his brother. Every morning, they checked in with each other, made sure they wore the same, exact outfits, right down to their shoes and belts and pinky rings. They had a good reason for doing this. The practice had kept one or the other of them from serving time ever since they were juvenile delinquents. It even let them get away with murder. Literally.

They had a long history of run-ins with the law, going all the way back to elementary school. But as close as they were, they never committed their crimes together. While one brother stayed home— say it was Chet—the other brother, Carl, would do whatever he wanted to do and didn't care who saw him do it. Eyewitnesses? Screw 'em. If anyone had the balls to admit they saw what he did, and if the cops bothered to arrest him, all his defense attorney had to do was parade the other brother in front of the jury and ask the witness, who was under oath, "Can you honestly say *without a doubt* that *this* isn't the Nickerson you thought you saw kick your husband repeatedly in the face?" The witness would inevitably stare at the brother, then at the defendant, who looked *exactly* like his brother, both of them wearing the same goddamn blue pinstripe suit and yellow tie with little blue anchors or something all over it, and everyone in the courtroom, including the jury, would know that the witness truly had no idea which Nickerson had committed the crime. Chet and Carl had "reasonable doubt" in their genes, twisted up in the double helixes of their DNA. It made them practically untouchable. Over the years, countless people watched helpless as one or the other of them committed whatever crime he felt like committing. Wouldn't even matter if he left behind DNA evidence, like saliva or hairs, because, as the brothers learned through a little research, their DNA was essentially identical from a forensic standpoint. As long as the twin perpetrating the crime didn't leave behind fingerprints, which would *not* be identical to his brother's, he was in the clear. Everyone knew one of the damn Nickerson brothers committed the crime, but *nobody* could ever say for sure which one it was. And *that* is reasonable doubt. And if you're a defendant, that's all you need. It's the reason one of the Nickersons had been able to walk into a crowded restaurant, beat some poor bastard to death with a crowbar, leave him covered with blood and linguini on the floor next to his table, and walk right out. Two dozen witnesses. No conviction. Drove the authorities nuts. As did all the cases in which a Nickerson was a suspect.

They certainly had to work at it, though. The furthest they ever went to keep their get-out-of-jail-free cards in their back pockets came when they were in their early twenties. After a night of heavy drinking, Carl somehow ended up in an alley behind a bar with three ex-marines who were passing through town but got totally hammered before they'd passed all the way through. The fight was ugly and animal, and one of the soldiers bit off Carl's left earlobe. The next day, Chet had his brother bite off *his* left earlobe in exactly the same way. After being identical for twenty-two years, there were seven hours or so when someone could have told them apart before they were identical once again. And they'd been that way ever since. Identical. And crazy.

Yeah, Stokes knew the Nickersons well enough. And they all got along OK. Stokes was never stupid enough to cross the psychopaths, and the Nickersons never seemed to think Stokes needed to be taught a lesson. Until now.

Stokes watched the brothers head toward him down the aisle. He saw the passengers instinctively shy away from them as they approached, even those passengers who probably had no idea who they were. They weren't that big, really. At around five feet ten inches, 180 pounds, they were a little shorter and a little lighter than Stokes. But they were both thicker all around, clearly having spent a good amount of time pumping iron. Also, where Stokes had a normal face with normal eyes, these guys had flint-hard faces with scary goddamn eyes. Imagine the most violent person you've ever seen, one given to fits of rage, and someone walks up to him and tosses a beer in his face for no reason. Imagine the look that would suddenly take hold of his eyes just before he started throwing punches or chairs or whatever else was handy. Well, the Nickerson twins had that look in their eyes all the time.

The bus didn't have an emergency door, and Stokes didn't have time to kick out one of the rubber-sealed safety windows, and locking himself in the bathroom would have bought him a minute or two, at most, so he just waited for the Nickersons.

"Stokes," one of them said. Stokes had no idea if it was Carl or Chet, and he knew better than to ask.

"Yeah," he said.

"Come on," Nickerson number one said. He jerked his head in a "let's go" gesture and followed his brother out of the bus, never glancing back, never doubting that Stokes would follow. Stokes pulled the backpack onto his shoulder and walked up the aisle. The looks on the faces of the other passengers weren't very reassuring. He wondered if those were the looks inmates on death row gave to the condemned taking their last walks.

Stokes stepped off the bus behind the Nickersons. One of the brothers nodded to a fat little man in a driver's uniform waiting nearby. The driver nodded back, scurried up the stairs into the bus, and quickly closed the door behind him. Clearly, he had been instructed not to leave until the Nickersons got there. And not surprisingly, the driver had complied, the fat little shit.

"Come on," a Nickerson said as he turned away. Stokes followed the two of them back through the station, toward the main doors leading to the street. As he did, he tried, as he'd been doing all his life, to see some difference between the two—a half inch of height, hair parted differently, a longer stride. He saw nothing. They were carbon copies, Xeroxes of each other.

"How'd you know I was here?" he asked. He'd already decided not to act intimidated. To be honest, he wasn't sure that he was. Maybe they'd beat the hell out of him. Maybe they'd even kill him. As for a beating, well, he'd had those and survived. And if they killed him, so what? He'd be dead and out of his misery. The only thing that really bugged him was the idea of them leaving him alive but taking his money.

He repeated his question. "How the hell'd you know I was here?" Nothing. The Nickersons just kept walking. Stokes kept following. "Come on, how'd you guys know I was on a bus?"

One of the Nickersons said over his shoulder, "Guy at the ticket booth gets a watch list from us. Names, with photos if we have 'em. People we wouldn't want to see leave town before we got a chance to talk to them. You know what I mean? We got guys at the local cab companies and a few at the closest airports, too."

"Hey," the other Nickerson said to the one who'd been speaking, "shut the fuck up, why don't you? Why're you telling him all our shit?"

The Nickerson who'd been so chatty shrugged.

Guy at the ticket booth? That son of a bitch Stokes had beaten up in high school? Shit.

"How'd my name get on your list? I've got a motorcycle. You guys must know that. You should've figured if I was leaving town I'd just ride out of here."

Chatty Nickerson said, "Your name's on the list. Doesn't mean we expected we'd find you here. Just means we don't want you leaving town when you owe us a hundred grand."

"What'd I say?" the other brother said. The first one shrugged again but fell silent. They were nearly to the front doors when the Nickerson who seemed less inclined to talk said to his brother, "Hey, you want some gum? I could use some gum."

Chatty nodded. "Yeah, gum sounds good."

They didn't ask Stokes if he wanted gum. He tried not to be offended as he followed them over to a vending machine. Non-Chatty checked his pockets for change and came up empty. He looked to Chatty, who did the same. They both looked at Stokes. Stokes dug into his pocket, fished out a bunch of change, and handed it over. Neither said thank you as they popped the coins into the machine and got themselves a pack of Wrigley's Doublemint gum. That was almost too much. Stokes thought back to the old Doublemint commercials, the ones featuring different sets of identical twins smiling like idiots as they engaged in a variety of entertaining activities—tennis, boating, whatever. He might have laughed if he wasn't in such serious trouble here. He watched

Non-Chatty try to open the pack of gum, struggling to get his fingernail under the little tab.

"Where are you guys taking me?" Stokes asked.

"Shut up," Non-Chatty said.

"Lot of witnesses on that bus. Remember, you guys were there together," he added, implying that they weren't going to be able to rely on the old "We're so identical that no one can tell us apart, therefore there's reasonable doubt" thing. They didn't say anything, just took turns fumbling with the pack of gum until one of them finally got it open. "Suppose when we're walking out I just start yelling about how you're kidnapping me?"

"We're not kidnapping you," Chatty said.

"Seems that way to me."

"Kidnapping's a sucker's crime. You never get away with it. There's always a witness. Unless you kill the hostage after you get the money."

"Still, it seems—"

Non-Chatty cut in. "We're not kidnapping you." He looked at his brother. "And are you gonna shut up or not?" He popped a stick of gum into his mouth and handed one to Chatty. "Here, you gotta work your jaw, do it on this." He slipped the pack into his pocket.

"Hey, that's my gum," Stokes said, just for the hell of it.

The Nickersons looked at him, then nodded for him to get moving again. He started walking. He looked across the expanse of the station and saw the trash can where he'd tossed the dead driver's cell phone. He thought about what Chatty had said about kidnapping being a stupid crime unless you killed the hostage at the end. He hoped whoever had kidnapped the little girl didn't think like that. Either way, it was out of his hands now. *Sorry, kid,* he thought. *I couldn't help you now even if I wanted to.*

A silver Cadillac Escalade waited at the curb in a no-parking zone. Chatty got behind the wheel and Non-Chatty motioned toward the back door as he climbed into the front passenger seat. Again, it never seemed to cross their minds that Stokes would try to run. And frankly, he wouldn't. Why bother? He wouldn't get far. He'd rather take his chances face-to-face. Maybe he could talk his way out of this. If not, maybe he'd get in a lucky punch or two.

When they were all in the vehicle, the Nickersons fastened their seat belts while Stokes waited for the car to pull away from the curb. He was thinking hard, trying to come up with a possible scenario that wouldn't end badly for him. They were pissed he was trying to leave town, that was for sure. Their father would probably be even more pissed. Stokes thought about giving them the ten thousand he owed right then, taking it out of the bag and handing it over, but they'd certainly want to see what else he had in the bag, thinking there might be more money, which there was. And they'd take it all, so screw that.

"Buckle your seat belt," Non-Chatty said.

"You're worried about my safety?" Stokes thought that was ironic, which was a word he was never sure he was using correctly, but he thought he knew irony when he saw it.

"Shit no, but if my brother screws up and hits a goddamn tree, you think I want you flying up here and splattering all over me? Now put on your seat belt and stop dicking around. You think we got all day to spend with you? You already interrupted our day by getting on that bus, making us come down here and pull you off of it. So cut the crap. We got places to be."

Stokes shrugged and did as he was told. He held the backpack tightly in his arms, but thinking that might look suspicious, he put it on the floor between his feet. The Nickersons must not have considered him much of a threat or they wouldn't have let him sit in the back by himself with his bag. Apparently, the thought that he might be carrying a gun never occurred to them. It should have, but they weren't terribly bright. Then again, he wasn't carrying. He never did. He didn't even own a gun. He didn't like them. Sure, he'd fantasized as a kid about being a gunslinger, fingers twitching near the handle of his Colt .45 as he stood in the dusty street, staring down the fastest gun in town while tumbleweeds rolled past and frightened townsfolk watched from the safety of their windows and doorways. But then he grew up. Guns were serious. They usually made things worse, not better. He wasn't scared of them, but he simply didn't want to do the kind of work or pull the kind of jobs where they were needed. Didn't think the risk was worth it. So he stayed away from them. Still, if the Nickerson boys had an ounce more brains between them, they would have at least searched him, and the bag, and found no gun but a lot of money. Stokes hoped they wouldn't wise up en route to wherever they were taking him.

Chatty pulled the Escalade away from the curb. Stokes was thinking hard. How was he going to get out of this with most of the cash and all of his bones intact?

"This about the money I owe your father?"

"What the hell do you think?" Chatty said.

"I think it is."

"Fucking genius."

"I have it."

Silence.

"I have it," Stokes repeated.

He saw Chatty's eyes flick up to regard him in the rearview mirror. Non-Chatty turned around. "Bullshit," he said.

"I'm serious."

"Then why were you skipping town?"

"I wasn't. I was going to Akron for a couple of days. Got some friends there who owe me money."

"Ohio?"

"Yeah, that's where Akron is."

"Bullshit."

"No, I'm pretty sure it's still there."

If either Nickerson got his joke or thought it was funny, he didn't let on. "You were skipping town, Stokes," Non-Chatty said. "Skipping out on your debt."

"I wasn't. Seriously. I have your money."

Non-Chatty squinted at him for a moment. Chewed his gum, his jaw muscles working. "Why didn't you pay then?"

"Due date's in two weeks. I still have time."

Non-Chatty chewed on that for a while, along with his Doublemint. "So you weren't skipping town?"

Stokes shook his head.

"So how much have you got then?"

After a brief hesitation, Stokes said, "All of it." He'd considered giving them only the ten-grand payment that was coming due soon and leaving town later with the rest, but then he'd have to look for Nickersons over his shoulder for the rest of his life, so instead he decided to pay them off entirely and start life somewhere with a clean slate—well, as clean as his slate could get.

"All of it?" Non-Chatty said. "The whole hundred thousand?"

"That's what I said."

"Bullshit."

"Jesus Christ, I said I have it. Do you want it or not?"

"You better not be lying."

"I'm not lying."

"Why should we believe you? Maybe we should just take you behind the old shoe plant and work you over a bit, like we were planning to do in the first place. Find out if you're lying."

"Well, shit, Carl, or Chet," Stokes said, "or whichever one you are, you can take me behind the old shoe plant and kick the shit out of me, or you can take me to where I'm keeping the money and I'll give you what I owe your dad. All of it. Every penny."

Non-Chatty thought about that for a moment. He looked at his brother. Chatty looked back at him. Then Chatty looked back at the road, which was a good thing because they were going fifty miles an hour now. Non-Chatty looked back at Stokes.

"Where's the money?"

Stokes told them where to take him. After a moment, Non-Chatty said, "Yeah, all right. But if you're lying, it's not gonna be a fun afternoon." Then he added, "For you, I mean. My brother and I will enjoy ourselves just fine."

Stokes had understood exactly what he meant.

They traveled in silence the rest of the way—well, not silence, really, not with two thugs chewing gum with their mouths open. The bus station wasn't far from the center of town, where Stokes had led them, so they arrived at their destination in just a few minutes. Chatty pulled the Escalade to a stop in a no-parking spot beside a fire hydrant in front of a Chinese restaurant. "Too Good Food" glowed in red neon in the front window. Stokes ate there now and then and was never sure if this was the name of the establishment or a testimony about the quality of its food.

"The money's in there?" Chatty asked, frowning.

"Yeah, it's in there. I'll go get it."

"Hold it," Non-Chatty said. "What're we, stupid? I'm going with you."

Stokes figured that would happen. He shrugged and got out of the car, taking the backpack with him. Fortunately, they let him.

"It better be here," Nickerson said as they walked toward the restaurant, the powerful aromas of the food that Stokes had to admit was indeed "too good" washing over them before they were within twenty yards of the place.

Inside, a little old Asian lady with a huge smile came forward to greet them, but Stokes walked right past her. Nickerson followed closely. Stokes walked between the tables and pushed through a swinging door, into the kitchen. A chorus of Chinese voices rose from the various cooks and servers, but he ignored them, scanning the room, then walked toward what looked to be an office in the back. He had no idea. He'd never been back there before. All the commotion drew an elderly Asian man from the office. He shouted in Chinese. Stokes held his hands out in what he hoped was a calming gesture. Nickerson watched him closely.

"It's OK, Pops," Stokes said. "Settle down. I'm back for the money you've been holding for me."

The wrinkled old man kept up a stream of agitated Chinese as Stokes brushed past him and stepped into the office.

"What the fuck's he chattering about?" Nickerson asked behind him.

"No idea. I don't speak Chinese." And, as Stokes already knew, the old man didn't speak English, which was one of the reasons he'd chosen this place. He crossed the office to an old desk against the back wall and opened a drawer. Acutely aware of Nickerson's eyes on his back, Stokes snuck a hand beneath his leather jacket and started removing bundles of cash from the waistband of his jeans, bundles he'd surreptitiously slipped out of the backpack and into his pants while he was in the Escalade's backseat. He hoped he'd counted it right, but he'd done it largely by feel, stealing glances down when he could, so he wasn't certain. He removed the last of the bundles from his jeans, shut the drawer, and turned around. He handed Nickerson the money. The old Chinese guy's eyes widened, seeing thousands of dollars apparently coming from his desk. His words ceased for a brief moment before tumbling out again, a hell of a lot more rapidly than before.

"It's OK, Mr. Chang," Stokes assured the old man, who didn't seem the least bit placated.

Nickerson eyed the money in his hands suspiciously. He stepped over to the desk and opened several drawers. Satisfied that there was no more cash to be had there, he headed out of the office, back toward the dining room, riffling through the money in his hands. Stokes followed. On Stokes's heels was an ancient and very upset Chinese man who may or may not have been named Chang.

The old man jabbered at Stokes and Nickerson all the way through the dining room and kept jabbering away at them from his doorway. Once they reached the Escalade, Stokes tuned him out. He wondered briefly if this episode would bring the old guy trouble from the Nickersons, but he didn't think so. Plus, he didn't care all that much.

The passenger window of the luxury SUV zipped down and Chatty leaned down and looked at them from behind the wheel.

"He really had the money?" he asked.

"Looks that way," Non-Chatty said. He looked at Stokes. "Why's that old guy still yelling at us?"

"Beats me," Stokes said. "He knew I'd be back for my money, so I don't know what his problem is."

Non-Chatty probably had a lot of questions—like why the guy was holding Stokes's money in the first place, and how he knew that Stokes would be back for it, when neither of them spoke the other's language—but in the end, all that seemed to matter to him was the money.

"Looks like a hundred and two thousand here."

Shit. Stokes thought he'd grabbed ten bundles of hundred-dollar bills. Must have grabbed a bundle of twenties, too. "Oh, that's a mistake. Give me back the two grand."

Non-Chatty nodded like that sounded reasonable to him. But he kept the money. "Guess you're paid up now."

He opened the passenger door and slid inside, placing the money on his lap. He fastened his seat belt.

"See you, Stokes," he said. "Nice doing business with you."

"Wanna give me a ride home?"

"Let me think about it."

Stokes watched the tinted window rise as the Escalade pulled away. He shifted the backpack on his shoulder and headed down the street to look for a pay phone so he could call a cab. He knew there was one in Too Good Food, but he didn't think he'd be welcome back in there for a while.

He spotted a cab idling in front of the drugstore on the corner, the "On Duty" light glowing on its roof. He walked toward it, feeling comforted by the weight of the bag on his back. Maybe twelve pounds of money. Sure, it was a $102,000 lighter now, but he'd managed to keep a lot of the money on his back while getting Frank Nickerson off of it. Equally important, he was still alive and in one piece. Things were OK. As he walked, he glanced at his watch. It was 4:49 p.m.

SIX

TWO HUNDRED FORTY-EIGHT THOUSAND DOLLARS. He'd counted it.

Jesus.

That meant the backpack originally held $350,000 before he paid off the Nickersons, which had been a shame. Still, $248,000 was a whole lot of money. What the hell? He'd call it $250,000. It was a nice round number, and it was close enough.

A quarter of a million dollars. Jesus.

He was sitting in the back of the cab, heading away from Too Good Food, on his way to his trailer on the outskirts of town. The route followed the one he'd just taken with the Nickersons, only in reverse. He'd go back past the bus station and out to where his twenty-five-year-old silver Airstream trailer squatted among even older trailers in the park. He thought about his trailer and smiled. He'd never done that before—thought about his trailer and smiled—but this time he could smile because he knew he'd soon be leaving the piece of shit tin can behind for good. Since he'd settled his debt with Frank Nickerson, he could return to the trailer for the last time, pack what little of his crap he wanted to take with him, if anything, and leave Shady Cross forever.

Two hundred fifty thousand bucks. In the first moments of the ride, the cabbie made a couple of halfhearted attempts at polite conversation. Stokes gave him nothing in return, and the guy got the message soon enough. He drove in silence and kept his eyes on the road. Still, Stokes put the backpack on the floor between his feet, far below the cabbie's sight line in the rearview mirror, and pulled out bundles of money, one after another. And there were a lot of them. Stokes knew that each bundle wrapped in a currency strap totaled a hundred bills of whatever denomination it contained. A lot of the bundles in the bag were hundreds, making each of those bundles worth ten thousand bucks. There were also bundles of fifties and twenties. Add them all together, he had $248,000. He began stuffing the money back into the bag, afraid the smell of it would waft through the little holes drilled into the Plexiglas divider separating him from the cabbie and make the man suspicious. Cabbies had been known to keep guns under their seats to protect themselves. Guns like that could also be used to rob a rich, stupid passenger.

Stokes fastened the flap on the backpack, the money safely stowed inside, and sat back. He smiled. He was thirty-six years old, and for just about every one of those thirty-six years he'd gotten the short end of the stick. But his life had abruptly spun on its heels and was finally heading someplace bright and sunny. Unconsciously, he squeezed the bag with his knees, perhaps to reassure himself that it was really there, it was really *real*. When he did, he felt a soft crinkle. The money wouldn't have crinkled. It was packed too tightly to crinkle. So what had crinkled?

He pulled the backpack onto his lap, checked the driver's eyes in the rearview mirror, and looked more closely at the bag. He knew the main compartment held nothing but the money, but there were also two outer pockets. He'd already been in one of them and found nothing but the dead guy's cell phone, which he'd thrown away.

He frowned. He zipped open the other pocket and reached inside. Pulled out an envelope, crumpled into a ball.

He should have just put it right back in the bag. Better yet, torn it in half and chucked it out the window. Instead, he lifted the flap of the envelope and pulled out a sheet of wrinkled white paper. A typed letter. He took a breath and read.

We have your daughter. We haven't hurt her but we will if you don't do exactly what we say. Tomorrow you're going to withdraw the $350,000 you stashed in your daughter's account, and tomorrow night you're going to give it to us. Every penny. It doesn't belong to you, it doesn't belong to her, and you're going to give it back. We'll tell you later exactly how and exactly when. Keep this cell phone with you at all times. We'll call you now and then to make sure you're behaving yourself and not doing anything stupid. We'll even let you talk to your daughter from time to time. If you fail to answer one of our calls, the girl loses a finger. We know you have the $350K so don't try to say you don't. It will only get your daughter hurt. If you say one time that you can't get the money, she loses an eye. You say it again, she loses the other one. You don't want to know what happens if you say it a third time. At some point we'll tell you exactly where to drop the money tomorrow night. When we have it, we'll tell you where to pick up the girl. If you don't show, your daughter is dead. If you go to the cops or the FBI or anyone like that—and we'll know if you do—she's dead. If anything happens to make us think this deal isn't going to go down smoothly, just *like we say, with no outside interference, she's dead. Don't screw us around. Get the money. Answer when we call. Show up where we tell you. Do all that and this ends okay. Screw us around and the girl dies. We'll call you soon.*

Without realizing he was doing it, Stokes glanced down at his watch: 4:52. Fifty-two minutes since he had ignored the kidnappers' call. He blew out a breath. This wasn't his problem. It sucked, but it wasn't his problem. He could forget about this. He had almost 250 grand in his lap, which would make it a lot easier to forget all about this. He looked out the window just in time so see the bus station drift past. In a few minutes, he'd be back at his trailer. In a few hours, he'd be on a plane or train or bus out of town forever.

Besides, they probably wouldn't even call again. He'd missed the four o'clock call. It might all be over already. The girl might be dead. Nothing he could do about that now.

Or she might not be. Maybe they just cut off her finger, like they threatened.

Then again, maybe they were going to do worse still.

Goddamn it, this just wasn't his problem. This was the dead guy's problem, and he certainly wasn't worrying about it anymore, so why should Stokes?

He squeezed the letter into a ball and dropped it on the floor of the cab before realizing it was evidence in a crime, evidence that could probably now be traced back to him somehow. He picked it up and stuffed it back into the outer pocket of the bag. As he did, his fingers touched something else in the pocket. He thought he knew what it was, so he withdrew his hand and zipped the pocket closed. He didn't want anything to do with what was in that pocket.

He paused. Sighing, he opened the pocket again, reached in, and took out a photograph. In it, Paul Jenkins—looking very much like he did when Stokes last saw him, only in the picture he was smiling . . . and alive—sat on a park bench beside a little girl with dark, curly hair, maybe six years old. She was a little chubby, with a nose that was a bit too big. She wasn't ugly or anything, but no one other than close family members or friendly liars would call her cute. Still, there was something about her eyes. A twinkle in them, maybe. Something. She was holding a stuffed frog that had the ragged, well-worn look of a favorite toy. She wore blue jeans with some kind of curvy, flowing stitching on them, a white T-shirt with a big daisy on it, bright yellow socks, and shiny silver sneakers. Stokes didn't want to look at the photo any longer, so he turned it over in his hands. On the back, in the lower right corner, was a date written in looping, childish handwriting, presumably the date the picture was taken. Eight months ago. Across the top, written in block letters—clearly different handwriting—someone had hand-written a message: "Found this in her backpack, in case you need a reminder to be a good boy."

The girl's voice, small and hopeful, said in Stokes's head, *Daddy? Are you coming to get me?* It said it again, then again. By the time he heard the words yet again, the voice was different, younger, a voice he hadn't heard in years.

He looked at his watch: 4:57. Almost an hour since their call . . .

Shit. Nearly a quarter of a million dollars.

Daddy?

A new life.

Are you coming to get me?

Goddamn it.

———

Stokes jammed yet another of Tom Whatever's twenty-dollar bills through the Plexiglas divider as the taxi jerked to a stop in front of the bus station. He didn't wait for his thirteen dollars in change. Backpack in hand, he burst from the cab and raced into the station. He looked at his watch: 4:59.

He ignored the stares directed at him as he ran across the bus station toward the trash can where he'd tossed the cell phone an hour ago. He'd already missed one call. Who knew whether they had made good on their threat. Who knew what they would do if he missed another?

Would they even call again at all?

Or would they just . . . ?

He skidded to a stop at the trash can, bent over it, and found a candy wrapper and an empty Pepsi can. That was it. No other garbage. No cell phone. Someone had emptied the trash since he'd thrown out the phone. Oh, shit.

As he stood, catching his breath, wondering if he was disappointed or relieved—after all, he'd tried now, right?—he became aware of a faint ringing. Definitely a cell phone. He looked around. Most of the people were still looking at him. None was reaching into a pocket or purse for a phone. Where was the ringing coming from?

The men's room door opened, and a gray plastic trash can on wheels rolled out, pushed by a sweaty guy in navy coveralls. The ringing grew louder as the janitor wheeled the trash can away from the men's room and closer to where Stokes was standing. Stokes covered the distance to the can in four long strides, wondering as he did why the hell the janitor wasn't more curious about the phone ringing in the trash can he was wheeling around. Stokes stopped the can and began pawing frantically through the garbage. The janitor looked surprised for a moment before shrugging and taking a seat in a row of nearby chairs, where he could watch from a safe distance.

The ringing continued as Stokes rooted through the trash, literally holding his breath as he pushed aside a half-eaten apple, old newspapers, cardboard toilet paper rolls, empty Styrofoam coffee cups, disgustingly moist paper towels, and a lot of unidentifiable nasty things until his hand finally closed around the smooth plastic of the cell phone. It had just finished another ring when Stokes flipped it open and raised it to his face. He tried not to think about where it had just been and why it was so sticky as he said, "Hello? Hello?"

The phone was silent a moment and Stokes thought he was too late. Finally, a man said, "You trying to kill your daughter? Where the hell have you been? We called you at four, like we said we would, then we tried you every fifteen minutes. We were about to give up and tie up the loose ends here, if you follow me." The voice sounded a little different than before. There was clearly more than one kidnapper; maybe they shared phone duty.

"Sorry," Stokes said, "sorry." Realizing that if he were truly the girl's father, he'd sound sorrier than he just had, he added, "Really, I'm so, so sorry."

"I thought you knew we were serious. I thought you said you watched the first video."

Video?

"You saw it, right?"

"Uh, yeah."

"You didn't like it, did you?"

It didn't sound like he would have, if he'd seen it, so he said, "No, I didn't."

"So how the hell can you make us send you a second one? My God, what's wrong with you? You watch that one yet?"

Second one? Oh, no.

"You don't think we're serious, Paul? Did you watch the second video?"

"I know you're serious."

"Did you watch the second video we sent?"

"No."

"Hang up and watch it. I'll call back in five minutes."

The line went dead. Stokes hesitated, then examined the phone for a moment. They said they sent two videos. Stokes's own cell phone was a relatively Stone Age model, without any bells and with, at most, one whistle, but he knew enough to know that the videos likely came in attached to either a text or an e-mail. Thankfully, there was a little button with the word "text" on it, so he pressed that and saw two texts in the in-box. Both had little icons of paper clips next to them. One had a time stamp of 10:09 a.m., and the other apparently came in at 4:12 p.m. . . . just under an hour ago, mere minutes after he missed the four o'clock call. He drew a breath and clicked on the first video.

The chubby kid, wearing a pink shirt with a purple heart stitched on it, sat on a bed, clutching the same tattered stuffed frog she was holding in the photo in the backpack Stokes was carrying, the photo the kidnappers presumably had sent to the girl's father with the ransom note. She was looking above the camera, which had to be the kidnapper's cell phone, probably looking at the guy holding it. It was a tight shot, just the kid sitting on the bed. Then she looked up and to her left as a shadow slid across the wall behind her. A hand reached in from out of frame and grabbed her left hand roughly.

"Ouch."

"Sssssh," the man off-camera said as he closed all but her little finger into his fist.

"We told you we'd know if you contacted the authorities, Paul. We told you we were serious. This is your fault."

The man reached down with his other hand, which held big scissors, maybe tin snips, and cut off her pinky. *Jesus.* The girl screamed. The camera phone recorded it all, maybe ten more seconds of hysterical shrieking before the screen went black.

Stokes thought he might throw up. He looked around to see if anyone had overheard the video, but that didn't seem to be the case. God, he was sweating so badly all of a sudden. He drew a deep breath and clicked on the second video. The girl was sitting on the bed like before, only now her hand was wrapped in a plaid dishcloth. Her eyes were puffy and red. It looked like she'd just woken up. Actually, it looked like she'd just woken up after crying herself to sleep earlier. She clutched her frog tightly. Stokes thought he saw blood on it. Her terrified eyes darted from the man with the camera phone to the person throwing another shadow on the wall, the one coming closer to her. She screamed and shrank away from the hands now reaching for her. She kicked but couldn't stop him from grabbing her left hand, unwrapping the towel. Stokes could see where her pinky should have been. She kept screaming as the man closed all but her ring finger into his fist, reached into a back pocket or somewhere—Stokes could see only his arms—and brought out the tin snips. The cries, already piercing, rose to a new level as the blades came together with a sickening snap-crunch. Maybe the bastards recorded ten more seconds of her screaming, like before, but Stokes snapped the phone shut. He was breathing as though he'd just run ten miles. He was dizzy. The phone rang in his hand. He opened it on the third ring.

"You watch the video?"

Stokes sucked in a gasping breath.

"You there?"

"I'm here," he finally managed to say.

"See the video?"

"I saw it."

"Now maybe you know how serious we are. I can't believe it took two fingers to convince you. But maybe we're on the same page now, though. Are we, Paul? Are we on the same page now?"

"Yeah. We are."

"Good. Believe me, we didn't enjoy that but you didn't give us a choice. Don't put us in that position again."

Stokes's breath was starting to slow. "I won't."

"We're trying to be patient with you, Paul. We're trying to work with you, right?"

Stokes said nothing.

"Aren't we?"

He seemed insistent, so Stokes said, "I guess."

"You guess? When you told us you had evidence about where you got all that money, evidence that could be bad for us, did we get all pissed off and hurt the girl? Did we just say 'fuck you' and break a few bones? No, we did not. We could have, but we didn't. And if we had, we'd still have the girl and you'd still want her back and we'd be right back where we started, only maybe the girl wouldn't be in such great shape any longer. But we didn't hurt her then. We realized you were just trying to protect your daughter. So we were nice enough to revise the deal. We agreed to let you give us the evidence along with the money. Wasn't that nice of us, Paul?"

Stokes rubbed his eyes.

"Paul?"

"Yeah. Yeah, it was nice."

"That's right, it was. So what happened?"

"When?"

"Why didn't you answer an hour ago? Or forty-five minutes ago? Or half an hour ago?"

Stokes didn't know what to say.

"Well?" the kidnapper said. "How the hell could you miss our four o'clock call? All we planned to do was call you now and then. *You're* the one who insisted we call every hour on the hour so you could talk to your daughter. And we agreed. And we also made it pretty damn clear from the start what would happen if we called and you didn't pick up. So what the hell happened?"

Stokes still didn't know what to say. He still didn't want to speak too much and give the kidnapper a chance to realize that the voice on the other end of the line wasn't the voice he'd first spoken with, the voice of the dead father. He had to say something, though.

"I'm really sorry," he said, speaking low. "I left the phone somewhere. Had to go back for it."

"She's going to run out of fingers sometime, Paul. When she does, we move on to something else. Is that going to happen? She going to run out of fingers?"

"No."

"Is this going to happen again? Because maybe we'll forget the fingers and take something else. Maybe we'll get creative. Or, shit, maybe we'll just kill her. How's that sound?"

"Please," Stokes said, struggling to keep his voice low, "don't hurt her anymore. I'm sorry. It won't happen again. I swear."

"Better not," the voice said. "Wanna talk to her?"

Stokes froze. He didn't want to talk to the kid. That was just a bad idea. She'd probably know right away he wasn't her father, and that could screw things up royally, put the girl in even worse danger than she was in. Plus, he just didn't want to hear her voice. He hadn't enjoyed hearing it in his head. He certainly didn't feel like hearing it live again. The problem was, if he were truly her father, he wouldn't just *want* to talk to her, he'd insist on it. And the last thing Stokes could afford to do if he wanted to help the girl was let the kidnapper know he wasn't her father.

"What the hell's the matter with you?" the guy asked. "You wanna talk to her or not? She's a little sad, of course, a little scared, and still in a bit of pain from the fingers, I think, but she can talk."

"Put her on," Stokes said.

A moment later, that damn little voice came on the line. "Daddy? Are you there? We kept trying to call you, but you didn't answer." Her voice was hoarse. From the screaming and crying, he knew. "They said they hurt me because you didn't answer the phone. I don't want them to hurt me again, Daddy. Can I come home soon? Please?" Stokes thought he heard a shuddering breath. Maybe it was a sob.

Stokes took a breath of his own. It was his fault. The second finger was his fault. Not the first one. That one was on her father, who obviously had ignored the kidnappers' warnings and contacted the authorities. Stokes didn't know if it was the cops or the FBI or whomever, but Paul clearly had called someone and the kidnappers, true to their word, had found out. And seeing as there didn't appear to be a mobilization of cops or agents looking for the kid, whatever man they had inside whatever department, agency, or bureau her father had called must have been able to nip things in the bud somehow as soon as Paul called it in.

"Daddy," the girl was saying, "can I come home soon?"

"Sure, Baby."

A pause on the line. "Baby?"

He realized his mistake. He shouldn't have used a pet name. He didn't even know her real name yet, and he sure as hell didn't know what cute little nickname her father had for her. Maybe he called her Princess, or Sweat Pea, or Sugar Bear. But judging by the girl's reaction, he never called her Baby. If the kidnapper noticed the girl's confusion—

"Satisfied?" It was the kidnapper's voice again. Stokes blew out a breath as quietly as he could. The kidnapper didn't wait for a response. "I'll call in an hour. You better answer. And you better have the money. You know where to be to get your final instructions. Now I'm going to tell you when to be there."

Huh? Wait a second. Stokes didn't know where to be. "Hey, hold on—"

"Be at that pay phone at one thirty this morning. If we see anyone hanging around there before then, we'll kill the girl. We'll tell you where to drop the money and the evidence. After we have it, we'll tell you where you can find the kid. Then we're done. Everybody's happy."

"But—"

The line went dead. Stokes closed the phone. A few people were still looking at him, but most had gone on their way. The janitor was sitting a few feet away, watching him. Stokes stuck the cell phone in his pocket and shoved the trash can with his foot, sending it rolling toward the janitor.

Pay phone? Stokes's mind was spinning. He had figured the kidnappers were just going to call the cell phone and tell him where to meet them. It never occurred to him that there was an instruction he'd already missed, something he was already supposed to know. But why send him to some pay phone to receive his final instructions when he had a cell phone? Stokes considered it. Maybe it made sense. They were probably going to send him from one pay phone to another, keeping an eye on him as they moved him around to make sure he wasn't working with anyone, communicating with someone during the process. Finally, when they were sure he was going it alone, as instructed, they'd tell him where to make the drop.

One of Stokes's problems, if he truly wanted to help the girl—something he was still struggling with a bit, if he had to be honest—was that he didn't know where he was supposed to be at one thirty to receive the drop instructions, yet he was obviously supposed to know that. They'd already communicated that to the dead father. Stokes couldn't play dumb and just ask them again. No father would forget that information. Somehow, Stokes would have to find out where that pay phone was located.

He had other problems, too. He was short $102,000 and the kidnappers sounded pretty serious about wanting every last dime of the $350,000 they asked for. Stokes had seen with his own eyes just how serious they were.

He also didn't have the evidence they were looking for, what-ever it was. He knew it wasn't in the bag with the money. That meant the father had planned to get it later. But from where? And what the hell was it?

Maybe it was time to confess that he wasn't the girl's father and he didn't have a clue about any evidence, but that he'd still be will-ing to give them the money in exchange for the girl.

But no, they'd been pretty damn insistent that nothing go wrong with their plans. And they'd demonstrated a cold brutality when something did. So Stokes simply wasn't ready to reveal that he didn't have enough money or the evidence they wanted. Maybe he could find both. Maybe he couldn't, in the end, but his best play for now was to continue to pretend to be the girl's father.

So he had to come up with another $102,000 before one thirty in the morning rolled around, and he had to figure out what evi-dence Paul was supposed to give the bad guys, and then find it. And it suddenly occurred to him where he had to go to start looking for both. He also knew that going there would be one of the stupidest things he'd done in his entire life, a life in which no one had ever accused him of being a genius.

SEVEN

THIS WAS ALL JENNY'S FAULT. Stokes had had time to give it some thought over the past twenty-two minutes, and he kept coming to the same conclusion. This was Jenny's fault. He couldn't blame his current situation on a little girl he hadn't seen in thirteen years, a girl he'd last seen when she was just two years old. And Jenny was next in the blame line, so it was her fault.

Back at the bus station, Stokes had gone against his nature, against everything he'd ever learned, against who he'd become after thirty-six years on this planet, and decided to help the chubby kidnapped girl. He'd give up the money—and, Jesus, it was a lot of money—to try to get the kid out of danger. There was nothing in it for him. He had no angle. He had nothing to gain and everything to lose—the money, the freedom it would buy, the dreams he could have realized with it, everything. But he was going to try to help the kid anyway.

He no longer had his bike, and he didn't want to take a taxi anywhere near where he was going, because that would leave a trail that could be followed by the cops later, so he'd stuck both arms through the straps on the backpack, fastened it securely on his back, and started to run. He didn't exercise regularly, but he was in decent enough shape. Ran once or twice a week when the weather was nice, like it had been lately. If he took shortcuts through a couple of parking lots and some woods, he probably would have less than two miles to run. It would be harder in the jeans, leather jacket, and lightweight boots he was wearing than it would be in sweats and sneakers, and the backpack full of money weighing him down didn't help any, but he'd manage. Shouldn't take long, which was good, because he was fast realizing that time was important in this.

It took him twenty-two minutes to cover the distance, twenty-two minutes during which he had nothing to do but run and think—regulate his breathing, watch his footing, and think. And the more he thought, the more certain he became that Jenny was throwing a wrench into the gears of his life yet again. Indirectly this time, maybe, but this was her fault nonetheless.

Stokes met her seventeen years ago, when he was nineteen. He'd dropped out of school three years before, kicked around aimlessly for a few years after that, getting into fights, getting into trouble, getting himself put on probation for trying unsuccessfully to rob somebody's grandmother at an ATM. The old woman screamed and Stokes ran, but not fast enough. Anyway, along came Jenny. Eighteen years old, pretty, hell of a sense of humor, the kind of person that other people wanted to be friends with. Well, women wanted to be friends with her; guys wanted something else. But everyone wanted to be around her. She didn't have to work at it; it just came naturally to her. Stokes truly had no idea what she saw in him. He knew he wasn't bad looking, but a girl like Jenny could have done better, especially if she started factoring in other traits, like potential and dependability and quality of character. Whatever it was she saw in him, it was something Stokes certainly didn't see. In fact, he was pretty sure it wasn't even there.

They dated for a year and he started getting into less trouble, started looking for real work, even started thinking about asking her to marry him. They moved in together, and things were pretty damn good for a while. Then one morning Jenny knocked his world off its axis with a little piece of news. Eight months later, Ellie was born. And when Ellie was born, everything changed. Forever.

Stokes knew what he was supposed to do, what the right thing was to do. And he did it. He stopped staying out with his buddies until the early morning hours. He stopped drinking too much. There were no more fights. He started taking his work more seriously, knowing he could no longer afford to grab his lunch pail and walk away from a job the moment he grew tired of it. He had to work steadily, put in overtime when he could, save money, save for a house, plan for the future. The thing was, Stokes had already started doing those things. Being with Jenny made it worth doing those things. He did them because he wanted to, wanted Jenny to be proud of him, wanted her to continue to see in him whatever it was he didn't see himself.

Then Ellie was born, and everything Stokes had been doing because he wanted to, he now did because he *had* to. And he resented it. It wasn't like he didn't like the kid, because he did. He loved her, actually. More than he thought he would. More than he thought he *could*. She was cute and plump and dimply and giggly, and when he held her while she slept and her little baby breath blew softly against his neck, and Jenny sat beside him on the couch, smiling at him, smiling at the father that had been inside the angry young man he'd been all along, well, in those moments he thought he had everything he could ever have wanted right there on that couch. But other times, when he was punching the clock, working yet another overtime shift at the warehouse, taking shit from his boss, telling his buddies he couldn't shoot pool that night because he needed to get home and give Jenny a break from Ellie, during those times he looked at beautiful Jenny and cute little Ellie and all he saw were manacles, twin iron manacles snapped around each of his ankles, grinding through the flesh down to the bone, chaining him to that house, that town, that life.

And then one day it all ended. He'd simply had enough. He'd tried, she had to give him that. He'd tried. So while Jenny snored softly, her dark hair fanned out across her pillow, while Ellie breathed her little baby breaths into the early morning air and dreamed of whatever two-year-old kids dream of, Stokes stuffed clothes into a duffel bag and slipped out of that house, that town, that life.

He drifted around, settled briefly in seven different states, moving on for one reason or another—because he'd grown tired of the place, because he'd heard of an opportunity somewhere else, or maybe because he'd needed to stay a step ahead of someone. And he'd hardly thought about Jenny or Ellie. It was like he'd thrown a switch in his mind. Turned off the light and shut the door. All that time, all those years, he never called her, never wrote. And he never heard of her trying to reach him. He knew what that said about him, about the kind of person he was. He'd come to terms with that a long time ago. He was that person for nineteen years before Jenny showed up. He was that same person while they were together, though he tried to be somebody else. Why wouldn't he be that same person after he left them?

Eventually, eight years after he walked out, he found his way back to Shady Cross. He didn't go to their old apartment. He didn't call their old phone number. After a couple of weeks, he finally asked around a little about her. He wasn't looking to get back together with her, didn't want to try raising a kid again. Besides, a woman like her, she wouldn't have been by herself for too long if she didn't want to be. So Stokes wasn't sure why he even asked about her. But in the end, it didn't matter because she and Ellie were long gone. Moved away within a year of Stokes's leaving and no one he spoke with had heard from her since.

Five years later, he had to admit that he thought about them now and then. In his mind, Jenny was still twenty-one, still full of youthful beauty, still quick to laugh her infectious, full-throated laugh. And Ellie was still two years old, toddling around on plump little legs, giggling at the silly faces and funny sounds he'd make, ready at the slightest invitation to throw her little arms around his neck and squeeze.

No, Stokes couldn't blame little Ellie for his being in this situation, for his giving up his chance at the good life to help out a six-year-old girl he'd never met, even though it didn't take Sigmund Freud to tell him that she had something to do with it. He knew it had been her voice he'd heard in his head, along with the voice of the little girl on the phone. But how could he possibly blame her? So he was forced to blame his ex-girlfriend—Jenny, who'd given him a daughter he never wanted but reluctantly loved anyway, loved as much as he knew how, which he knew wasn't even close to enough in the end. Because of that little two-year-old girl he hadn't seen in thirteen years, he was standing where he was at that moment, back on the deserted stretch of road where all this started nearly four hours ago.

Stokes was standing at the spot where the dead guy's car had entered the woods. His legs were heavy from his run, and he was sweating despite the crisp evening air. There were no cars in sight. It wasn't even six o'clock in the evening, but the sun was far below the treetops, getting ready to set for the night, and the road was growing darker by the second. Still, Stokes could see the dented guardrail on the other side of the road. His twisted Yamaha lay in a shallow depression twenty yards in the trees beyond, covered with leaves. He turned back to the woods in front of him, looked deep into them. The trees were thicker in there. What little light remained in the sky had a hard time falling all the way to the ground. From where he stood, he couldn't see the dark car that he knew was wrapped around a thick trunk thirty feet into the trees. The car with a little girl's dead father inside.

Stokes took one last look up and down the road, then walked into the wooded darkness.

EIGHT

BRITTLE LEAVES CRACKLED AND CRUNCHED under Stokes's boots as he moved through the dim light. Out on the road, dusk was in full bloom. Here in the woods, darkness had taken hold.

It had been risky as hell coming here. If someone had found Paul's car, the place would have been alive with cops and curious onlookers and maybe a reporter or two crawling all over the place like ants swarming over a fried chicken wing left on a picnic blanket while everyone was off playing volleyball. And Stokes wasn't terribly eager to be connected with this accident, seeing as he had caused it.

But he was alone. Except for the dead guy, of course, who wasn't far ahead.

Another few steps brought the dark, vaguely car-shaped hulk into sight. It was as he remembered it, misshapen, smashed up against a fat tree. He regarded it for a moment before approaching the driver's door. The driver was as Stokes remembered him, too, still smashed and still dead. Only now he looked even more dead. His eyes were still open and staring, but the skin Stokes could see through the blood covering most of his face had dulled to a waxy gray.

He hadn't wanted to return here. Only an idiot would return here. But he didn't know what else to do. If he was going to try to figure out where he was supposed to be at one thirty that morning, and if he had any hope of finding the evidence the kidnappers wanted, he had to start here. And he had to move quickly. Time was moving faster than he remembered it ever moving before. He had to get to work.

He walked around to the passenger side of the car, dropped the backpack onto the soft carpet of leaves under his feet, and used his shirttail again to open the door without leaving fingerprints. The dome light glowed as Stokes slid into the passenger seat and he picked up a crumpled napkin from the floor and used it to turn off the light so no one passing by would see it and decide to investigate. Then he used the napkin to open the glove compartment, where he found a flashlight. He clicked it on and turned it toward the dead man.

Paul Something-or-Other was still slumped over the steering wheel, just like he'd been when Stokes had first seen him. Stokes reminded himself never to get into another car that didn't have working air bags. He reached over and pulled on the body's shoulder, trying to move it back against the seat. The guy didn't seem to want to move—well, he'd probably have given anything to be able to move again—and Stokes was getting resistance from the body. He pulled a little harder and the corpse suddenly popped back from the steering wheel with a wet sucking sound. Stokes lowered his light and saw in its beam an open, ugly wound in the body's chest. He looked at the steering wheel, which was made of hard plastic. The top half of it had broken off in the violent impact. The driver had clearly been thrown forward into the wheel, snapping it, and the broken part still attached to the steering column had slammed into him, shattering his breastbone, punching into his chest. Stokes glanced again at the raw, ragged, bloody gash. He took a breath, then reached up and slipped his hand into the guy's jacket pocket, ignoring the stickiness his fingers encountered as they crept around in the folds of fabric. He was looking for a wallet. He needed to know the guy's full name if he was going to continue to pose as him, in case it came up in conversation with the kidnappers.

He found the wallet in a breast pocket and opened it. Sixty-four bucks. It wasn't a hundred thousand, but it was a start. He pocketed it. No other pieces of paper in the wallet, nothing that looked like "evidence" Paul could have used against anyone, and nothing with an address for the pay phone written on it. Damn. He shined the flashlight on the guy's driver's license. Paul Douglas Jenkins. Thirty-four years old. Two years younger than Stokes, who was going to continue to get older, at least for a while longer, while Paul Jenkins was not. Stokes noted the address on the license. It wasn't in one of the more expensive areas. This tracked with the idea that Jenkins might have stolen the $350,000, which Stokes had suspected. So did the fact that ten-year-old Nissan Altimas, like the kind Stokes was sitting in, weren't exactly the first choice of the rich and famous. Yeah, Paul must have stolen the money. For some reason, this bothered Stokes.

He slipped Jenkins's wallet into his own pocket and shined the flashlight on his watch: 5:38. Just under eight hours before he had to be at a pay phone somewhere. He steeled himself and checked the rest of Jenkins's pockets, one by one, looking for a written address. Nothing. He played the flashlight beam around the car's interior, searching for something with an address written on it, and also for whatever evidence Paul had unwisely threatened the kidnappers with—files, a notebook, a computer disk, maybe a little tape recorder. But he saw nothing of the kind, which was a big disappointment. As for the pay phone's address, maybe Jenkins never wrote it down. Maybe the kidnappers told it to him and he simply committed it to memory. But Stokes had to do something, so he kept searching. He checked the trunk and found nothing helpful. He slammed the trunk lid and climbed back into the passenger seat.

He sighed. He'd come up empty in his search, but he still had work to do here. Though it would become more unlikely the darker it got, someone could find this car in the next couple of hours. And they'd call the cops. And if the kidnappers truly had an informant in the police department, they'd know Paul Jenkins was dead and reasonably assume that they weren't going to get their money. And then they might kill the kid. So Stokes absolutely could not let the cops know Jenkins was dead. He thought for a moment. He couldn't move the car, couldn't hide it any better than it was hidden, but he could try to make it harder for the cops to figure out whose car it was. Sure, they'd have a body, but if Jenkins hadn't worked for the government or been in the military, and hadn't been arrested—which the average person hasn't—they shouldn't have his fingerprints on file, which would make it more difficult to ID his body. And all Stokes needed was a few more hours.

He opened the glove compartment again and removed the vehicle registration and stuffed it in his pocket. He walked back to the trunk and got a screwdriver he'd seen there moments earlier and used it to remove the license plates. Then he opened the driver's door and found a sticker he knew he'd find on the car's frame, a sticker that would be hidden when the door was closed. It listed information about the vehicle, including the vehicle identification number, or VIN. He used the screwdriver to scratch out the information on it. Next he would—

He froze. Cocked his head, listening. He heard it again. Voices. A flashlight beam stabbed through the darkness, struck a nearby tree, and started a slow, probing crawl toward him.

Shit, shit, shit.

Cops? He couldn't tell.

He had to get the hell out of there. Grab the backpack from the ground on the other side of the car and run like hell.

But he hadn't finished removing the car's identifiers. The kidnappers would find out Jenkins was dead, which was very bad for the kid.

Stokes could still bolt, though, and get away with the money. He still had a chance at a new life.

But the kid would have no chance at all.

He hesitated. For too long.

Daddy?

He should just run like hell. No time even to grab the bag any longer. If he was going to get away clean, he had to take off *now*. Still, he hesitated. The goddamn kid. And, he had to admit, the money.

The voices were close in the darkness now. He heard footsteps through crackling leaves. The flashlight was crawling closer. Too close.

It was over. He wasn't going to get away. And now maybe the little girl wasn't, either.

NINE

WHOEVER WAS COMING THROUGH THE dark woods was getting close now. Stokes's last chance to get away cleanly had come and gone. As the flashlight beam bounced off the tree in front of him, the tree that had stopped Jenkins's car and his life, Stokes crawled quickly through the open driver's door, scrambled over Jenkins's dead body, and positioned himself in the passenger seat, slumped over the dashboard. The damn bag of money was on the ground outside the passenger door. He'd worry about that later, if he got the chance. At the moment, he was worried about the fact that he was sitting there, the picture of health, in a wreck of a car beside a driver who had been turned to raw hamburger. That was going to look suspicious.

He heard footsteps stop outside the car. He sensed the flashlight beam striking the tree again, then playing over the crumpled hood. Stokes took a chance. Without moving anything but his arm, he reached over, slid his hand under Jenkins's jacket, groped along the sticky shirt, and finally reached the open chest wound. He took a shallow breath and dug his fingers into a hole in the flesh, his knuckle scraping on jagged bone. He pushed his fingers in, sinking them into the congealing bloody mess inside, then pulled his hand back, covered with gore. He let his head slide down just a little, resting his forehead on the dash, and brought his hand to his own face. He wiped the mess on his cheeks, his nose, his chin, suppressing a violent urge to vomit. Then he was still. There was no sudden commotion. They hadn't noticed his movements.

It wasn't a bad plan. It hadn't been a lot of fun, poking around inside a corpse, and sitting there with his face covered with a dead guy's blood and gore wasn't the way he wanted to pass the time, but all in all, it was a decent idea. The gore served double duty, making Stokes look like a victim of the crash while also disguising his face, which could be useful so long as the people outside weren't cops, who would certainly arrest him as soon as they realized he wasn't actually injured and had the dead guy's license and vehicle registration in his pocket. But if they weren't cops and he got the chance to grab the bag and run, the blood and whatever-the-hell-else he'd pulled from Jenkins's chest and smeared all over his face might keep whoever was standing outside the car from identifying him later.

This was nuts. *He* was nuts. This whole situation just wasn't his goddamn problem.

Daddy?

Shut up, kid.

Stokes had his face turned away from the window. The voices were very close. Through half-closed eyes he saw a flashlight beam creep around inside the car. He heard one of the voices again.

"There it is." A male voice.

"Man, they look messed up," a second voice said, also male.

Based on what little he'd heard, Stokes didn't think they were cops. They sounded young. But still, he waited.

"What's this bag on the ground?"

"Check it out while I call 911."

He'd heard enough. He let out a loud, dramatic groan and turned his face to the window, directly into the flashlight beam, careful to keep his eyes mostly closed so he wouldn't lose his night vision completely.

"Jesus Christ."

"Holy shit."

The flashlight dropped to the ground. Two young men, teenagers from the looks of them, backed away from the car. The fear on their faces was almost comical. They stopped, looked at each other, then looked back at Stokes. Then they squared their shoulders, trying to look unaffected by what they were seeing.

"Shit," the taller of the two said, "that one guy's still alive."

The other kid pulled a cell phone out of his coat pocket. "We gotta call the cops."

Stokes didn't want that. Moving only his arm, he nudged the door open so they could hear him better. "Please," he groaned, "come here."

The kids hesitated before slowly stepping forward.

"I need your phone," Stokes said.

"I gotta call the cops," Shorty said. "You need an ambulance, man. You're pretty jacked up."

"Please," Stokes said, raising his head briefly before letting it drop to the dashboard again. "Please give me your phone. I may not make it. May not . . . live long. Need to call my wife. Tell her . . . good-bye."

Shorty looked at Tall, who shrugged. "His funeral, right?" Tall said.

Shorty still looked unsure.

"Please," Stokes croaked. He added a hacking cough for good measure.

"Shit, give him your phone," Tall said.

Shorty stepped up to the car, handed his phone through the open door. He watched as Stokes struggled to sit up, fumbling with the phone. Stokes punched a few random digits, then paused. He turned his head weakly to look at the kids.

"Did you find the guy on the bicycle?" he asked.

They frowned.

"What guy on a bicycle?"

"The one we hit with our car. Did you find him?"

"We didn't see any guy on a bike."

"We hit him a few hundred yards back, I think," Stokes said. "Please . . . you have to go find him. See if he's OK." He coughed again.

"I should call the cops," Shorty said again.

"I'll call them. I'll say good-bye to my wife, then call 911. You go look for the cyclist." Stokes gave a gasp loaded with fake pain. "He might need help. My buddy here is dead and I don't know if I even have a chance, but the guy we hit . . . maybe he can be saved. You gotta find him."

Shorty eyed his phone in Stokes's hand.

"My phone . . ."

"I'll make the calls. You'll get your phone back."

"But . . ."

Stokes fixed him with a hard gaze. "I'm dying here . . . and some poor guy might be dying on the road up there . . . and you're worried about your phone?"

The kid looked confused. Maybe he was worried about losing his cell phone. More likely, he was afraid Stokes would die before he called 911, and then everyone would wonder why the hell he'd given a dying man his phone without first calling the cops himself.

"Where am I gonna go with it?" Stokes asked. "I'll be here when you get back. Hopefully, I'll still be alive. Now please, go look for the guy we hit." He let loose a horrible, wracking cough. "For God's sake, *go*."

The kids scurried away, scrambled through the trees, back toward the road, their flashlight bobbing before them. How the hell had they found the car? It was practically dark out, and Stokes thought he'd wiped away all traces of the tire tracks. Whatever—he needed to move. Stokes kicked open the door, stood, and wiped down the kid's cell phone with the bottom of his shirt before letting it fall to the forest floor and stomping on it, grinding it beneath his boot.

"Sorry, kid."

He got to work, figuring he'd bought himself only a few minutes before they'd be back. Or maybe they'd flag down a passing car, borrow a cell phone from the driver. Whatever, Stokes had to move fast. He hurried around to the driver's side again, leaned into the car, and shined his light into the tight corner where the dashboard and the windshield and the side of the car all met. There he saw the small metal plate with the VIN stamped into it. He tried to get the screwdriver under it to pry it up, but couldn't. So he used the sharp edge of the tool to scrape at the number. He dug at it as hard as he could for a minute before leaning back and inspecting his handiwork. He had completely obliterated five of the seventeen characters, and had badly damaged two others. Maybe this would slow down the identification of the car; maybe it wouldn't. But he'd tried. He knew there could be another VIN stamped somewhere else on the Altima's frame, but if there was, he didn't know where and didn't have time to hunt for it. He hurried around to the passenger door again so he'd be closer to the bag of money, and dropped into the seat there. He leaned over, turned the key to the "off" position, and plucked the keys from the ignition. He removed the only key that looked like it could have been a house key, then stuck the car key back into the ignition and turned it back to the "on" position. He used the napkin again to wipe his prints off the keys still on the ring.

Then he sat for a minute and thought, acutely aware of the seconds zipping by. Yeah, he'd done all he could. He was ready to go. He looked at his watch: 5:53. They'd be calling in seven minutes. He switched off the flashlight, stuffed the license plates into the bag next to the money, and picked up the backpack. He took a last look at Paul Jenkins.

Doubt started to creep into his mind. The cops were going to find the car. The kids would eventually bring them, probably sooner than later, and they'd ID the vehicle, probably fairly quickly. Or hell, maybe one of the cops even knew Jenkins personally somehow. Played golf with him or went to the same barber. Whatever. The point was, if he left the body in the car, they might figure out who he was in time to kill the deal, and maybe the girl, too.

Stokes sighed. There was nothing else to do. He had to take the body with him. Even if they identified the car, without the body they wouldn't know for certain that Jenkins had died, and the kidnappers therefore might believe that their chance for a payday was still alive. Yeah, Stokes had to take the body. He should have just done that to start with, but who the hell thinks about dragging a corpse around?

Just when he'd made up his mind, he heard the kids' voices again.

Goddamn it.

He dropped the backpack on the ground, where it had been when the kids were there a few minutes ago, and slipped back into the passenger seat. He let his head flop back against the headrest, closed his eyes, and tried to think of another goose chase to send them on so he could slip away with the body while they were gone.

Footsteps approached. He couldn't hear what the kids were saying, but they were getting closer and the words were becoming more distinct. He opened his eyes a crack and saw the flashlight beam bouncing his way again.

"I'm telling you, we were talking to him," one of the voices said. Sounded like Tall.

"Bullshit," someone said. Stokes frowned. Didn't recognize the voice.

"He's alive, Kevin," Shorty said. "Royally messed up, but alive. I gave him my phone so he could say good-bye to his wife."

They were almost to the car. Stokes heard the new kid, Kevin, start to respond. "But I thought . . ."

"Yeah, yeah," Tall said, cutting him off, "the driver's dead as hell, but the other guy's still alive. At least he was when we left him here."

"But . . ."

The flashlight hit the side of Stokes's face. He turned slowly into the light and smiled weakly.

"Thank God you're back," he whispered, acting even closer to death's door than he had before.

He looked at Shorty. Wasn't sure what he was going to tell him about his phone. Stokes slid his gaze from Shorty to Tall, then moved it over to the new guy, Kevin. Kevin was staring back at him with a mixture of emotions on his face that Stokes couldn't categorize. He was looking at Stokes, but he spoke to the other two.

"I swear to you guys, I looked in this car half an hour ago."

Uh oh.

Kevin turned to the others. "Dudes, there was only one guy in there."

Well, Stokes certainly hadn't seen that one coming.

TEN

STOKES DIDN'T HAVE TIME TO think. It looked like the three teens had independently come to the same conclusion—that they needed to run away as fast as they could. Stokes couldn't allow that, so he sprang from the car with far more speed and agility than the kids could have expected from a guy with one foot in the grave. Before they could move, he stepped right up to them, looked down at them from his solid, six-two height, and held the screwdriver up in front of their eyes.

"See this?" he asked.

They nodded.

"Think I could do serious damage to you guys with it?"

They nodded again.

"Think I could kill you with it?"

More nods.

"Good. Don't run and I might not have to use it. Got me?"

Emphatic nods that time.

"Look at me." They did. He knew what they saw. A big guy with a face slick with blood. Intense eyes, probably, because Stokes felt like there was intensity in his eyes. Probably made him look even scarier. And the pointy screwdriver in his bloody hand certainly wasn't making him seem any more friendly. "Look at me," he repeated. "You think I'd hesitate to stick one of you boys if you piss me off."

They shook their heads that time.

"So you're not gonna run, right?"

They shook their heads again. But Stokes wasn't convinced. Tall and Shorty looked ready to bolt the second they got the chance. Stokes looked at the three of them in turn, sizing them up. One of them might have been old enough to drive, possibly two, but they were all wispy things. Shorty looked to be thirteen at most. Without warning, Stokes shot his hand out and grabbed his shirt. Pulled him close. Held the screwdriver against his throat. The other kids tensed but didn't move. Smart kids.

"This is your little brother, right?" he asked Tall. He'd seen a resemblance.

Tall's frightened eyes were on the screwdriver. He nodded.

"What about you?" Stokes asked Kevin.

"Friend."

"I don't wanna hurt anyone," Stokes said, "but I definitely will if I have to. Now, I want some answers. If I think you're lying, the kid gets stuck. If you make me stick the kid too much and he's no use to me anymore, I grab one of you and start sticking again. So don't lie to me, OK?"

They nodded again.

"What's your name?" he asked Tall.

"Chris."

"Chris what?"

"Parker."

"Address?"

Chris gave him an address Stokes knew was nearby. Sounded plausible.

"You drive?"

Chris nodded.

"Let me see your license."

The kid pulled a wallet from his back pocket, removed his license, and held it out.

"Hold it up for me. I got my hands full."

Chris held it up so Stokes could see it.

"A little light here?" Stokes said.

Kevin leaned forward—didn't step forward, but leaned as far as he could without actually getting any closer to the maniac with the bloody face and the sharp screwdriver—and shined the flashlight on the license. Chris had been telling the truth. Stokes turned to Kevin and was about to speak when the cell phone in his pocket rang.

Shit. Stokes understood what had driven Paul Jenkins to insist on receiving a call from the kidnappers every hour on the hour until this was over . . . why he felt the need to hear his daughter's voice every time . . . but goddamn it, these calls could be inconvenient. He wished like hell he just could say, "Hey, guys, I've been thinking about it. Calling me every hour is a lot to ask. Maybe just give me a ring every three or four hours. That's probably enough." But he couldn't say that. The real Paul Jenkins would never have said that, and Stokes needed them to believe he was the real Paul Jenkins.

The phone rang again. Shorty looked up at him.

"Mine, not yours," Stokes said. "Yours is broken." He pushed the sharp tip of the screwdriver tight against Shorty's throat, making a slight indentation in the soft flesh.

"I gotta take this call," he said. "You guys make a single sound, I push this through the kid's neck, you hear me?" Without waiting for an answer, he looked hard at Shorty. "You move, you die, OK?" Shorty nodded.

Stokes released his hold on the kid's shirt, kept the screwdriver hard against his neck, and pulled Jenkins's cell phone from his pocket with his free hand. He flipped it open on the fourth ring, keeping his eyes on the three kids.

"Hello?"

"Why's it take you so long to answer the phone, Paul?"

"Sorry," Stokes said.

"Here's your six o'clock call. The girl's doing all right."

Stokes knew what was expected of him.

"Let me talk to her."

The kidnapper didn't respond. A moment later, the little girl's voice came on the line. "Daddy?"

He reminded himself not to call her Baby. "Yeah, it's me. You OK?"

Silence on the phone for a moment. "Daddy? Is that you?"

Jesus Christ. He had to put a stop to that. He prayed the kidnappers couldn't hear his half of the conversation. "Listen, kid," he said quickly, "your daddy's gonna come get you, but you gotta help him. You gotta pretend I'm him, OK?"

The girl said, "But where—"

He cut her off. "Don't ask where your daddy is. He's working hard to come get you. But you gotta trust me. You gotta pretend I'm your daddy, OK? If you don't, your daddy can't come for you. You have to believe me." Stokes heard the urgency in his voice. He was probably scaring her silly, but he had no choice. "You understand, kid?"

A pause. "Yes, Daddy."

Stokes blew out a breath.

"That's enough for now, Paul," the kidnapper's voice said. "Got the money?"

"I'll have it."

"You better. And you've got this evidence you claim to have?"

"I do."

"OK. Talk to you in an hour."

The line went dead. Stokes shoved the phone into his pocket and grabbed Shorty's shirt again. Looked at the kids, who were staring at him, questions in their eyes.

"Forget all that. Where was I?" He thought for a moment. "Oh, yeah." He looked at Kevin. "Don't suppose you have your driver's license yet, do you, Kevin?"

To his surprise, Kevin nodded. Christ, had the kid even hit puberty yet?

"OK then," Stokes said. "You know the drill."

Kevin took out his license, held it up for Stokes, shined the flashlight on it. Kevin Joseph Shapiro. Also lived nearby.

Stokes nodded. "OK, guys. Last question. You call the cops yet?"

Kevin shook his head. Chris hesitated before shaking his, too. He was holding back.

"Try that again, Chris. You call the cops yet?"

Chris sighed. "I didn't call them, but when Kevin came to our house a little while ago, told us he found a wrecked car out here, my mother was in the room. The three of us ran out before she could tell us not to. She might call the cops. Especially if we're not back soon."

Stokes almost smiled. The kid had made his point. Pretty smart. Mom knew where they'd gone and would start to worry if they didn't come back soon. And Stokes believed him. Still, just in case the mother hadn't called 911, he said, "OK guys, here's the deal. You never saw me here. Understand? No one knows I was here but you, so if the cops find out about me I'll know it came from you guys. Remember, I know your names. I know where you live. They find out about me, I'll come for you. And I'll be carrying something bigger and sharper and a whole lot scarier than a screwdriver, you hear me? You do *not* call the cops. If your mother already did, you tell them nothing about me. You came here, found a wrecked car, end of story. I wasn't here. The car was empty. Got it?"

They'd been nodding during his instructions, but the last one stopped the bobbing of their heads.

"Empty?" Chris said.

"That's right."

"What about . . . him?" He nodded toward the car.

"The car was empty," Stokes repeated. "Maybe you saw blood, but you didn't see a body. And you sure as hell didn't see me. You understand?"

They looked confused.

"I need to know that you understand. That you'll do what I'm saying. That you understand what will happen if you don't do what I'm saying."

Chris and Kevin nodded. Stokes looked down into Shorty's face.

"You understand?"

Shorty swallowed hard and nodded. He was scared out of his mind. Stokes felt a little sorry for him.

"You do as I say and you'll be all right." He released Shorty, who moved quickly to his big brother's side. Chris put a protective arm around his shoulders.

"You don't do exactly what I say," Stokes added, "I'll be seeing you real soon."

They looked at him. He could see they believed him.

"Now get the hell out of here."

They hesitated a fraction of a second, then ran, kicking up leaves as they sprinted toward the road. Stokes turned back to the car. And Paul Jenkins. He groaned inwardly as he walked around to the open driver's door. He unfastened the guy's seat belt and wrestled the body from the car. It wasn't easy. The guy was nearly Stokes's size.

Similar build, which might come in handy if he needed to get close to the kidnappers before they realized that he wasn't Paul Jenkins. But though their similar sizes might be helpful later, Stokes would have preferred Jenkins to be a dwarf at the moment. He struggled with the big corpse, which was literally dead weight. When the body was on the ground, Stokes retrieved his bag of money and hiked it up onto his back, then picked up the flashlight and stuck it into his rear pocket. He returned to the body, struggled to get it into a sitting position—which was made more difficult by the rigor mortis that had clearly begun to set in—then groaned and staggered as he hoisted it up onto his shoulder for a fireman's carry. *Shit*, the guy was heavy. Stokes wasn't exactly a weakling, but he was surprised at how hard it was to carry a dead body. He switched the flashlight on, then stumbled away from the road, farther into the woods, the dead body heavy on his back.

If the three kids didn't tell the police what they knew, Stokes's removing the body from the car should confuse the cops. Even if they figured out the car belonged to Jenkins, and even though there was a lot of blood inside it, if Jenkins was missing, they couldn't be certain he was dead. And if they weren't sure, the kidnappers couldn't be sure—especially if Stokes kept posing as the father in their hourly calls.

Stokes trudged through the dark, chilly night, the corpse on his back slowing his steps. Still, he walked as quickly as he could, ever aware of time bleeding away. He still had so much to do, so much he needed to figure out. And he knew the consequences of failure.

He shifted the body on his shoulders, got a more secure grip, and continued his march through the cold woods, the unwanted image of the kidnappers cutting off the little girl's fingers, the sounds of her screams, playing over and over again in his head.

ELEVEN

STOKES'S FEET WERE FREEZING. IT had been twenty minutes since he trekked, with a dead body on his back, through the small but mercilessly cold stream in the woods. Fortunately, the woods, which were on land preserved by a conservation organization interested in saving some frog or turtle or something, backed right up to the rear the trailer park on the edge of town, where Stokes kept his Airstream. He knew the woods well, having cut through them on more than one occasion—usually moving quickly to avoid someone or other he'd seen coming down the road toward his trailer, someone looking for him, maybe to arrest him, or to try to hurt him, or to squeeze money out of him . . . money he most likely owed but didn't have. Stokes had known the stream was there. So he'd hauled Jenkins's body for fifteen difficult minutes, dying for a rest but pushing on, knowing that his trail wouldn't be tough to follow until he came to the stream. He stepped into the goddamn cold water, hoped it wouldn't rise above the tops of his boots, was terribly disappointed in that regard, and slogged downstream for a hundred yards or so, praying he wouldn't slip and tumble into the frigid water or, worse, snap an ankle on a slime-slick rock. He was doing anything he could to slow down any pursuit of him that might develop. Cops coming upon Jenkins's car would see the tracks he'd left leading into the woods. They'd think it was Jenkins himself who had, by some miracle, walked away from the crash. They'd probably think he was disoriented, walking farther into the woods instead of walking thirty feet back to the road. The important thing would be that they thought he was still alive. As long as there was doubt, the kidnappers would have that doubt, too, and they might not abandon their plan to trade the girl for the money and the evidence.

Stokes had exited the stream, lugged Jenkins's corpse up the slope on the other side, and carried him another minute or two until he found a dense growth of evergreens, where, *finally*, he was able to dump the body and the Altima's license plates. Then he headed toward his trailer park. He'd intended to run there, but someone seemed to have replaced the blood in his legs with cement. So he walked for a while, trotted a little when he could, walked again, and trotted some more. Soon enough, he came to a chain-link fence, which he climbed over, into the rear part of Forest View Trailer Park.

He looked at his watch: 6:51 p.m.

He cut through properties as needed, wending his way past giant tin can after giant tin can, each of them somebody's home. He had just reached the back of his trailer when he caught a muffled squawk from out front. He knew that sound. He hated that sound. It made him turn and start back the way he'd come. Then he heard the goddamn door of the goddamn trailer behind his bang open, and Charlie Daniels, Stokes's goddamn neighbor—no relation to the singer—stepped around his trailer with a full Hefty bag in each hand. He dropped one of the bags, noisily tipped the metal lid off a metal trash can, letting it bang off the side of the metal trailer and clang to the ground. He dropped the bag into the can and looked up.

"That you, Stokes?" Daniels said far too loudly. He wasn't too bad a guy—he asked for a little too much now and then as a neighbor, a favor here or there, but all in all he was OK. Still, Stokes just didn't need this right now.

"Yeah, Charlie, it's me."

Stokes hurried back over to his trailer, peeked around the side, lifted the lid off his own trash can out of sight of Charlie, and placed the backpack in quietly. He replaced the lid even more quietly.

"What are you doing sneaking around out here, Stokes?" Daniels asked.

Stokes ignored him, moved quickly along the back of his trailer, and walked around the other end. He nearly bumped into a cop coming the other way, as he suspected he would after hearing the radio squawk in front of his trailer, and after his neighbor had banged the hell out of his trash can and had spoken to him, calling him by name, loudly enough for everyone in the park to hear.

Stokes tried to look surprised to see Sergeant Millett, who had questioned him at the police station last night and that morning.

"Officer," Stokes said.

"Sergeant," Millett corrected.

Millett was a big guy, Stokes's height, probably a few pounds heavier, those pounds looking like nothing but muscle. He was two years older than Stokes, which Stokes knew because they were both local boys, with Millett two years ahead of him in school. Of course, Millett finished high school, got into the academy, and became a cop, while Stokes dropped out, got into trouble, and would never be a cop.

"Right," Stokes said. "Sergeant. Sorry. Guess you're looking for me."

"That's right."

"How come your shirt's unbuttoned like that? Can't you get into trouble for being out of uniform or something?"

"I'm off duty."

"Oh." Stokes knew that wasn't good. If he was giving Stokes a hard time off the clock, he must have been really invested in his case.

"Whose blood is that?" Millett asked.

"Blood?"

After stashing Jenkins's body in the trees, Stokes had trotted back to the stream, dipped his hands into the frigid water, and rinsed Jenkins's blood and other gory stuff off his face and his leather jacket. But, he now saw, he'd gotten some on his shirt.

"It's mine. My blood."

Millett's hard eyes appraised him for a moment, looking him up and down.

"You don't look injured."

"Bloody nose. I'm fine now. Thanks for your concern, though."

Millett fell silent. Stared Stokes down. Stokes knew what he was doing. He was trying to be intimidating. He wasn't saying anything, hoping Stokes would get nervous and try to fill the silence and, in the process, say something stupid and incriminating. But Stokes merely stared silently back until Millett finally spoke again.

"Thought you might want to know that the guy whose house you robbed last night, the guy whose head you bashed in with a brass bookend that's now missing, the guy who spent the rest of last night and all day today in critical condition, well, the doctors aren't sure he's going to make it."

"Thanks for coming all the way here to tell me this, but it's got nothing to do with me. I'm sorry some guy got his head dented, but it's not my problem. I didn't have anything to do with that, like I spent most of last night and all of this morning telling you."

Millett stared at him for a moment. "Looks like you might have killed the guy."

"No I didn't."

"You smashed his skull in last night and he might die any minute now."

"Or he might recover. Whatever. It's got nothing to do with me."

Stokes didn't like the look on Millett's face. He really did seem to be taking this personally, like the injured guy was his father or something. Maybe it was because Stokes had wised off a bit during the interrogation. Who knew? Stokes should have been smarter than that, but Millett had pissed him off. Nothing Stokes could do about that now. But no goddamn way was he going down for this one. They were pretty sure he'd broken into a couple of houses over the past few weeks—and they were right, he had, trying to raise enough money to keep Frank Nickerson and his psycho sons off his back—but he absolutely was *not* going to let them lay this one on him, especially not if the homeowner ended up dying. Shit, there were other people in this town who could have pulled that job. Why were they picking on him? They had nothing but a suspicion. If they had more, they never would have let him go, not with the guy clinging to his life by a thread. And Millett wouldn't be here right now, in a desperate attempt to make Stokes say something stupid. Or maybe he hoped his steely glare would make Stokes crumble and confess. Well, he was going to be disappointed. He'd have to find someone else to pin this on.

"Look, Sergeant, you know me. Knew me growing up, maybe heard a few things about me around town since then. We both know I'm no angel, but I've never hurt anybody who didn't try to hurt me first. Check my sheet, ask around about me, you'll find that's true."

"First time for everything."

"You're trying to sweat the wrong guy. Meanwhile, the right guy's out there laughing his ass off at you. Now, you guys kicked me loose, so leave me alone."

"The guy you put in the hospital?" Millett said. "I've known him all my life. He and my father were best friends. He's my godfather. So you picked the wrong house last night, Stokes."

Well, that explained a few things.

"I didn't pick any house last night, Sergeant."

Millett tried the tough-guy-glare thing for a few more seconds. He actually wasn't bad at it. But when Stokes didn't wither under it, the cop sneered and looked Stokes up and down again. His eyes landed on Stokes's boots, which were still wet from his trudge through the stream. And his feet were still freezing.

"Where you coming from?" Millett asked.

"Sorry, but that's not your business."

Millett's jaw muscles twitched. Stokes stared back at him. At that moment, the cell phone, Paul Jenkins's goddamn cell phone, rang in Stokes's pocket. Had it really been an hour already? The phone rang again and Stokes must have reacted in some way, shown his anxiety, because Millett raised his eyebrows, smiled a little, and said, "You gonna answer that?"

"Up to me whether I do or not."

"Guess it is."

The phone rang a third time. Millett just stood there. Stokes looked at his watch. Straight up seven o'clock. Another ring. Stokes stepped to his left to move around Millett. Millett slid to his right to block his path. Stokes didn't bother trying to go back the other way. The phone rang a fifth time. Millett waited. Stokes took the phone from his pocket and flipped it open.

"Hello," he said, turning his back to the cop.

"Your hourly call, Jenkins," the kidnapper said.

"Thanks."

"Got the money yet?"

"I will soon."

"I know you will, because you got a pretty good idea what happens if you don't. Wanna talk to the kid?"

"Of course."

Stokes turned away again and started walking. He could hear Millett following him around the corner of his trailer. He could feel the cop's eyes on his back. Knew he was listening to every word Stokes said. When Stokes reached the other corner of his trailer, Millett sped up and stopped in front of him.

"Daddy?" the little girl said on the phone, her voice tinged with faint hope.

"No, it's still me," Stokes said, "but remember, you have to pretend I'm your daddy."

A brief pause. "OK . . . Daddy." Her voice was different from a moment ago, sadder. She'd hoped she'd be speaking with her father again. But she was smart enough to play along. He only hoped the kidnappers hadn't noticed her change in tone.

"Good girl," Stokes said, and Millett's eyebrows knitted. "Keep it up. This will all be over soon. I promise. Are you . . . OK?"

A sniffle. "I guess, Daddy. My hand hurts a lot, though."

"I'm sorry—"

Stokes heard a fumbling on the other end of the line, then the kidnapper said, "OK, Paul, are we—"

"What will all be over soon?" Millett asked.

"Who's that?" the kidnapper snapped.

"Nobody," Stokes said quickly. "Just some guy standing nearby. I'm in public right now."

"Who's that on the phone, Stokes?" Millett asked, too loudly.

"What'd he say?" the kidnapper asked. "Who the fuck is with you, Paul?"

"Jesus, nobody, all right, nobody." He was addressing both of them. "I'm just in public is all," he said into the phone.

The kidnapper was silent for a moment. "Just get the money. We'll be heading into the home stretch soon. Then you'll have your little girl back, almost as good as new. Talk to you in an hour."

Stokes closed the phone and slipped it into his pocket. Millett leaned back against the side of the trailer. "What's gonna be over soon?" he asked as he absently reached down and began drumming softly, steadily on the metal lid of the trash can beside him—the trash can where Stokes had stashed the money.

"Not your business, Sergeant."

"Who's the 'good girl' you were talking to?"

"What?"

"You said 'good girl.'" Millett noticed a crumpled piece of paper on the ground at his feet. He picked it up, uncrumpled it, and gave it a quick scan with his eyes. Stokes wasn't worried about what was on the paper. Probably a bill. More likely an overdue notice. Either way, he wasn't worried about what was on the paper. What he was worried about was what Millett was going to do with the paper, which he was crumpling again.

"This is my personal life, Sergeant."

He held out his hand for the ball of paper. Millett looked at the hand, then reached down and lifted the lid off the trash can. Stokes focused all of his energy on not letting his eyes stray to the bag of money that he knew was fully visible now.

"In fact," he continued, willing Millett's eyes to stay locked on his own, "this is my property you're standing on, not yours, so I'll have to ask you to get off it. My feet are cold and wet. I need to put on some dry socks. Have a good night."

He moved past the cop, hoping Millett's eyes would follow him. An agonizingly long moment later, he heard the clang of the lid dropping back onto the can, followed by Millett's footsteps behind him. As Stokes stepped up into his trailer, he expected to hear the cop say something like "I'll be watching you," but he said nothing. Probably thought it would sound like a cheesy line from a bad movie, which it would have. Stokes closed the door. When he parted the little curtain on the little window in his kitchen, he saw Millett walk over to his cruiser and lean against it, his eyes on the trailer.

Man, Stokes did not need this.

TWELVE

STOKES FORCED HIMSELF NOT TO look out through the trailer's curtains again. He didn't want Millett to see him looking. Didn't want to seem anxious. He was anxious as hell, of course. Anxious that Millett wouldn't leave soon, because Stokes still had a lot to do to help the kid. Anxious that the cop would get bored simply standing out there staring at the trailer, and might start poking around, eventually looking in the trash can where Stokes had hastily dumped the backpack stuffed with money. That probably would have been an illegal search, as the cans were on Stokes's property and not set out at a curb for pickup, but Stokes didn't think that little inconvenience would stop Millett. Anyway, Stokes didn't want to make Millett more suspicious than he already was, so he stayed away from the window, slipped into a pair of warm, dry socks, and popped the top of a Budweiser. Then he figured he should keep a clear head, so he finished only half of the beer—the first time he remembered ever doing that. While he puttered around, growing more anxious with every passing second, he listened intently for anything that sounded like Millett was rooting through his garbage. After fifteen minutes, he heard the powerful engine of the police cruiser as it roared to life, then listened as it grew fainter. Stokes peeked out the window and watched until the car's taillights disappeared around a bend in the dirt road. The second it was gone, he burst from the trailer and hurried around the corner to his trash cans. He tore off the lid of one can, panicked when he saw nothing but his garbage inside, then realized he'd dropped the bag in the other can, where he found it safe and sound.

Stokes shouldered the backpack and walked up the dirt road, past a few of his neighbors' places, and knocked on the metal door of one of the more dilapidated trailers in the park.

"Who's that?" a man inside asked, his voice deep and gruff.

"Since when am I psychic?" a woman responded.

The trailer's door opened. A woman stood in the doorway in dark-gray sweatpants and a light-gray sweatshirt that Stokes knew had once been white. She was in her early thirties and not too unattractive, despite the fact that her looks had passed their expiration date, which had come earlier for her than for a lot of women who didn't live life as hard and fast as she did. When she saw who had knocked on her door, her eyes widened and her mouth dropped.

"Who's there?" the man repeated.

She hesitated before blurting, "A neighbor."

"What's she want?"

"It's a he, and why don't you gimme a second so I can find out?" The look of surprise on her face was replaced by anger and confusion. "What the hell are you doin' here?" she said, keeping her voice low. "My husband's home, for Christ's sake."

"Relax, Joyce," Stokes said quietly. "I'm not here for that. I need a car."

"What?" Her face screwed up in greater confusion. Her eyes were squinted, and her mouth distorted into a squashed oval. Looking at that mouth, Stokes felt a moment of revulsion at the things he'd let it do.

"I need to borrow your car, OK? I'll have it back by morning."

"My husband's here, you moron."

Had she been this charming around lunchtime last Wednesday, while her husband was at work? If she had been, he hadn't noticed.

"Look," Stokes said, his voice barely above a whisper, "I wouldn't ask if it wasn't important."

The husband spoke again, his bass voice rumbling. "Joyce, who the hell is at the door and what does he want during my dinner-time?"

Looking at Joyce, listening to her talk, listening to her husband talk, Stokes realized that they should be on a poster somewhere for trailer trash. Most of the residents of the park were nice, decent people, people who had good, steady jobs, kept their homes neat, their little patches of lawn tidy, people who were just like most other people in their little neighborhoods full of houses—the main difference being that these people's homes could be hitched to a truck and driven away. But Joyce and her husband were walking punch lines of a hundred different trailer park jokes. Actually, that was why Stokes had taken up with Joyce in the first place. He couldn't have gone to any of the other reasonably attractive residents of the park for what he went to Joyce for. Stokes now saw a hard truth staring him down—he was far more like Joyce and her husband than he was like the more decent people in the park.

"Listen, Joyce," Stokes whispered, "I don't know anybody else here that well and I really need a car. It's an emergency, OK? What do you say?"

"It's Bobby's truck, not mine. You know that. I can't let you take it."

She'd been letting him take a lot more than that at least twice a month going on half a year now, but Stokes didn't point that out. He was about to ask again when footsteps sounded in the trailer. Bobby came around the corner. He stood about five five and wouldn't crack 140 on a scale with his pockets stuffed with rocks.

"Stokes?" he said. "It's late." His freakishly deep voice was as amusing as always, coming out of the tiny little mouth in his tiny little head.

"Yeah, sorry about that. But listen, Bobby, you got a truck, right? A pickup? I'd like to borrow it."

Bobby looked like he was trying to decide whether to just shut the door in Stokes's face or whether to laugh first. Before he could decide, Stokes spoke again.

"I'll give you forty bucks if you let me use it."

That got Bobby thinking. "I need that truck for work in the morning. Suppose you aren't back with it by then."

"I will be."

"Suppose you aren't."

"I will be. I'll be back by two this morning, three at the latest."

"Suppose you aren't."

Stokes wasn't sure what else to say. Bobby's record sort of got stuck on a groove there. Then, suddenly, he knew exactly what to say.

"Well, I suppose if for some reason I didn't get back in time, you'd have to call a cab, right? That might cost you another twenty bucks, I guess. Making it sixty total."

"Might cost me another forty."

"Forty for a cab? Don't you do body work at Tucker's place on Sycamore? What's that, a mile from here?"

Bobby shrugged. "Could be traffic."

Stokes sighed. "Eighty bucks then?"

"Plus there's the gas you'd be using tonight. My gas."

"Another twenty."

"Should cover it."

"So, a hundred?"

Bobby thought about it and nodded. Stokes could see he'd enjoyed sticking it to his neighbor. Which was fine, because Stokes had been having an OK time himself sticking it to *his* neighbor, who happened to be Bobby's wife.

"Get the key," he said. "I'll get the hundred from my trailer and come right back."

Bobby disappeared inside. Joyce winked at Stokes, which yesterday might have given him a little charge, and closed the door. He walked away, slipped behind a dark trailer nearby, and took out his wallet. Between what he had left of Tom-from-Pittsburgh's money and what he took from Paul Jenkins's wallet, there was a hundred forty-two bucks inside. He removed five twenties, waited long enough to make it seem like he'd gone all the way to his trailer and back, then walked over and knocked on Joyce and Bobby's door again. Bobby opened it. He held up a hand with a car key on a ring dangling from his finger. Stokes pushed the money into his free hand and reached for the key. Bobby pulled it up, out of Stokes's reach, which wasn't easy for a five-foot-five guy to do to a six-foot-two guy, but Bobby was up in his trailer and Stokes was a couple of steps below him. Bobby chuckled and handed the key to Stokes. The whole thing annoyed Stokes, and he thought he might come back and give the jerk's wife one more ride, even though he'd already decided he wasn't going to spend any more afternoons with Joyce.

Stokes turned without a word and headed over to Bobby's rusty, dented Ford F-150 pickup. Tossed the backpack in, got behind the wheel, turned the key, and was satisfied with the sound of a healthy engine. As he pulled away, he glanced over at Bobby, who was still standing in the doorway of his trailer. Joyce had joined him. He stood there with his little arm around the waist of his cheating wife. Stokes flipped him off.

THIRTEEN

IT WAS QUARTER TO EIGHT when Stokes pulled Bobby's truck over to the curb in front of Jenkins's modest house in his modest neighborhood. It was a two-story colonial, not terribly big. Probably had three bedrooms, two and a half baths. Definite fixer-upper that no one had gotten around to fixing up.

Stokes stared at the house and, for the first time, a question popped into his mind that probably should have popped into it hours before. Where was the kid's mother in all this? Was she sitting inside that house, waiting for her husband to bring their daughter home? Were they divorced? Did she even know about any of this? Or did she maybe die of some accident or disease a long time ago? Stokes looked at the dark windows of the house, too dark this early at night for anyone to be inside. He eased Bobby's pickup along the street and left it in front of the house two doors down, then walked back to Jenkins's house with the backpack slung over a shoulder.

He looked around, saw no one watching, and moved swiftly up the front walk. He knocked on the door, just to be sure. A moment later, he rang the bell to be doubly sure. He wasn't worried about an alarm system. This wasn't the neighborhood for it. And there weren't any alarm company stickers in the windows and no alarm company sign sticking out of the scraggly little plants by the front door. Still, he peeked in a window by the door, into the front hall, and was pleased not to see an alarm panel there. He slipped Jenkins's key—which he hoped was indeed his house key—into the lock and turned it. The door opened. Stokes stepped quickly into the house, shutting the door behind him. He moved into the living room and pulled the drapes closed, then walked back through the hall and did the same in the TV room. Then he flicked a switch on the wall, turning on a ceiling light. This wasn't the middle of the night. No one knew Jenkins wasn't coming home. Lights on in the house wouldn't look suspicious.

The house itself wasn't in the best shape, with old and faded wallpaper, worn carpets, and outdated lighting fixtures, but it was neat and clean. No junk lying around, no magazines scattered on the coffee table, no ashtrays full of cigarette butts on the end table. The TV remote sat on top of the television. Throw pillows were positioned neatly in each corner of the sofa. Either Jenkins had a maid, which he didn't appear to be able to afford, or he and his daughter kept the place well. Stokes saw a bookshelf in one corner, an array of kid's toys tidily lined up on its shelves—pink things, cuddly things, colorful things—and he remembered why he was there. Seeing the toys made the weight he was carrying a little heavier, and he wasn't thinking about the backpack he'd been lugging around all day. He looked at a stuffed panda on the bookshelf and was reminded of the girl's ragged stuffed frog.

He saw the girl's face again, dimpled, smiling this time, not scared at all—saw it on top of the bookshelf where a row of pictures of her stretched from one side to the other. She was grinning in each one. One looked like it was taken in a park. Another at a birthday party. In yet another she stood ankle deep in the surf in a pink floral one-piece bathing suit, squinting in the bright sun, mugging for the camera. And there she was as a baby with a smiling brunette, probably her mother. And in another one she was a little older, sitting on the knee of an attractive blonde. Maybe *that* was her mother and the brunette was an aunt, though the brunette's hair color was closer to the little girl's. And there were more pictures on the wall. A baby picture, the little girl on a pony, the girl standing beside a snowman twice her height. The goddamn snowman had an honest-to-God carrot for a nose. In most of the shots, she was with the blonde again, who must have been her mother after all. And naturally there were a few of Jenkins with his daughter, the two of them smiling wide. He wondered who took those pictures. In them, the ones with her father, the girl seemed to be smiling the brightest. Or maybe that was Stokes's imagination. Either way, he felt a pang of guilt.

He heard her little voice again. *Are you coming to take me home?*

No, kid, he's not. But I'm working on it.

He got busy. He was looking for three things. First, he hoped to find whatever evidence Jenkins had on the kidnappers. And since he didn't have the slightest idea what that might be, he hoped it would be in a big file with the word "Evidence" stamped on it in red capital letters. Failing that, he had to hope he'd find something that looked to Stokes's admittedly untrained eye to be evidence of . . . well, of some kind of wrongdoing. He was a shady character himself, so he might be able to recognize something like that. Second, he was looking for something, anything that might tell him the location of the pay phone where he was supposed to be at 1:30 a.m. to receive final details from the kidnappers. Third, he was looking for a $102,000, though he didn't have high hopes of finding it in the couch cushions or under a mattress.

Stokes started in the living room, pulling open drawers, checking the sofa, searching the bookshelf, looking anywhere Jenkins might have intentionally placed or accidentally dropped a piece of paper with the pay phone's address on it, or where he could have hidden evidence of some kind. No luck. He searched the TV room with the same result. And everywhere he looked, more pictures of the girl.

In the hall closet, he searched coat pockets. He didn't see any women's coats, which told him that the girl's mother didn't live there. He moved quickly. He could practically hear a clock ticking. Leaving the closet, he passed an ancient grandmother clock and realized that he *had* been hearing a clock ticking.

In the kitchen, he checked every drawer and cabinet, looked at every scrap of paper stuck by magnets to the avocado-green refrigerator, or by thumbtack to a little bulletin board above the toaster, and didn't find what he was looking for. He tried to ignore the cute little drawing of a cowgirl riding a dinosaur the girl had made with crayons. Stokes even lifted the lid on the trash can in the corner and dug around through Jenkins's garbage until he was satisfied that he hadn't written the address down and later thrown it away. Nothing. He struck out in the downstairs bathroom, too.

He took the stairs two at a time, realizing he had to move faster. Bathroom at the top of the stairs. Low priority at this point. To his right, Jenkins's bedroom. He searched it quickly but thoroughly and found nothing—no evidence, no pay phone address, no money . . . unless he counted the seventy-two cents in change he found on Jenkins's nightstand next to yet another framed photo of Jenkins with his daughter. Stokes pocketed the coins and moved on. He decided the master bathroom was also a low priority and skipped it for now.

His hopes rose when he entered a second bedroom, which Jenkins used as an office. He rifled through the desk and a filing cabinet and, unfortunately, didn't come across the pay phone's address or anything remotely resembling evidence of anything. He likewise failed to find $102,000. He flicked on the computer, saw that it needed a password, and turned it off again. He didn't know anything about computers.

Damn it.

He sighed. One last door off the hall. One last room left to search. Had to be the little girl's bedroom. If he struck out in there—and it didn't seem likely that Jenkins would leave the location of the pay phone in his daughter's room—then Stokes would have no choice. He'd have to come right out and ask the kidnapper in the next phone call where he was supposed to be at one thirty. He could pretend to have written it down and lost the paper, forgotten the address. It would look suspicious, but he was running out of options. He needed to—

His thoughts were interrupted by the cell phone ringing in his pocket. He automatically glanced at his watch. Eight o'clock on the dot.

Wherever you are now, Paul, Stokes thought, *you're killing me with all these phone calls.*

He opened the phone. "Yeah," he said.

"You holding up OK?" the kidnapper asked.

"You care?" Stokes spoke more freely, figuring that if his voice hadn't yet alerted them that he wasn't Paul Jenkins, it wasn't going to. They'd talked enough times that it was probably *his* voice now, and not Jenkins's, that they associated with the girl's father.

"Watch yourself, Paul. We still have your little girl. We could hurt her again."

"Sorry," Stokes said quickly. Again, he knew what was expected of him. "Let me talk to the kid."

Silence. Stokes immediately realized his mistake.

"The '*kid*?'" the voice on the line said.

Stokes tried to recover. "Yeah, my daughter," he said quickly. "Let me talk to her."

A pause. "Your daughter."

This wasn't going well. "Yeah, let me talk to her. That's the deal, right?"

Another pause. "Paul, is this really you?"

Oh, shit.

"Of course it is. Now I want to talk to my daughter." He needed to do better here, to fix this. He tried for bluster. "So help me God, if you've hurt her—"

"We already hurt her, Paul. You know that. Or should, anyway. The question is, how much more do we hurt her."

Stokes realized he was sweating. His heart was beating like a ferret's.

"Please, let me talk to her."

"Who?"

"My daughter."

"Your daughter?"

"Yeah, my daughter."

"What's her name?"

"What?"

"Tell me your daughter's name, Paul. Simple question, you gotta admit."

Oh, God. He had no idea. Was it Ellie? No, that was Stokes's real daughter, and she'd be in high school now. What the hell was Jenkins's daughter's name?

"Hell," the kidnapper continued, "even if you're actually a cop or FBI agent you'd know her name. So who the hell are you?"

"I'm her father," Stokes said as he strode the final few feet down the hall toward what he now prayed was the kid's room and pushed open the door.

"Paul—if that's really your name—I'm waiting. And I'm picking up a knife."

Stokes looked frantically around the room. Definitely the little girl's room. Pink shit all over the place. Dolls on the bed. Stuffed animals in a corner. Posters on the wall of ponies and puppies.

"Time's up, Paul. I'm hanging up now."

"Amanda," Stokes blurted.

He saw the name stenciled in primary colors on a toy chest in one corner. Amanda. The first "A" was green, the "M" was red, the second "A" was yellow, the "N" was blue, and so forth. Amanda. Please, God, let it be Amanda. Please don't let that toy chest be something Jenkins picked up from a thrift shop and hadn't bothered to stencil his own kid's name on.

After a long moment, the kidnapper said, "Good guess."

"Come on, I know my own daughter's name. I just got flustered. I'm under a lot of pressure here. This is all pretty stressful, you know."

Stokes became dimly aware of the sound of a car door closing nearby. Then another.

The kidnapper was quiet.

"Let me talk to Amanda," Stokes demanded.

"In a minute." Silence again.

The pleasant chime of a doorbell sounded in the foyer, floated up the stairs and down the hall to Stokes. He moved to the window overlooking the front lawn and saw a police cruiser in the driveway. He'd heard two car doors closing, meaning there were two cops standing on the porch right now. Two cops who'd seen a bunch of lights on in the house and who therefore would surmise that someone was inside.

Stokes's mind started spinning like it was on a carnival's Tilt-A-Whirl. They must have found Jenkins's car. Had the teenagers he'd threatened in the woods ignored his warning and spilled their guts? No, probably not. If the police knew Jenkins was dead for certain, and that somebody had threatened three teenagers and then apparently stolen Jenkins's body, and then they came and saw lights on in his house, they'd be a lot more forceful in their approach. Who knew? Maybe the teens' mother had indeed called the cops. But Stokes believed that the kids had kept their mouths shut so far. He also believed that the cops hadn't yet found Jenkins's body. But they definitely had identified Jenkins's car somehow. Knew it was his, but they didn't know where Jenkins was.

The doorbell rang again. The cops would wonder why whoever was in the house and using all the lights wasn't answering the door. Then they'd think about the blood in Jenkins's car. Then they'd kick down the door.

Or they'd just turn the knob and walk in, because Stokes hadn't locked it behind him.

"Paul?" the kidnapper said in his ear. "Got a question for you."

The doorbell rang a third time. It was immediately followed by a loud knocking, which in turn was followed by a cop yelling, "Police, open up."

"Paul, if that's really you, are you still there?"

"Is anyone there?" one of the cops called.

"I'm here," Stokes said into the phone as he turned and fled Amanda's room. He ran down the hall and into Jenkins's bedroom just as the front door opened downstairs.

Stokes could picture the cops downstairs. Eyes scanning the rooms, hands on their guns, or maybe they had their guns drawn already. Thick, muscular young men, top students at the academy, young but up-and-coming in the department, crack shots with their weapons. Stokes slipped into the master bathroom and closed the door behind him to help hide any sound he was going to make. He moved to the window he'd seen when he peeked in here a few minutes ago. He tried to raise it but found it difficult to do with the phone in one hand.

"Here's my question, Paul," the kidnapper said.

"Listen, can I call you right back?"

"No."

Stokes tucked the phone into the crook of his neck, against his shoulder, and tugged with both hands at the window, which stubbornly refused to rise. He heard heavy footsteps clomping around downstairs. He knew they'd clomp up the stairs at any moment.

"Can you call me back in a couple of minutes then?"

"I thought you wanted to talk to Amanda. Now you want me to call you back. Doesn't sound like a concerned father to me."

He heard the cops' voices again. Might have been right at the bottom of the stairs. Stokes still struggled with the window sash.

"Let me talk to her, then," he said.

"Like I said, I got a question first."

The window flew up suddenly, less quietly than Stokes had been shooting for. He didn't think the sound had carried far, though. He raised the screen and peered out and saw roof just a few feet below him.

"OK," he said as quietly as he dared without making the kidnapper suspicious, but as loudly as he dared without alerting the cops to his presence. "What's your question?"

"OK, Paul, tell me . . . what's the song you sing to Amanda every night when you tuck her in bed?"

"Huh?"

"Amanda says you make up your own silly words to a certain tune. So what's the tune?"

The question brought Stokes up short. He was about to start climbing out the window. He stopped for a moment. *Oh, no.*

"Paul?"

"Hold on a second," he said quietly. "I didn't catch that. Bad reception, I guess. Let me move a little."

He put the phone on the top of the toilet, next to the backpack, and climbed up on the toilet seat. He thought he heard footsteps on the stairs. Not racing up, but climbing stealthily. He climbed out onto the roof and reached back inside for the bag and cell phone.

When he had them, he pulled the window down and lowered the screen, leaving it open half an inch. He crept as quietly as he could away from the window. The roof's pitch wasn't too bad, so he was confident enough of his footing. He turned a corner of the house and climbed to the roof's peak, out of sight of the window. He could just see the police cruiser in the driveway. He sat on the peak with the phone to his ear and the backpack in his lap.

"You there?" he asked into the phone.

"I'm here. How's the reception?"

"Better. Are we finished here? Can I talk to Amanda now?"

"You still haven't answered my question. I've got a problem, see? I heard from a reliable source that your car was found in the woods, smashed to hell. There was blood all over. But no Paul Jenkins. They tell me you might have got knocked silly, wandered off into the woods. So I've gotta wonder what happened, right? Whether you might be dead. And if you are, then who the fuck am I talking to, right? Who the fuck have I been talking to for the last few hours?"

The bad news was that this pretty much guaranteed that the kidnappers had a source inside the police department at least, and if they'd been telling the truth about that, they might have been telling the truth about having a source in the FBI, too. The good news, though, was that they seemed willing to believe that Paul Jenkins was still alive and that Stokes was, indeed, Jenkins . . . as long as he was able to prove it.

"You see my problem, Paul?"

"Sure," Stokes said. "Yeah, I had a car crash. Some idiot ran me off the road. I've been walking all day. Satisfied?"

"Not at all. You keep avoiding my question."

Damn it. "What was it again?"

"The tune you sing to Amanda every night, making up silly words."

"Oh, yeah."

Stokes's mind was back on the Tilt-A-Whirl, whipping around, spinning, dipping, twirling—

"Paul? I think we're done here."

Stokes had seen something. In the girl's room. He knew he had. If he could just remember.

"Bye, whoever the fuck you are. I'm gonna cut the kid's throat now."

"Wait—"

The line went dead.

Jesus Christ. The kidnapper hung up.

Stokes sat with the silent phone at his ear for a moment, irrationally hoping he'd somehow hear the kidnapper's voice again.

What have I done?

He lowered the phone and stared at it.

Jesus Christ, I've killed her.

Stokes heard the front door close. He sat, staring stupidly at the phone.

I should have just gone to the cops. Should have taken my chances and gone to the cops, told them about all this, let them handle it. Maybe their inside man would have been off duty or out on a call or something. At least the kid might have had a chance. At least—

Voices from below jolted Stokes back into the moment. He crab-walked quickly away from the peak, out of the sight line of anyone below. When the phone rang in his hand, he snapped it open halfway through its first trill and prayed the cops below hadn't heard it.

"Hello? Hello?" he half whispered. "I'm here. Hello?"

Stokes heard car doors open and close. A powerful engine rumbled to life.

"Are you there?" Stokes asked desperately.

A moment of silence on the line. "I'm here."

Stokes almost sighed with relief but realized that this call might have been made to inform him that Amanda was dead. Stokes watched the police car pull out of the driveway and head off down the street.

Stokes took a breath. "Did you . . . is Amanda OK? Please, tell me you didn't . . ."

"Not yet. We figured maybe you really are just nervous, having bad cell reception, whatever. So you get one more chance. Now answer my question."

"Your question?"

"You really do want her dead, don't you? Tell me the name of the tune you sing to her at night with your stupid made-up lyrics."

Stokes closed his eyes and brought the girl's room to his mind again. There had to be something—

"Paul? Time's up."

"We sing a lot of songs, OK? Just give me a second."

The kidnapper sighed. Sounded like he was disappointed. "I really didn't want to have to do this. Good-bye."

"Twinkle, Twinkle, Little Star," Stokes blurted, suddenly remembering the glow-in-the-dark, star-shaped stickers stuck to the ceiling above her bed and the star-shaped night-light on her bed table. It had been nothing more than a guess. A guess met with silence. Stokes held his breath.

Finally, the kidnapper spoke. "Hold on."

Stokes heard muffled voices on the other end of the line, then the kidnapper was back on again.

"OK, here's another one. What's her favorite stuffed animal?"

Stokes pictured the room again. He wanted to go back inside and look around but he knew the kidnapper wouldn't let him stall long enough to get there.

"Paul? Her favorite stuffed animal. She says it's on her bed at home right now."

Stokes blinked sweat from his eyes. He tried to remember what stuffed animals he'd seen on her bed. A duck, maybe? And he thought there might have been an elephant. Possibly. *Shit.*

A couple of seconds ticked by. Though he needed to concentrate on nothing but the question before him, nothing but Amanda's favorite stuffed animal, he couldn't help but think that the cops would be back soon. He'd left the lights on in the house, the front door unlocked. And Jenkins's car was wrecked and he'd disappeared. Yeah, the cops would be back. He needed to get away from there.

"Oh well," the kidnapper said, "you can't say we didn't give you a chance."

"Her favorite stuffed animal?" Stokes asked.

"Yeah."

Stokes was about to try to buy more time, as risky as it was, time to run through the things he'd seen in her room again, when he blurted, "Her stuffed frog."

Stokes hoped he was right. He remembered the tattered stuffed frog Amanda was clutching in the photograph of her with her father, the one the kidnappers had sent to Paul and that Stokes still had in his backpack. And she was clutching the same frog in the videos the kidnappers had texted to the phone Stokes was carrying. The stuffed toy was ragged and worn. It had clearly been hugged and dragged and cuddled and slept with for years. It wasn't in her room. It was with Amanda right now. It was a trick question. At least Stokes hoped it was.

"OK, Paul. You got that one. One more question, just to be sure. What's Amanda's favorite food?"

"Chicken noodle soup," Stokes answered immediately, recalling the inordinate number of cans of chicken noodle soup he'd seen while searching the kitchen cabinets. Had to be two dozen of them, stored neatly in stacks and rows.

After a moment of silence, a moment that stretched longer than Stokes was comfortable with, the kidnapper said, "OK, good enough. But you've got to get your shit together, Paul. Sounds like you're starting to lose it. Here's Amanda."

Stokes closed his eyes and exhaled.

"Daddy?" the girl said. Her voice still hadn't regained the enthusiasm of the first conversations, when she still thought she was speaking with her father, but she was trying. Stokes had to give her that.

"Good girl, Amanda," Stokes said. "You'll be home soon, OK? Be brave."

"I will."

Then the kidnapper had the phone again. "By the way, Paul, I hope you'll be able to get your hands on another car later. You'll need one."

"I will." After a second, he added, "I'm going to borrow a friend's."

"Good. It's almost over. Everything goes smoothly, Amanda's with you at two thirty this morning, just six and a half hours from now."

Stokes wanted to ask the address of the pay phone, but he knew he couldn't now. Any hope he'd had of asking had gone out the window when he'd aroused such serious suspicion in the kidnappers. Though they'd moved on, they might be harboring lingering doubts about him. He couldn't do anything to fuel their suspicion further.

Stokes realized the kidnapper was still speaking. "I mean, your daughter will be in your arms as soon as we get the evidence and the money, of course. You'll have the money, right?"

"I will," he said, knowing full well that he was no closer to figuring out where to be at one thirty, no closer to finding the evidence, and no closer to coming up with the 102 grand he was short on the ransom.

FOURTEEN

STOKES KNEW THERE WAS A good chance the cops would return to Jenkins's house soon. They'd searched the place quickly but must not have found anything suspicious, or they'd have stuck around, called for backup. Fortunately, Stokes hadn't ransacked the house as he searched. He'd opened drawers, then closed them, opened kitchen cabinets, then closed them. No one would know he'd even been there, unless they dusted for prints later. Which they might. They'd certainly be back, though, when they found Jenkins's body. Possibly even sooner.

He was about to stand, to make his way down from the roof of Jenkins's house, when he looked up into the sky. It was a clear fall night. It was peaceful up here. He wished he could just sit down, forget all this. Better yet, take the money to the airport and fly to Mexico. There were a hell of a lot of stars up there tonight. It was so quiet he could have fallen asleep right where he was. He hadn't realized how exhausted he was, how the events of the day had worn him down. It was peaceful up on the roof. He couldn't hear ticking, though he knew time was pressing on. And he didn't hear Amanda's voice at the moment. Or Ellie's. He looked at his watch. He knew he should get moving again soon, but he had no idea where to go. Or what to do.

He couldn't remember when he'd seen so many stars. He couldn't recall the last time he'd really looked at them.

Amanda liked to hear the "Twinkle, Twinkle, Little Star" tune. Her father sang it to her before bed every night, substituting silly words for the real lyrics. He smiled. Her dead father. Who Stokes had killed. He stopped smiling. It was an accident, but he'd killed him nonetheless.

It was a clear night. He wondered if Amanda could see the stars from wherever she was. Stokes looked up at them, pinpricks of light in the black night. He recognized a few of the constellations. Pisces, Andromeda, Cassiopeia. He looked at a few other groups of stars, remembered his father pointing out the constellations they made. Rags the Dog over there. Quackers the Duck. Toots the Train. Stokes recalled being very young, looking for his father a few times to say good night, finding him sitting in a lawn chair in their dark, weed-choked backyard, smelling like beer. He'd ask about the stars, and his old man would point out the constellations. The Shovel. The Boot. Bozo the Clown. Stokes thought he still might be able to find some of them. But he knew now that his father had made them up. Not to entertain his son with goofy, fake constellations, the way Paul Jenkins made up silly lyrics for Amanda, but because it amused him to lie to his kid. He was drunk and he'd tell Stokes the name of another con-stellation and he'd chuckle to himself. And Stokes believed him. He believed him because five-year-old kids believe their dads. It wasn't until a few years later, after his father was long gone, that he learned the truth. The man knew the names of three constellations. The oth-ers were lies, like many things he'd told Stokes when he was a boy, including "This hurts me more than it does you" and "I'm just head-ing to the store for some smokes, I'll be back soon."

Stokes knew that if it hadn't been for his mother, he probably would have grown up to be a truly screwed-up individual—well, even more screwed up than he was.

He sat up. Hmmm. He grabbed the backpack by a strap, made his way back to the bathroom window, and crawled inside.

He hurried down the stairs and into the living room, where he remembered seeing a few faux leather photo albums lined up on a bookshelf. He pulled one out and flipped through. Mostly they were pictures of Amanda, or of Amanda and Jenkins together. Beneath every photo was a caption made with a label maker. Good old organized Paul. There were captions like "Amanda—first day of kindergarten" and "Amanda and Daddy—camping on Memorial Day weekend." Stokes flipped quickly through the pages before moving on to a second album. As soon as he opened that one, he hit pay dirt. The first picture was of a slightly younger Paul with a slightly younger Amanda on his shoulders. Beside him was a pretty blonde, the same one he'd seen before. The caption read, "Mommy, Daddy, and Amanda at the zoo." Stokes looked at little Amanda's dark, curly locks and figured she must have gotten her hair from her dark-haired father.

The next photo in the album was the one Paul needed. It was of just Paul and the woman. They were sweaty and tanned, holding drinks in their hands. According to the caption, this was "Paul and Nancy in New Mexico." Amanda's mother's name was Nancy. Maybe she knew something about all of this. Even if they were divorced, would Paul have left her completely in the dark about their daughter being in such danger? Maybe he told her where he had to be at one thirty, just in case something went wrong, in case he didn't come home, in case someone had to go look for him.

Stokes hurried back upstairs to Jenkins's office. He opened a drawer where he'd seen credit card bills and bank statements, neatly organized, bound with rubber bands. He pulled Paul's checkbook from the top desk drawer and flipped through it. If the woman were dead, he'd find nothing. If she were alive, he'd find—

And there it was. A September 28 entry in the check registry for check number 932, written for six hundred dollars. Next to the dollar amount, Paul had written "Nancy—October alimony." He picked up the phone on Jenkins's desk and dialed local directory information, asked for a Nancy Jenkins. The operator checked without success, broadened her search, then informed Stokes that there was no one by that name in this area code. So Stokes knew she'd either moved out of the area or changed her name. He dug into the drawer again, came out with Jenkins's bank statements. They were stored in their envelopes. He looked at the postmark for the most recent statement. October 14. He opened the envelope and pulled out the statement. As he'd hoped, Jenkins's bank returned his canceled checks to him. Leave it to superorganized Paul Jenkins to pay an extra fee for the service. Stokes thumbed through the checks, found number 932. It was made out, in extraordinarily neat handwriting, to Nancy Filoso. Maiden name, most likely, or perhaps she'd remarried.

Stokes opened the top drawer of the desk again and removed Jenkins's leather address book. He turned to the *F*s and found Nancy's address and phone number. Stokes finally had some good luck. She lived in town, just a few miles away. Hey, he wasn't half-bad at this. Like a TV detective, maybe.

He hoped to hell Nancy and her ex-husband were still close, that he had told her what was going on. Stokes feared that he might not have wanted to worry her, that he'd planned to bring their daughter home without her knowing of the danger their little girl was in until it was over and Amanda was home safe and sound. But maybe he did tell her something. And maybe, if Stokes was really, really lucky, she had some money lying around for emergencies. Either way, Stokes had nowhere else to turn, no other ideas.

He peeked through the curtains, hoping he wouldn't see cops out there. He didn't. He walked downstairs, left the lights on, the way the cops had seen them, and walked out the front door, down the walk, and up the block to Bobby's pickup.

On the drive to Nancy Filoso's house, he dialed her number on the cell phone the kidnappers had provided. A woman answered and Stokes asked for Ms. Filoso. She said that she was Ms. Filoso. He said, "Well, Nancy Filoso, your name was selected at random to receive a free weekend at a time-share in North Carolina." The woman stopped him, saying that she had no interest in time-shares. Stokes hung up. He wasn't going to be able to sell her a time-share in North Carolina, but at least he knew she was at home tonight. And he'd found that out without having to tell her over the phone that her ex-husband was dead, which she certainly didn't know, or that her daughter had been kidnapped, which she may or may not have known.

———

Nancy Filoso's house was less than three miles from where Paul Jenkins lived. It was a small ranch, looked like a two-bedroom from the outside, in a lower-middle-class neighborhood. The house and yard were immaculate. The white picket fence out front gleamed brightly in the moonlight, as though it had been painted just that afternoon. The lawn and flower beds were well tended.

Stokes left Bobby's pickup at the curb instead of pulling into the gravel driveway and walked up to the house along a walkway where not a single weed poked through the cracks between the bricks. He rang the bell and looked at his watch: 8:37. He rang the bell again and was rewarded with the sound of footsteps from inside. Stokes detected movement to his left and saw a little curtain flutter in a narrow window beside the door. A moment later, he heard the clack of a lock disengaging and the door opened just an inch or two, not even as far as the security chain would allow. A woman's eye peered through the crack. It was bright blue and opened wide.

"Are you hurt?" the woman—presumably Nancy—asked.

"Am I—huh?"

"Did you have an accident? I can call 911 for you."

"I don't know what . . ." He trailed off. He remembered the blood on his shirt. He should have changed it back at his trailer. "Oh, the blood, yeah. It's not mine."

Nancy's eye squinted in confusion. And suspicion.

"Whose is it?"

"It's your husband's. I mean, your ex-husband's. Your ex-husband Paul's."

The eye went wide again. The one he couldn't see probably did, too.

"God, has something happened to Paul?" She hesitated. "Did . . . did you hurt him?"

"No," Stokes said quickly and a tad untruthfully. "No, no, no. But we need to talk about him. About Paul. And your daughter."

Stokes heard her gasp. He was botching this badly. He knew she'd be freaked out, but he didn't want her to freak out until after he was inside, when she couldn't just slam a door in his face if she wanted, when she'd have to hear him out at least a little. But he'd mentioned her daughter, which was sure to get her worked up.

"Listen, if you've hurt Amanda—"

"Jesus, no, I didn't. I swear. Please, just let me in. I think . . ." He paused, unsure if he should say it. He probably shouldn't. Not like this. But he did. "I think your daughter may be in danger. Please, let me in."

"Danger?" Panic was bleeding into her voice. "I'm calling the police."

"Bad idea," Stokes said quickly. "That could get her killed."

"What are you saying? You'd hurt a six-year-old—"

"I'm trying to tell you," he said desperately, "it's not me. I just want to help."

The eye appraised him for a long moment before the door finally closed. Stokes heard the chain slide free, then the door opened again.

The photo of Nancy Filoso at Paul Jenkins's house hadn't really done her justice. Clear blue eyes and honey-gold hair. She wasn't even wearing makeup—she was, however, wearing an unflattering, baggy flannel nightshirt—yet she was still sexy. She wasn't necessarily beautiful in a cover girl way—more like the girl next door, which was a phrase Stokes had heard enough times but never really understood because no girl like this ever lived next door to him.

He realized he was nearly on the verge of staring. She was standing to one side of the doorway, waiting for him to enter the house. He did, moving past her, through the door, which opened right into the living room of the small home.

"Please," she said, the word cracking with emotion. "Is Amanda in danger? What happened to Paul?"

"Can we sit down?"

"Can't you just tell me—"

"Sit down first, OK?"

She hesitated, her pretty face a portrait of worry.

"Please," he said. "Just have a seat."

"But Amanda—"

"Just sit, OK? Please."

She blew out a breath, nodded, and walked quickly into the living room. Stokes instinctively checked out her ass as she did. It didn't disappoint. She shoved aside a jacket that had been flung over the back of an armchair. As she did, her bottom moved out of Stokes's view, so he looked casually around the room. The neat and clean state of the yard and exterior of the house didn't extend inside.

Nancy Filoso wasn't nearly the housekeeper her ex was, and Stokes wondered idly whether this had led to some of the arguments that ultimately drove them apart. In addition to the jacket carelessly tossed on the chair, there were stacks of magazines and newspapers littering the coffee table, a pile of unfolded laundry on the sofa, an empty glass on an end table, and of the only photos in the room— three framed pictures of flowers that hung in a row on a wall—not a single one hung straight. Then he was back to checking out her ass as she moved the laundry to the floor. She motioned him to the now-empty armchair. She took the sofa. Stokes slid his backpack from his shoulder and placed it on the floor at his feet.

"Now, please," she said. "This is driving me crazy. Please tell me what's going on." He thought her hands might have been shaking. She looked close to tears.

He nodded. Took a breath. No easy way to do this. "Your husband, I mean your ex-husband, is dead."

Surprise and horror took over her face. He felt awful, and that was without her knowing that *he* had caused Paul's death. He hoped she never would. He certainly wasn't going to tell her.

"This is his blood," Stokes said.

"My God . . . Paul."

"There was an accident," he said, "a car accident. Paul swerved to avoid, uh, someone coming the other way . . . or something . . . and, well, he hit a tree. Killed him right away, I'm sure. I doubt he suffered. The car was pretty badly—uh, anyway, I don't think he suffered."

"What about Amanda?" Nancy said, her voice shaking. "You said she's in danger. Was she in the car?"

"Oh, shit, no. Shit, I'm sorry, no. I'm pretty sure she's OK."

"Pretty sure?" She was nervously rubbing her hands up and down her thighs, and her nightshirt had ridden up just a little. Stokes realized he was probably going to hell for noticing that at a moment like this. Of course, he was bound for hell anyway, once his ticket was punched.

"Really," he said quickly, "I think she's OK. She wasn't in the car, I mean. She's not dead. Paul was alone in the car."

"I'm not getting you," she said desperately. "Amanda wasn't in the car, but she's in danger? Help me understand this, *please*. Where is she? What danger? Just tell me what's going on."

Stokes sucked in a breath, tried to gather his thoughts so he could lay out the situation clearly and concisely. "She's been kidnapped."

And he thought she'd looked frightened before. "*Oh my God. Kidnapped? Amanda?*"

"I guess you didn't know, then."

"No, I . . . . Why would anyone kidnap Amanda? I don't . . . What do they want? Do you know what they want?"

"They want this," he said, nudging the backpack in front of his chair with his foot. The bag fell over and a few stacks of bills tumbled out. Thousand-dollar bills. Nancy's eyes were wide. Stokes leaned down and shoved the bills back in.

Nancy opened her mouth to speak and the doorbell rang. Stokes looked at Nancy. She looked back, confused. She obviously wasn't expecting anyone.

"Who is it?" she called.

"It's the police, ma'am."

Oh, shit.

Stokes leaped to his feet, and words started streaming out of him like water from a fire hose. "They've found your husband's car, look, you have to trust me, your daughter's in danger, she's been kidnapped, and I'll explain it all to you after the cops leave, but you can't tell them about me, or your daughter, and you have to pretend you haven't heard about Paul because you shouldn't know about that yet, you have to pretend you think he's still alive because they can't know that he's not, and you definitely can't tell them about me, because if you do, or you tell them about your daughter being kidnapped, then Amanda will be in even more danger, but I have the ransom money Paul was going to pay them, it's in this bag, and I'm gonna use it to get her back, so don't worry about that, and oh, by the way, your husband's body wasn't with the car when the cops found it, I moved it, the body, not the car, and I'll explain that later, too, but you really do have to trust me, so please just listen to the cops, act surprised and upset, which you obviously are, and get rid of them as soon as you can because time is running out on me here, running out on me and on your daughter."

He paused and looked at her and tried to catch his breath.

A polite knock at the door. "Ma'am, please open up. I need to speak with you."

Nancy looked at the door, then back at Stokes. He felt her blue eyes sizing him up, which was never a good thing for him.

"I know you have no reason to trust me," he said quickly, quietly, and urgently, "but you gotta believe me. I want to help Amanda, but if you tell the cops any of this, I can't. And this is real serious. They might kill her. Please, believe me."

The bell rang again.

"Kill her?" she said in a strangled whisper.

"We don't have time for this. What's it gonna be?"

"Ma'am?" the cop at the door said. "Are you OK in there?"

Nancy was clearly torn. Stokes tried hard to look sincere. He had no idea if he was pulling it off, but he doubted it, seeing as he hadn't had much practice being sincere and therefore had no idea how he looked the few times that he actually was.

"Please, Nancy, you don't know what I've been through just to be here right now. I want to get Amanda back, and I need your help with that."

The bell rang again.

Nancy struggled with indecision.

He pleaded with his eyes. She looked like she desperately wanted to trust him.

Finally, she nodded.

"Go into the kitchen. There's a pantry by the fridge. You can hide in there. I'll hear them out, play dumb, answer their questions, and let you know when they're gone. And then you need to make me understand exactly why I sent them away instead of telling them all of this, or I'll call them right back."

He exhaled in relief as he bolted for the kitchen. He saw the pantry, right where it was supposed to be, and slipped inside. He pulled the door nearly shut, leaving it open a couple of inches.

Thank God she believed him. He knew he sounded crazy. Must have looked it, too—disheveled, with blood on his shirt, probably a wild look in his eyes.

The bell rang again, followed by a loud knocking. He thought he even heard the cop call to her again. Why the hell didn't she just open the damn door already?

Just when Stokes thought maybe she went to put on some clothes or something, she finally let the cop in. He could barely hear her voice, apologizing for taking so long, explaining that she'd been about to step into the shower. Then he heard a man's voice, a cop introducing himself. Apparently, he was alone. He was explaining how they'd found her husband's car. There was a lot of blood in it but no Paul. And someone had worked hard to make it difficult for them to identify the car, so it looked like foul play. He was just starting to ask another question when he stopped, seemed to be listening for a moment, then spoke quietly, too quietly for Stokes to hear what he was saying.

Stokes frowned. He pushed the pantry door open another few inches, leaned his head out to hear better. And he heard Nancy speaking, her voice soft, her tone urgent.

"He's got blood on him," she was saying, "and he said it was Paul's. He probably killed him. He's hiding in the kitchen right now."

Thanks a shitload, Nancy.

FIFTEEN

"I THINK HE MIGHT BE dangerous," Stokes heard Nancy say to the cop at her door.

Stokes may not have been the quickest thinker around, but two options came to him in a blink: he could either run for it, burst from Nancy's pantry, fly out the back door, and hope he could lose the cop as he raced on foot through the neighborhood, or alternatively, he could take the offensive, which is what he did without making a conscious choice. It was just instinct—an instinct that wouldn't let him run away without the quarter of a million dollars sitting in the backpack in the living room with Nancy and the police officer.

He bolted from the pantry and was through the kitchen in four strides. He'd come without warning and was moving fast. Nancy hadn't expected it. The cop hadn't yet understood the situation. And suddenly there was Stokes, all 190 pounds of him, charging across the living room. The cop—thank God there was indeed only one—looked up at the last second and reached for his belt, where he had all sorts of things that could hurt Stokes—things like a baton, pepper spray, and, of course, a gun—but Stokes was on him before his hand found any of those things. Stokes lowered his shoulder and slammed into the cop, a little like a linebacker, but more like a guy who had experience fighting his way out of trouble. His shoulder plowed into the cop's chest and the impact knocked the man back into the closed front door. His head smacked off the solid wood with an ugly sound, and he slid to the carpet. Stokes threw a punch that he realized only a split second after it landed was unnecessary. The impact of the guy's head with the door had knocked him unconscious. The punch, which landed on the poor bastard's cheek, had been overkill. And now Stokes's whole hand stung. He turned to Nancy.

"Nancy, what the hell?"

The woman backed up a step, her eyes wide with fear, and stumbled over a pair of her shoes. She landed hard on her ass, her nightie flying up high on her thighs, exposing delicate white panties that Stokes barely noticed.

"Get up," he said. "And sit down. On a chair, I mean."

She moved over to the armchair he had occupied earlier.

"Stay there." He looked back at the cop, unconscious on the floor. "*Shit.*"

He jammed the heels of his hands into his eyes and rubbed hard, trying to relieve tension that hadn't been there twenty seconds ago.

"Shit," he said again, with true feeling.

He'd just assaulted a cop. Millett was gonna love this.

"You have any idea what you've done here?" he asked her.

She was silent.

"Goddamn it." He started pacing. He had to do something. The cop would wake up eventually. Unless he was dead. Oh, man, Stokes hadn't considered that. Maybe he'd done far more than assault a cop. Maybe he'd killed one.

He walked over to Officer Martinson—the cop's name, according to the little plastic nameplate on his chest—and put his hand in front of the man's mouth. He felt breath.

With a warning look at Nancy, Stokes took a couple of sets of plastic ties off the cop's belt—plasticuffs, he thought they were called—and secured Martinson's hands, then his feet. He took the guy's belt, which held his radio, along with his gun and a few other cop goodies, and put it on an end table by the sofa.

Stokes wasn't sure, but he didn't think Officer Martinson had gotten a good look at his face. Just in case he'd been lucky in that regard, he took a black shirt from the pile of laundry Nancy had moved earlier to the floor and blindfolded the cop with it. He used a pair of Nancy's black tights to gag the man. He wiped sweat from his forehead as he worked. He was in deep and dangerous waters now, with swift currents tugging him toward jagged rocks.

He had to do something. The cop would wake up eventually and Stokes couldn't be there when he did. And if he didn't wake up soon and radio in, more cops would be here before Stokes knew it. And it would be all over for him . . . and for little Amanda Jenkins.

Things had gotten very bad very fast.

Stokes turned back to Nancy.

"Goddamn it," he said, "you really screwed up here. Why the hell'd you tell him about me?"

She had her arms wrapped around herself, her breasts resting on her forearms. She shook her head, looking like she might cry. "I don't know you. You show up with blood on your shirt, tell me it's Paul's, that he's dead. You tell me Amanda's been kidnapped. I'm confused, scared, and I don't have any idea who you are. You tell me I can't talk to the police about you, which only made me more scared. What was I supposed to do?"

"Goddamn it, Nancy, you made things a whole lot worse." He was pissed, but he couldn't truly blame her under the circumstances, if he really thought about it. So he didn't think about it. He stayed pissed. "Goddamn it."

"I'm sorry," she said. "Please don't hurt me." She was shaking. She was scared. Of course she was scared. Some guy she'd met ten minutes ago just knocked a cop cold in her living room. She was probably having a hard time thinking of anything good that could come of that. Realizing this didn't do much to take the edge off his anger, though.

He walked over to Nancy, sat on the coffee table in front of her. She shied away.

"Listen to me," he said in the calmest voice he could muster. "I wasn't lying, OK? Everything I said is true. Paul died in a car crash. Your daughter's been kidnapped. I plan to get her back. But I need your help. Are you listening?"

She took a shuddering breath and nodded.

"OK, first, you have to understand something. The cops are not our friends in this. You just have to believe me about that, OK?"

"Why not? If Amanda's been kidnapped, we should go to the police, right? Or the FBI?"

"Look, I don't have time to go into all this right now. Just believe me, if you want your daughter back again, you can't tell anyone about this, at least not until it's all over and you have her back."

"I don't understand. They can help. They can get my little girl back for me."

"Look, the men who took your daughter say they have someone in the police department, and I have good reason to believe them. And if they were telling the truth about that, they might have been telling the truth about the FBI, too. True or not, we can't take the chance on making a mistake. Trust me on that."

She didn't look convinced.

"Look," Stokes continued, "Paul made that mistake and he regretted it. After that, he was trying to handle this by himself when he had his accident. That's why I've got two hundred fifty thousand dollars in that backpack there, money I'm gonna exchange for Amanda." He looked for the backpack where he'd left it and saw that Nancy had moved it around behind the chair before she opened the door for the police.

"Two hundred fifty thousand dollars?" she said.

"That's right. And I'm going to trade it for Amanda. So no cops, you got it?"

She hesitated.

"If we call the authorities," he added, "Amanda's as good as dead. I really believe that. And I need you to believe it, too, understand?"

Finally, she nodded.

"OK," he said. "Now, I told you that I'm gonna get your little girl back, and I am. But I need some information. First, you didn't know anything about this, did you?"

Her eyes were unfocused. She looked like she was having a tough time processing all this.

"Nancy, please. You gotta get with it here. You gotta help me out." He shot a glance at the unconscious cop. "We're running out of time."

She blinked a couple of times, nodding a little to herself.

"Nancy?" he said. "You didn't know anything about this, did you?"

She shook her head. "About the kidnapping? No. Paul didn't tell me. He probably didn't want to worry me." She looked on the verge of tears again. "Oh, my little girl." She lowered her face into her hands. Thankfully, it didn't look like she was crying, just holding her face in her hands, struggling to keep it together.

"This seems like a silly question right now," Stokes said, "but you don't have a hundred thousand dollars lying around, do you?"

She looked up. "What?"

"Maybe hidden somewhere. A little nest egg. Emergency fund. Nothing like that?"

"A hundred thousand dollars?"

"Actually, a hundred and two. I'm a little short right now. Paul had the money but I gave a little away."

"A hundred and two thousand dollars?"

"Well, maybe not so little. But look, if I hadn't, I wouldn't be here right now, and Amanda would have no chance, OK? So I guess you don't have that kind of money, huh?"

She shook her head again.

"You got anything here? Any money to speak of?"

"Maybe sixty dollars in my wallet."

He sighed. It was what he expected, but he had to ask.

"OK, here's the main reason I came. Did Paul say anything to you about having to be somewhere tonight at one thirty? Anything at all?"

"Tonight? No, nothing."

"Think about it. Think hard. He didn't tell you he had to be someplace specific tonight, someplace people should look for him if he, uh, didn't make it home? Nothing like that?"

"No, I'm sorry. What does that have to do with getting Amanda back?"

Damn it. He ran a hand through his hair.

"Shouldn't we be doing something?" she asked. "Shouldn't you get going, get started doing whatever you're going to do to bring her home?"

"Yeah, I should. I mean, I will."

"When? You do have a plan, right? Please tell me you do."

"I'll figure it out, don't worry about it. But listen, I need help with part of this. I don't think I can come up with a hundred and two thousand dollars, and unless I do, Amanda's gonna get hurt. Is there anyone you can call? Any friends who might loan you the money?"

"I don't have any friends who have that kind of money. And you're saying you have to meet with them tonight. Who has that kind of cash lying around their house?"

He'd struck out. Coming here had not only been a waste of time, a precious commodity at the moment, it was a disaster. He'd assaulted a cop, bound him with his own plastic ties. He'd face serious charges for that when this was all over, unless he was lucky enough that the cop hadn't gotten a good look at him *and* Nancy here helped him out by saying he'd worn a mask or something so she didn't see his face. Shit.

He shook his head to clear it. It didn't work. He'd really hoped Paul had told Nancy where he'd be going tonight. Now, as suspicious as it would sound, especially after raising their suspicions earlier, he might have to ask the kidnappers where he needed to be at one thirty and take his chances. He'd wait as long as he could in case they mentioned it in passing, but if they didn't, he would have no choice but to ask. It was a big risk. And if it turned out to be a mistake, little Amanda would pay the price.

Nancy was watching him.

He was about to ask another question but the kidnappers' call stopped him.

"This is them," he told her. "Their nine o'clock call. Don't say a word."

"But—"

"*Sssssh.*"

He kept one eye on Officer Martinson, who was still unconscious, as he pulled the cell phone from his pocket and flipped it open.

"Hello," he said.

"Answered on the second ring this time. I'm honored. Got the money?"

"Yeah, I got it."

"All of it?"

"Enough."

Silence.

"Listen, Paul, don't pull any shit with us. We know you have three hundred and fifty thousand. You think we don't know where it came from? Did you think we wouldn't want our money back? So don't screw around with us. You try to save a few bucks in this, it'll cost you something you can't replace. We're not kidding here."

"I'll have it all."

"You better. We're gonna count it, while you wait, and if you're a dime short, we'll kill her and maybe you, you got it?"

"Yeah. You'll have all of it."

"And your evidence, of course."

"Yeah, yeah, that, too."

More silence.

"Let me talk to Amanda," Stokes said.

A moment later, the little girl's voice came down the line. "Daddy?"

"Good girl," he said. "You OK?"

"My hand still really hurts . . . Daddy."

"Is that Amanda?" Nancy asked.

"Ssssh," Stokes hissed at her.

"My hand's all wrapped up in a bandage," the little girl said, "and they gave me medicine but it still hurts."

"I know, Amanda. We'll get you to a doctor soon. He'll make it stop hurting. And Amanda, remember, don't—"

"Don't what?" It was the kidnapper again.

A sudden inspiration struck him. It was a long shot, but he'd hit a long shot once before. At the track. Blew the money on a new stereo system, which was stolen a month later, but it showed him that long shots sometimes come in. "Let me talk to Amanda again."

"No."

"Put her on."

"Fuck you."

"No, pal, fuck you. Now let me talk to my daughter one more time."

125

The silence on the phone was cold. Stokes felt a tension crackling down the line, like the moment just after lightning has struck and you're waiting for the next ear-splitting crack of thunder.

"Not the right time to grow a pair, Jenkins," the kidnapper said. "Want me to cut off her whole fucking hand?"

Stokes took a deep breath. "I'm sorry," he said. "I really am. I'm just tired, I'm under a lot of stress, and I'm worried about my daughter. Can I talk to her one more time? Please? I just want to tell her that everything's going to be OK. She sounds scared." Nothing. "Please?"

After a long pause, Amanda came back on.

"Daddy?"

"Listen, Amanda, you've been in the room with those men when they've called me, right?"

"Huh?"

"Every hour they've been calling me, thinking I'm your daddy. You've been in the room with them. So listen, OK? This is important. Do you remember anything about a pay phone? Did you hear where your daddy was supposed to be tonight to get a phone call later?"

"A phone call?"

The kidnapper was going to grab the phone back any second.

"At a pay phone. Did you hear them say anything about a pay phone? Please, Amanda, think. And hurry."

"Ummmm . . ."

Shit. She didn't know. He heard the kidnapper say, "Gimme that," at the same moment he thought he heard Amanda blurt, "Laundro—" At least he *thought* she said that. He wasn't sure.

"What the hell was that all about?" the kidnapper asked.

"Just making sure Amanda's OK, telling her I'll see her soon."

"Didn't sound like that."

"Look, this is almost over, right? I'll take care of the money. You take care of my daughter. Everybody will get what they want. OK?"

After a moment of silence, the kidnapper said, "Talk to you in an hour," and ended the call.

A Laundromat. Shady Cross had a few that Stokes knew of, but only one had a faded billboard he'd seen somewhere around town declaring it to be the only twenty-four-hour Laundromat in Shady Cross. So Laund-R-Rama was where he needed to be at one-thirty. He hoped. If he'd heard Amanda right, and if Amanda had been correct, that's where he had to be to get the kidnapper's phone call.

Stokes looked at Martinson. Still napping.

"Is Amanda all right?" she asked, her voice shaking. "Is she OK?"

"Yeah, I talked to her. She sounded fine."

"You said something about getting her to a doctor."

"She's fine, Nancy, really. She bumped her knee and she's crying about that. I told her a doctor would make it better to give her something else to think about other than her situation." She seemed to buy that so Stokes continued. "Now listen, did you know your ex-husband had three hundred and fifty thousand dollars in an account for your daughter?"

"What? Three hundred and fifty thousand dollars? Are you sure?"

"Trust me."

"My God, no, I didn't. I had no idea he had that kind of money. He's an accountant. Makes eighty thousand a year."

An accountant? Stokes nodded, thinking. It was starting to make sense.

"Did Paul ever talk about his clients?"

"His clients? Which ones?"

"Did he ever give you the idea that he was keeping the books for questionable people?"

She was thinking. "Like criminals?"

"Exactly."

"Yeah, maybe he hinted that he had at least one client like that. He wasn't very happy about it, but it's hard to turn down paying clients, you know?"

"He say who it was?"

She shook her head. Stokes frowned. Jenkins was probably into something illegal. Either he helped out with some creative accounting and was rewarded well for it, or he stupidly cooked the books and tried to hide a hell of a lot of money from the wrong people. They were certain he had $350,000, so he must have stolen at least that much from the kidnappers. Paul simply got his hand caught in the cookie jar, and they wanted their cookies back. Every last crumb.

"Paul ever tell you about important files he kept somewhere, somewhere other than his house?"

Nancy shook her head. "Anything not at his house would be at his office."

"That's what I figured. Where's that?"

"The Emerson Building downtown."

"I don't suppose you have a key to his office there?" Stokes asked without much hope. Why would Paul's ex-wife have that?

"No, sorry. Besides, you couldn't get in there, even with a key, unless you also had the accounting firm's office security code. Without that you can't get past the reception area on the firm's floor."

Stokes shook his head. The Emerson Building was one of the newer buildings in Shady Cross. It had alarm systems and security guards. That was a dead end. If Jenkins kept the evidence there and had planned to pick it up later, Stokes wasn't going to get his hands on it.

"Nancy, do you own a computer?"

"Sure."

"Go get me a computer disk, OK? I don't care if it's blank."

She hurried off down the hall. Stokes looked over at the unconscious cop. He was going to have to do something about the guy. But what? He couldn't leave him here with Nancy. She might be inclined to free him, perhaps worrying that she might get into trouble herself if she kept him bound, which she would. And even if she didn't free him, he'd certainly have radioed in his location before he came to the door. Other cops would be coming when they didn't hear from him. No, Stokes couldn't leave him here. Which meant he had to take him with him. Which meant he'd be kidnapping an officer of the law. Kidnapping is a serious goddamn crime. Kidnapping a cop is probably ten times worse. Oh, man, things were spinning out of control.

Who the hell was he kidding? He'd never had a single thing under control tonight.

Still seated on the coffee table, he leaned over, grabbed his backpack off the floor, and slung it over his shoulder. He'd take it out to Bobby's pickup, pull the vehicle into the driveway, right up to the house, and dump Martinson in back. As soon as this was all over, he'd let the cop go and pray the guy had never gotten a decent look at his face.

Nancy returned and handed him a silver object, the length of his little finger.

"This OK?" she asked.

"What is it?"

"A thumb drive." He stared at her blankly. "It's like a computer disk."

"Oh." He stuck the drive into a pocket of the backpack. "I'll be right back," he said as he started toward the door.

"Wait . . ." She looked worried.

"I'll be right back. I promise."

He pushed the cop away from the door and hurried outside. When he came back after stowing the bag in the truck and moving the vehicle into the driveway, Nancy was standing in the living room in a tight pair of jeans and a sweatshirt the same shade as her baby blue eyes.

"I'm coming with you," she said.

"The hell you are."

"The hell I'm not. How do I know you're not going to decide to just take off with the money?"

"I could have done that hours ago and saved myself a shitload of trouble."

"Yeah, but how do I know you're not going to change your mind? No offense, but there's too much at stake for me to trust you. Amanda's my daughter, not yours."

Letting her come along would be a bad idea. But she was right. Why should she trust him? And even if she did at first, she might start to get antsy and call the cops after all. She didn't know how serious the kidnappers were, and he wasn't about to show her the videos of Amanda being maimed to prove it.

"All right," he said. "But you have to listen to me. And do what I say. If I tell you to stay out of the way, you do it. Got it?"

She nodded. "I just want to get her back safe."

He was starting to get a headache.

"Help me carry this guy to the garage."

Stokes took the cop's arms and Nancy took his legs and they half carried, half dragged him down the hall, then down three concrete steps into the garage. Nancy hit a button and the garage door cranked open. Stokes had backed the truck right up to the door. He grabbed a canvas tarp he spotted on a shelf and folded it under the cop's head. No reason to give the guy a concussion if the drive got a little rough. Finally, he pulled the cop's car keys from his pocket and slipped them into his own. He didn't want Martinson to try to use them as a weapon or to slice through his bonds.

They hurried back inside. Stokes grabbed the bag of money and the cop's utility belt—complete with gun, baton, pepper spray, and the like—and headed for the garage again. Nancy went down the hall.

"I'll be right back," she said. "Just grabbing a few things."

Stokes walked through the garage, slid behind the wheel of the truck, and dropped the bag of money and the cop's belt on the floor of the cab. He briefly considered taking off before Nancy returned, hoping he could trust her not to do anything to jeopardize Amanda's life. He didn't want to put her in danger, too, by bringing her along. But Amanda was her daughter. The choice was hers. Besides, she might even help out somehow. You never know. Plus, she was nice to look at.

A minute later, she appeared at the passenger-side window, a small duffel bag hanging on her shoulder.

"What's in there?" he asked.

"A few things. Extra clothes for Amanda, my wallet, a flashlight. I even grabbed a first aid kit."

"You must have been a Girl Scout." He had a mental flash of her in the uniform, but filling it out as she would now.

"I didn't know what we might need," she said, "so I just grabbed whatever I thought might be useful."

"Good thinking. Listen, it won't be fun for you, but I think you should ride in the back. If he wakes up, bang on my window."

"What will you do?"

"Beats the hell out of me. But I'll have to do something, right?"

She threw her bag into the bed and climbed in after it. When she was settled, Stokes pulled out of the driveway. Again, the irony in this situation was evident to him. To get one kidnapping victim back, he'd kidnapped someone else. A cop, no less. The poor guy was just doing his job and didn't really deserve a knot on the back of his skull, the headache he was going to wake up with, or, when he did wake up, having to do so in the bed of a pickup truck, bound and gagged. On the other hand, the guy *was* a cop, so Stokes's sympathy didn't run too deep.

Stokes hadn't figured out exactly where he was going, only that he had to get away from Nancy's house. Martinson hadn't been awake to check in with his dispatcher so the rest of the cops would get suspicious soon. Stokes had briefly considered taking the cop's car, but realized that it probably had a LoJack-type device, a transponder or something that would tell the authorities exactly where it was, and therefore, where *he* was. So he stuck with Bobby's truck and tried to put some distance between them and Nancy's house, all the while considering his options.

He couldn't come up with any good ones.

SIXTEEN

STOKES DROVE OUT OF NANCY'S neighborhood. Within a few minutes they were traveling along a road with a few scattered houses, not truly part of any neighborhood, just houses lined up along the road. He didn't have much of a plan. He figured he'd stash the cop in the woods somewhere, someplace fairly remote. If he got the chance later, he'd call the police and tell them where to find their buddy. Every once in a while as he drove he'd lean a little so he could see Nancy in his rearview mirror, and every now and then the moonlight hit her and he'd realize that she was even prettier now than when he first saw her, the moonlight bathing her face, the wind whipping her hair into a yellow storm. He let himself fantasize for a moment about how beautifully this could end. He saves the girl. He's a hero. She loves him for it and they live happily ever after. Perfect. And pure fantasy—one he wasn't even completely certain he'd want to come true. He hadn't done such a great job of settling down the first time he'd tried it.

Without warning, he hit the brakes, jerked the wheel, and bounced up a driveway. He looked at the house illuminated in his headlights. Windows completely dark. The place was small, didn't even have a garage, and there were no cars in the driveway or on the street out front. It was the "For Sale" sign on the lawn that attracted him. It looked to Stokes like the owners had moved out before they could sell. He got out of the truck and peered in a front window. No furniture. And no alarm system he could see. A realtor's lockbox for the house key hanging on the front-door knob. Stokes looked to his left, then his right, and saw that the houses on either side of this one were each a good fifty yards away. This would work.

He drove the truck around the back of the house, parked it, and got out.

"He didn't wake up?"

"Slept like a big baby," Nancy said.

Without the wind blowing her hair around, it hung shapelessly. She didn't bother to fix it, which Stokes liked about her. Just a quick shake of her head to clear stray strands from her eyes. She looked tired, though. And worried.

"She'll be OK," he said. "I promise."

She smiled a small smile and nodded.

"Wait here a second."

Stokes walked over to the house and, as quietly as he could, smashed a windowpane on the back door with a rock. If he'd had his lock picks with him, he could have been neater about it. And quieter. He knocked out the glass shards that remained in the opening, then reached through and unlocked the door from the inside. He walked back to the truck, reached into the cab, took Martinson's gun from its holster, and stuck it into the back of his jeans.

"Think you'll need that?" Nancy asked.

"Hope to hell I don't, but I'd rather have it if I do."

Together, he and Nancy slid Martinson to the end of the truck bed, where Stokes bent down so they could work the unconscious cop onto Stokes's shoulder. His back was starting to ache from all the people-lugging he'd been doing.

Stokes carried the guy, all two-hundred-or-so pounds of him, into the dark house, down a dark hall, and into a dark bedroom, which he made darker by pulling down the window shades after depositing Martinson on the floor. His shoulders throbbed. His legs burned. He went back into the hall and was nearly to the back door when he heard sounds coming from inside the house. When he reached the bedroom again he found that Martinson had woken up and was struggling ferociously against his bonds, grunting like an angry, desperate wild animal into his gag. When he heard Stokes's footsteps, he tipped his head back, trying to see underneath his blindfold.

Stokes deepened his voice in an improvised and somewhat pathetic attempt to disguise it and said, "Stop that."

The cop didn't. He grunted louder as he strained to break free.

Stokes added, "I've got your gun and it's pointed at your balls, so shut up or you lose your boys."

The gun was still in the back of his jeans but the cop didn't know that, so he shut up and stopped struggling.

"Listen, Officer," Stokes said in a quiet, faux-deep voice, "this seems like a shit situation, but it isn't as bad as you think. I don't want to hurt you. I will if I have to, but I don't want to. Why, you ask? Well, I've got nothing against you personally, except the fact that you're a cop, but that's not enough to make me want to hurt you. Also, I know I'm in deep shit for this and I don't need the added trouble that hurting you more than I already have will bring. You understand?"

Martinson tilted his head up, again trying to see under the bottom of his blindfold. That was good, Stokes realized, because it probably meant he hadn't gotten a look at Stokes's face earlier. Of course, he might have simply been trying to figure out where he was, assessing his situation.

"Now," Stokes continued, "I'm gonna leave you here for a little bit, a couple of hours at most, then I'll let your police pals know where to find you. I just need you out of the way for a while, that's all."

Martinson shook his head and tried to speak.

"I don't really want to hear what you have to say, Officer, and I don't have time to explain this any better. So that's the situation. Deal with it."

Stokes appraised the cop.

"Sorry about this," he said as he used another plastic tie to secure the cop's wrist bond to his ankle bond. He figured the guy might be able to scoot around the floor a little if he tried hard enough, but hog-tied as he was now, he wouldn't be able to stand or open the door, which Stokes was going to close. He might free himself eventually, but it would probably take a while and Stokes only had to make it through another few hours. Satisfied, he headed back outside.

Nancy was sitting in the passenger seat of the truck with the door open. Her duffel bag was in her lap. His bag of money was between her feet.

"Ready to go?" she asked.

He looked at the backpack on the floor. The flap was closed but not fastened. He reached in and picked the bag up by a strap.

"Did you look in here?"

She hesitated. "I had to see it." She paused. Stokes waited. "It's what caused all this," she added. "It's what put Amanda in danger. I wanted to see it, that's all."

Stokes nodded. "Well, it's what's going to save her now," he said, wishing he felt as confident as he tried to sound.

He started for the driver's door.

"Was that him?" Nancy asked suddenly.

"What?"

"Was that the cop making that noise?"

"What noise?"

"It just came from inside the house. Glass breaking maybe?"

"Shit, I'll be right back." Stokes slung the bag over his shoulder and headed for the house.

"Toss me the keys. I'll start the truck and turn it around."

"Just give me a second." He ran into the house and through it until he came to the door to the bedroom where he'd left the cop. It was still closed. Maybe the guy had slipped out of some of his bonds somehow. Or maybe all of them. Maybe he was waiting just inside the room, waiting to take Stokes down the second he stepped into it. To hell with it, Stokes thought. He didn't have time for this. He kicked the door open and saw Martinson right where he'd left him, though his gag was starting to slip. Stokes walked over to secure it better. He knelt down and untied the gag, intending to slap it right back on him, tied tighter this time. As soon as the gag was out, Martinson said, "I don't have to tell you, buddy, that you're in a mess of trouble."

"No," Stokes said, "you don't."

"So why don't you cut me free now?"

"Sorry, I've still got some work to do."

"You're really screwed, pal, you know that? You're going to prison for a long time."

"Yeah, I know."

They were silent for a moment. Stokes looked at his watch: 9:44 p.m.

"Here's the thing, Officer. I'd love to end this. I'd love to let you go. It sure as hell wasn't in my plans to have to bring you along, stash you here. But I'm doing something important tonight and I can't have you screwing it up. You're not gonna believe this, but I'm trying to do something good. And it's not even illegal. I'm trying to help someone. A little kid."

"What are you talking about?"

Stokes probably shouldn't say anything, especially given that this cop theoretically could be the kidnappers' inside source in the police department. But Martinson wasn't going anywhere anytime soon, so it couldn't hurt if Stokes shared a little. Besides, if the guy wasn't on the kidnappers' payroll, and if he believed Stokes, maybe they'd go easier on him when they arrested him later.

"A little girl's been kidnapped," Stokes said. "I gotta get her back."

Martinson seemed to be thinking that over, probably trying to decide whether it was total bullshit.

"Who's the little girl?"

"Just a kid. I don't know her. Never even met her."

"Then why are you trying to help her? Just a Good Samaritan?"

"Not me. And don't ask me why. I'm not completely sure myself, but I have my suspicions."

Martinson tipped his head back again, trying to see Stokes.

"Stop that," Stokes ordered.

"How do you plan to get her back?"

"Give the kidnappers the money they want."

"How much?"

"Almost two hundred fifty thousand, three fifty if I can manage it."

Martinson snorted and Stokes knew he thought he was getting snowed. "Where are you gonna get that kind of money?"

"I already have most of it. Got it from the girl's father. He had the money with him when he had a car accident."

Martinson shook his head.

"I don't care if you believe me, but the kid's dad died today. You got kids, Officer?"

The cop said nothing.

"Come on, you got kids?"

"One son."

"You love him to death, right? Tuck him in at night, read him stories, all that stuff?"

"None of your business."

"What? You don't love him? You don't tuck him in?"

The cop hesitated. "He lives with his mother."

"Oh. You probably have pictures of him everywhere, little drawings he made at school hanging on your fridge, all that stuff, right?" Stokes thought about all the photos of Amanda at Jenkins's house.

Martinson nodded. "All over my house. What's your point?"

"You'd do anything for him, right?"

"Of course."

"Well, this kid's dad would have done anything for her, but he's dead. I'm stepping in. Somebody's got to."

Stokes reached for the gag.

"Wait," Martinson said quickly.

Stokes paused.

"If this is true, call the police. This is our job, not yours. It isn't your problem."

"Yeah, I keep telling myself that."

"So call them. They can help."

"I can't do that," Stokes said.

"Why not?"

He thought about the video of the kidnapper cutting off Amanda's finger. And he thought about how the kidnappers knew very quickly that Jenkins's car had been found and that Jenkins hadn't been. "The kidnappers have a source with the cops. They say they'll kill the girl if anyone goes to the authorities."

"Bullshit."

"It's true. I know it for a fact. The kid's dad already tried it, and they cut off one of her fingers. They say they have someone with the police and the FBI, too. I'm actually not sure whether the father called you guys or the Feds, but I know the kidnappers cut off her finger because of it. I'm not going to make the same mistake."

Martinson was silent for a moment. Probably wondering whether it was possible that one of his fellow cops was that dirty. He thought for quite a while, so he clearly didn't reject the idea out of hand.

"Listen," he said, "cut me loose. If you're not lying, I'll forget all of this. We'll get the girl back, just you and me, and I'll forget this ever happened. I swear to God."

Stokes wished he could believe him.

Martinson added, "If what you say is true, that little girl is counting on you. Don't try to cowboy your way through this. Don't do it alone. Let me help."

He seemed completely sincere. But though the odds were against it, it was still possible that Martinson was the kidnappers' inside man. And even if he wasn't, there was a good chance that as soon as he was cut loose, he'd try to arrest Stokes. So as much as Stokes wanted to believe the guy, as much as he would have liked to have the cop's help in all this, he just couldn't take the chance.

"Sorry," he said as he lifted the gag and fitted it snugly into place in Martinson's mouth. As he made sure it was tight, the cop continued to plead with him. He didn't seem to be pleading for his own sake, though; rather, he seemed to want more than anything to help save Amanda Jenkins. Confident that Martinson wouldn't be heard if he tried calling for help, Stokes stood.

He paused. Something bothered him, something the cop had said. He wasn't sure what, though. He heard a sound behind him and turned. Nancy walked through the door.

"What's taking so long in here?" she asked.

He couldn't shake the feeling that there was something wrong, something he was missing.

She bent down and picked up the backpack he'd left on the floor. "I've got this," she said. "You almost ready to go?"

He hesitated. Something wasn't right.

Nancy looked at him with those beautiful eyes, and then he had it.

"Yeah, let's go," he said. "I'll take the money."

He held his hand out for the bag. Nancy was starting to hand it to him when she suddenly shifted her eyes past Stokes, to where Martinson was supposed to be sitting on the floor, and said, "You better sit back down." And Stokes, feeling like a fool almost the instant he began to turn to check on Martinson, felt a sudden, solid blow to the back of his head. The room jerked to the side of his vision, then disappeared from his sight altogether, along with everything else.

SEVENTEEN

STOKES WAS LYING ON A hard floor. Someone was digging through his pockets. He heard a faint jingle, then footsteps fading away. A moment later he heard a car door slam. His head hurt like a bastard. He opened his eyes and, thank God, saw his backpack lying a few feet away. The flap was open. He could see inside. He blinked. There should have been money in there. Almost a quarter of a million dollars. Instead, he saw a few articles of clothing and a big, clunky metal first aid kit the size of a fishing tackle box. It was probably the first aid kit that had momentarily stunned him.

Goddamn Nancy. He struggled to his knees, expecting the truck's engine to turn over any second outside. It didn't. He put his hand on the wall for support and got to his feet. He was dizzy for a moment, but it passed quickly enough. He wished it had taken his headache with it. He felt behind him for the gun and found it still snugged into the waistband of his jeans. Thank God it hadn't gone off and shot him in the ass when he fell. He left it tucked where it was. He didn't want to shoot Nancy.

He hurried through the house and out the back door, where he saw her, with her duffel bag over her shoulder, stepping out of the truck. She had just begun to run when he called her name. She turned and he started toward her. She must have realized he'd catch her with ease because she jumped back into the truck and yanked the door closed. He saw her push down the locks.

"Open the door, Nancy," he said through the closed window.

"Fuck you."

Sweet little Nancy had a nasty side.

"Looks like you took the wrong keys out of my pocket," he said. "Took the cop's keys, left me the truck key."

"I know that now, asshole."

"So I could just unlock the door myself, you idiot. You might as well save me the trouble."

After a moment's hesitation, she did as instructed.

"I'm gonna pull this door open now," he said. "I don't think anyone in these other houses is close enough to hear you scream if you try, but I don't want to find out. So if you scream, I'll knock you out, you understand?"

She nodded. He opened the door. She opened her mouth. Stokes didn't know if she was going to scream or not, but he slapped her in the face anyway, just in case. He didn't take any pleasure in hitting a woman. He'd seen too much of that when he was a kid. He didn't want to do it a second time, and he told her so. "So don't make me," he added.

She rubbed her cheek and nodded. He took the bag from her lap, the one she'd transferred his money into, and dragged her out of the truck by her arm. He led her back inside the house, to a second bedroom, and shoved her into a corner. He pulled all the window shades down and pointed to a rolled-up area rug that the house's prior owners had left behind.

"Sit down."

She did. He rubbed his eyes.

"How much, Nancy?"

She glared at him but said nothing.

"How much?"

There was something not very beautiful in those previously beautiful eyes. "How much for what?" she asked.

"How much did they pay you to sell out your own kid?"

He'd started having suspicions just before she clocked him a few minutes ago. He'd just finished speaking with Martinson, thinking about the guy loving his son who lived with his ex-wife, and there's the cop with pictures of his kid all over his house. And Jenkins, Amanda's father, he had pictures of his daughter everywhere. No matter where you stood in his house, you were never out of sight of a picture of Amanda. And then he remembered that Nancy didn't have any pictures of Amanda displayed in her house. Not in the living room anyway. Just three crooked photos of flowers on the wall. And he didn't remember seeing any in the kitchen, either. So he'd started to wonder, and while he was wondering, she decked him and tried to run with the money.

Stokes shook his head. "Jeez, you were good. I thought you were really going to cry a couple of times."

She said nothing. He took a few of the cop's plastic ties from his pocket and started to truss her up. She struggled a little, but gave in soon enough. While he worked, he said, "I'm trying to figure out why you told the cop I was hiding, back there at your house."

He remembered that though he'd left his backpack in front of the armchair he'd been sitting in, when he came back out of the kitchen he'd noticed she had moved it behind the chair.

He said, "I guess you were hoping I'd be arrested and hauled off, and you'd be left with a quarter of a million bucks. Probably planned to blow town with it." She remained silent. A moment later, she was bound hand and foot. He stared down at her, sitting on the rug, looking up at him with darkness in her eyes.

"I'm gonna check on the cop," he said. "Don't move a muscle." He opened the door, went across the hall to where he'd left

Martinson, and returned a few seconds later with his backpack, her clothes spilling out of it.

"I don't have time for bullshit right now," he said, "not if I wanna try to help Amanda . . . your goddamn daughter, by the way."

He needed answers. He knew she'd switched the contents of their bags a little while ago when he first brought the cop into the house alone, but that was all he knew.

"You don't give a shit about her, do you?" he asked as he dumped the backpack out.

She said nothing, merely stared at him. But it wasn't a blank stare. Something ugly was swimming in the dark depths of her eyes.

Finally, she spoke. "That's a lot of money you have there . . . you know, you never told me your name."

"Right on both counts."

Stokes said nothing more as he knelt and began removing the money from her bag and stuffing it back into his backpack.

After a moment, she said, "Maybe we can make a deal."

"What kind of deal?"

She licked her lips, and Stokes—if he'd had more of a conscience, he would have been ashamed—found the sight enticing.

"Well," she began, "how about we split the money and go our separate ways?"

He fastened the flap on the backpack and stood. "I've already got all the money. Why should I split it with you?"

"OK, don't give me half. Give me a third of it."

"You still haven't told me what's in it for me."

She shrugged her shapely shoulders. "Anything you want."

"Yeah? Anything at all?"

"Anything you can dream up. Any fantasy you've ever had but have been too nervous or polite or embarrassed to ask for. Anything at all."

A small flick of her eyes toward the front of his jeans weakened his knees.

"We'll get a motel room," she said. "We can do whatever you want for however long you want to do it. When we're done, I take my money, you take yours."

"And you want a third? Shit, Nancy, I admit I wouldn't mind taking you for a spin, but I gotta say, and no offense here, but nothing I can dream up is worth eighty thousand bucks."

"You should talk to some of the men I've been with," she said as she gave him a smile that felt almost like oral sex. "You want a taste of what I'd be bringing to the table?" she asked, looking up at him. "I'll give it to you right now. Let you make an informed decision."

"But . . ."

"No risk for you, not while my hands are tied together. No obligation to buy on your part. Just a chance to see what you'll be getting for your money."

"But . . ." he said again.

"Yes?" She smiled. Her eyes said, "I've got him."

"What about Amanda?" he asked.

She jerked her head back as though he'd slapped her again. Disgust clouded her face. "She'll be fine."

"They might kill her."

"They're not gonna kill her. If they don't get the money, they'll let her go. They said—" She cut herself off.

Stokes shook his head. "Thanks for the offer, but I'm gonna have to pass."

A wave of rage rippled across her features before disappearing again, leaving her face looking much like it did when Stokes first saw it tonight, only somehow it didn't seem so attractive.

"Now, what did the kidnappers tell you?" he asked.

Her jaw muscles clenched. Thunderheads roiled in her eyes, which turned a darker, dangerous blue.

"You're worried about Amanda?" she asked. "Hell, what's she to you? Have you ever met her? Had you even heard of her before today?"

He shook his head. "Nope, but somebody's gotta get her back, and it turns out that somebody is me. Now I've gotta get a move on here, Nancy, so start talking. I already know you're somehow involved in all this. Start with this, though: Where the hell did Paul get three hundred and fifty thousand dollars? And don't give me the bullshit you tried to give me back at your house."

"Fuck you."

"I thought we covered that. I'm not interested. Now answer my question."

"Fuck you."

After hitting her outside, he hadn't wanted to do so again. But he was running out of time and had no choice. He slapped her hard.

"I don't have time to screw around anymore. Answer my questions. You don't, things get worse as we go on. The slap becomes a punch, the punch becomes a kick, my fist becomes a pistol butt, and soon you aren't so pretty anymore, you understand?"

She looked into his eyes, tried to gauge the man in front of her. She gauged pretty well because she soon dropped her eyes and nodded.

"OK," he said. "The money. Exactly where did Paul get it? He steal from his clients?"

"Paul handled a lot of people's money. He's been skimming for years."

Stokes shook his head. Even though he'd been pretty sure that was the case, he hadn't wanted to be right. He'd wanted Paul Jenkins to be everything he himself was not: honest, hardworking, a good family man. Stokes had hoped he was wrong, that the kidnappers were wrong, that Jenkins had earned the money honestly. Now that he learned the truth, he was disappointed. But it shouldn't have surprised him. Look at the prize he'd married. None of this changed his thinking about Amanda, though. She deserved to be saved.

"Keep going," he said.

"He put a lot away over the years, I guess. I didn't realize how much while we were married."

"When'd you figure that out?"

She hesitated. "I kept a key to his house after I moved out. Anyway, I had some suspicions, I guess, and I started to wonder if I couldn't get a court to raise my alimony if I found out for sure how much he had. So I snuck into his house one day and went through papers in his office. I found some financial records, account statements, and questioned Paul about them. We argued. Finally, he told me what he'd done, but he said he'd done it for Amanda. He told me he had three hundred and fifty thousand dollars in an account for her that only he could access."

"And that wasn't good enough for you? That Amanda's life would be a little easier for her one day. You had to have a cut, too."

"Why should his daughter have so much while I have so little?"

His daughter?

"You mean your daughter, don't you?" Stokes asked.

She shook her head. "She's Paul's daughter. With his first wife. Amanda's real mother died when Amanda was a year and a half old."

Well, that explained a shitload, right up to Nancy's blonde hair and little Amanda's dark hair, which Stokes just assumed she'd inherited from her father. He remembered a photo at Jenkins's house of baby Amanda in the arms of a smiling brunette—Amanda's biological mother.

"And you never quite warmed up to the girl, I guess," Stokes said.

She shrugged. "Not really."

"What'd you do after you found out about the money?"

"I made Paul give me more alimony."

"You blackmailed him."

She shrugged.

"And then what? It still wasn't enough, so you found some guys to kidnap Amanda? Your own stepdaughter?"

She said nothing. He was tired of screwing around, so he slapped her again.

"Ow, *shit*."

He still didn't like hitting her, but by being such a horrible creature she was making it a little easier on him, for which he was grateful.

"Answer my questions and don't jerk me around. Next time you get knuckles. You obviously told someone about the money. How else would the kidnappers know to ask for exactly three hundred and fifty thousand? So who'd you tell?"

She was silent. He raised a fist. She shrank back and raised her bound hands in front of her to ward off the blow that didn't fall.

"That was your last warning," he said. He wasn't proud of himself, but he needed answers fast.

She took a deep breath. "I gamble sometimes. On horses. I lost a lot. Too much, so I borrowed more to win it back. Lost again. Borrowed a little more and lost that, too. Then I couldn't get any more loans. And I couldn't pay back what I owed, either."

"Who'd you borrow from?"

"Some small-timer, I thought. But when a couple of guys came around asking for the money, they made sure I knew whose money I'd really been playing with."

He waited. Had to be either Leo Grote or Frank Nickerson.

"Leo Grote," she said.

"And to save your skin you told them about the money Paul had in an account for Amanda."

She nodded. "It was Grote's money anyway," she said. "Paul did some work for him."

"That's who Paul stole from?"

She nodded.

"You said you didn't know who any of Paul's criminal clients were."

She shrugged again.

No wonder the kidnappers were so insistent on getting the entire $350,000. Paul had stolen it from them, and they wanted it all back.

"So you told Grote about the money," Stokes said.

"Well, I told his guys. They told me that if I helped them get it, they'd cancel my debt."

"And you knew Paul would give it all to them to protect Amanda."

"Every penny."

"So why didn't they just grab your ex and beat him until he gave them the money?"

"I told them that wouldn't work, at least not as well as kidnapping Amanda would. Paul might have risked his own neck to hang onto his money, especially when he'd collected it for her, but I knew he'd never risk his daughter's life."

Hell, maybe Jenkins was an OK guy after all. At least he cared about his kid.

"So you and Grote's guys worked out the kidnapping thing together. They'd get their money, you'd get Grote off your back. How much were you into him for?"

"Eighty-five thousand."

"What about the rest of it?"

She said nothing.

"Don't tell me. They were gonna split it with you."

She shrugged. Stokes did the math in his head, which took a little while. He got hung up once and had to start over. Finally, he said, "That's something like a hundred thirty grand for you, and the same for Grote. Jesus, you're a sweet thing, you know that?"

"Fuck you."

"They cut off two of her fingers, you know."

"What?" Her voice caught the tiniest bit as she said it.

"Yeah, your friends cut off two of Amanda's fingers. Nice people you're in bed with, huh?"

Nancy's eyes softened around the edges for a moment, then hardened like quick-drying cement. "She'll be OK."

"Sure she will, Nancy. Keep telling yourself that until this is all over. Now, who'd you cut the deal with?"

"What do you mean? Grote, I guess."

"No, no, Grote had to OK the deal, I'm sure, but who'd you work the plan out with?"

"I never got their names."

He knew some of Grote's men, from when they'd all had the same boss. Grote would probably want guys he trusted on something as delicate and dangerous as a kidnapping, guys who had been with him for a while, so there was a decent chance Stokes knew them.

"What'd they look like?" he asked.

She thought for a moment. "There were two of them. One was a big, dark-skinned guy. Not black, I don't think, but real dark complexion. Muscular. Black tattoo on his neck, I think. Some kind of swirly design."

He nodded. Iron Mike, they called him, after Mike Tyson, the boxer.

"And the other guy?"

"Real ugly. Tall, stocky, gold tooth on one side of his mouth, I think."

Danny DeMarco. Stokes knew him, too. Leg breakers, both of them. Enjoyed their work far more than he ever did.

Stokes thought about the scam. He was a little surprised by it, surprised Grote would go for it. Sure, it turned his eighty-five grand into, what? Over 215 grand? And actually, despite what they'd told

Nancy, she never would have seen a dime of that money, so Grote was probably really looking at the whole $350,000, which was something like four times what Nancy owed him.

But Grote had plenty of money already and kidnapping was risky, like one of Nickerson's psycho sons had said to Stokes earlier that night. Unless you kill the hostage, there's always a witness. He wondered if Grote even knew about the deal at all. It sounded like maybe Iron Mike and DeMarco were doing this off the books. Maybe they planned to snatch the kid, collect the ransom, give Grote the money Nancy owed him, and pocket what was left. Assuming they cut Nancy out entirely, like he suspected they would, they'd each be something like a 130 grand richer and Grote would be none the wiser. Then again, guys like Iron Mike and Danny DeMarco don't do much thinking on their own. They don't have the brains for it, and they don't, in the end, have the balls for it. They had to know that if Leo Grote found out they'd crossed him, they wouldn't have any balls at all, at least not for long. No, the more Stokes thought about it, the more he realized that Grote must have OK'd the deal after all.

He asked, "Paul ever tell you about any evidence he'd collected against Grote, maybe as an insurance policy? Evidence of Grote's criminal activities?"

Nancy shook her head.

"All right. Any idea where the exchange is supposed to take place tonight? Where Paul was supposed to drop the money? Where he was supposed to pick up Amanda?"

She shook her head.

"Give me the truth."

"I swear to God, I don't know."

"Am I supposed to be at Laund-R-Rama to get my phone call at one thirty tonight?"

"I don't know. Really."

"OK."

He stood and started for the door.

"So?" she said.

"So what?"

"So what about me?"

"What about you?"

"You're leaving me here? Like this?"

"Oh yeah," he said. "I forgot."

He went back to her, pulled out another of the plasticuffs, and used it to connect the ties binding her wrists with those binding her ankles.

"What the hell?" she said.

Stokes pulled the plastic ties tight, drawing her hands down near her feet. It didn't look to Stokes like a comfortable position in which to spend a few hours.

Life's rough.

"You can't just leave me like this."

"Sure, I can. Don't worry, when the cops come for Officer Martinson, they'll find you, too."

He faced the door, which he'd left open. He'd also left open the door to the cop's room across the hall a few minutes ago.

He called out, "So, did you get all that, Officer Martinson? Grunt once for yes and twice for no."

He heard a single, muffled grunt. It wasn't loud, but he heard it clearly in the empty, echoing house. No doubt the cop had heard Nancy clearly enough, too.

Stokes said, "Looks like you just confessed to conspiracy to kidnap your own stepdaughter."

She spit at him. He didn't care.

"You may not give a shit," he said, "but I'm gonna get Amanda away from Grote's men. I'm gonna bring her home." He had no idea, though, to what home he'd bring her. Both her biological parents were dead, and her stepmother, who didn't care about her anyway, was going to have a new home herself in an eight-by-ten-foot cell.

She glowered at him. "I'm thirsty."

"You'll live."

"I need a drink."

"Join the club."

"Come on," she said, "I'm thirsty."

"The cops can give you a drink in a few hours."

"I have to pee."

"Don't let me stop you."

"You asshole."

He bent down, removed her sneakers, and yanked off her socks, which he tied together and used to gag her. He stood and looked down at her. Her eyes were wild. Her face red with rage. Incredible how she'd completely lost her looks in less than an hour.

He walked away, shutting the door behind him.

Outside, he got back into Bobby's truck. He pulled around the house and back onto the road. A couple of minutes later, the cell phone twittered in his pocket. Stokes didn't have to look at his watch. It would say it was exactly ten o'clock. He opened the phone.

"I'm here," he said.

"You got the money, right?" the kidnapper asked. Stokes wondered whether it was Iron Mike on the other end of the line or Danny DeMarco.

"I got it," Stokes said, then felt a flash of fear that the kidnappers would suddenly change the plan on him, tell him to meet them right now . . . with the money and Paul's evidence against them. He assumed they had their reasons for waiting until later, though . . . probably fewer potential witnesses or cops around, or something like that . . . and he prayed that those reasons were compelling enough for them to stick to their game plan, because he sure as hell wasn't ready to meet with them.

"Just a few hours until you see your daughter again," the kidnapper said, and Stokes breathed a mental sigh of relief.

"I know," he said. "Put Amanda on."

"She's sleeping. Want me to wake her?" Stokes thought it might have sounded more like DeMarco but he couldn't really tell.

"Wake her," Stokes said. "I need to know she's OK."

"You don't trust us?"

"Well, I know kidnappers are usually a trustworthy bunch, but I'd still like to talk to Amanda."

Stokes could almost hear the kidnapper shrug. A moment later, a little sleep-filled voice said, "Daddy?"

"I'm here, Amanda. And I'll be there soon to take you home. Now go back to sleep, OK?"

"OK . . . Daddy."

The kidnapper took the phone. "Talk to you in an hour, Paul."

"Wait."

"What?"

Stokes swallowed. "There's been a slight change of plans."

A pause. "Really? Because I don't remember changing them."

"*I'm* changing them." Stokes held his breath.

After a moment of silence, the kidnapper said, "You think so, huh? What change are you suggesting, Paul?"

"I'm not going to drop the money and the evidence and hope you tell me where to find Amanda."

"You're not?"

"No. I want to see her before I give you anything. I need to know she's still alive, that she's OK."

"Fuck you, Paul. Listen to me—"

Stokes interrupted but tried to keep from sounding overly confrontational. "No, you listen to me," he said, then quickly added, "please." He continued. "I don't care about the money. I just want Amanda back safe. So I'll give you the money, and all the evidence

I have, but I won't do that unless she's there for me when we meet, ready to come home with me. OK? I see her, I give you the money and the evidence, and you give her to me."

Stokes waited through a cold silence. He began to sweat. A moment later, mumbled conversation drifted across the connection. Finally, the kidnapper said, "Fine, Paul. We'll do it your way. I'll call in an hour."

Stokes would try to give them the entire $350,000 they wanted. Also, he'd give them the blank thumb drive and tell them that it had Jenkins's evidence on it. By then, they'd know he wasn't Paul Jenkins, so he'd tell them that Jenkins was dead. He hoped they'd accept the money and take the thumb drive and let him go with the girl. And if they unfortunately had a laptop at the meeting place and could verify that the thumb drive didn't contain the evidence they were expecting, he'd apologize and explain that he'd searched Jenkins's house and hadn't been able to find any evidence, and that Jenkins, being dead, was beyond being able to give it to them or, more importantly, to the authorities. And if they seemed inclined to kill Amanda and him anyway after all that, he'd try to convince them it just wasn't necessary. Stokes just wanted the girl, and the girl just wanted to go home. And her real parents were dead and her stepmother didn't give two shits about her, so there was no one to care about bringing anyone to justice.

It was a lousy plan, but it was all he had.

He looked down at the cop's gun lying on the floor of the truck, secured in its holster again on Martinson's belt. As he drove, his eyes kept returning to the weapon.

EIGHTEEN

STOKES FELT LIKE HE'D MADE a little progress. He thought he knew where to be to receive the one thirty call. And he'd been able to convince himself that the kidnappers wouldn't really care about the evidence, whatever it was, once they learned that Jenkins was dead. His big problem was that he still had only $248,000 and Grote's guys had made it crystal clear that showing up with a penny less than the $350,000 Paul stole from Grote was not going to be acceptable. And $102,000 was a lot more than a penny. So he needed to come up with that amount in just under three and a half and hours. He wasn't factoring in the forty-odd dollars he had left of Tom What's-His-Name-from-Pittsburgh's money, the cash he took from Paul's wallet, or the seventy-two cents he found on his nightstand.

If he wanted to come up with a lot of money fast, he had only a few options of varying levels of viability. The first option was to borrow it. The odds of one of his acquaintances having that kind of money within easy reach were very, very low. And if, by some miracle, his acquaintances did have that kind of money on hand, the chances of them loaning it to Stokes were even lower. No, if he were going to borrow $100,000, he knew . . . as he always knew . . . that it would have to be from either Leo Grote or Frank Nickerson.

He considered Nickerson first. The problem was that Stokes had just taken almost a year to erase a $75,000 debt, a debt that an unconscionable interest rate had inflated to $100,000 by the time Stokes paid it back earlier that very afternoon. Plus, his sons had no doubt voiced their opinion that Stokes had been trying to leave town without settling that debt before they hauled him off a bus. So he didn't like his chances of getting the money from Frank Nickerson. Besides, the guy wasn't likely to be in a giving mood if Stokes knocked on his door after ten o'clock at night.

Stokes turned his thoughts to Leo Grote. The irony would be that the money Stokes would borrow from Grote would be paid back to the bastard only hours later as part of the ransom for Amanda Jenkins. The problem was, Stokes had a history with Grote, and not a pleasant one, so he didn't like his chances of getting big bucks from old Leo, either. In fact, the last thing Grote said to him was something like, "Stokes, I hope you realize how lucky you are that you're only going to end up with a few broken bones tonight, because I really ought to punch your ticket, you know? So good fucking riddance, and if I ever see your face again I'll probably just have you killed, so stay the fuck out of my sight." So Grote wasn't much of an option, either.

All of which forced Stokes to consider a third option. Which was why he was sitting in Bobby's truck, parked a short way up a side road into the woods, hidden from the main road, a quarter of a mile from his trailer park. He'd leave the truck where it was and enter the park on foot. After the unpleasant little surprise of finding Sergeant Millett waiting for him at his trailer a couple of hours ago, he couldn't risk driving right into the place. But he nonetheless needed to go in.

He used a flashlight to make his way through the trees to the trailer park again. He hopped the chain-link fence and moved through the park, sticking to the shadows where he could, staying off the roads as much as possible in case one of his neighbors was up late and had nothing better to do than sit at his window, watching the dirt road in front of his trailer. Stokes was slinking from shadow to shadow, two rows of trailers over from his—which was likely far enough in the event Millett had decided to camp out in front of Stokes's place all night—and was about to duck behind Mrs. Grandison's trailer, when he heard someone call his name in a half whisper, half yell. It was Charlie Daniels—still no relation to the singer—calling to him through the dark. Stokes must not have been as stealthy as he'd intended to be.

Stokes ignored Daniels and disappeared behind Mrs. Grandison's trailer. Daniels called again.

Jesus Christ.

Stokes hurried around the trailer and across the road, where he found Daniels parked in a lawn chair in front of his place, a can of beer in one hand, a lit cigar in the other. Stokes was now on the road parallel to the one he lived on, where Millett may have been sitting in his cruiser at that moment, waiting for Stokes to come home—perhaps waiting to arrest him.

He tried to keep the frustration out of his voice as he quietly said, "Hey, Charlie."

"Hey, Stokes."

"How about keeping our voices down, OK? Don't want to wake the neighbors, right? Or end up with a citation from that Nazi Barrington."

Bill Barrington was tasked with enforcing the rules of the trailer park—rules pertaining to how long your grass could be, whether you could have pink plastic flamingos on your property, what type of holiday decorations you could have, when they could be put up, and when they had to be taken down. He seemed to take secret delight in flexing the muscles his position of authority had put on his skinny, sixty-five-year-old frame, and handing out the occasional citation.

Daniels nodded. "Yeah, we should keep our voices down. Don't want to bother the neighbors, like you say. Or the cops who were knocking on everybody's doors an hour or so ago, asking about you. Or the ones who went through your trailer."

Stokes hesitated. "Yeah, don't wanna bother them, either."

They were silent for a moment. Stokes cursed inside his head—really loudly inside his head. He couldn't go back to Bobby's truck now. They'd be looking for it. He was glad he'd taken to keeping the backpack with him wherever he went.

Daniels took a swig of beer. "Looks like you're in trouble."

Stokes nodded. "Cops still around?"

"Been gone a little while now."

"They were in my trailer?"

"Yup."

Stokes nodded again, thinking. Sounded like Millett came back again and brought friends with him. And a search warrant. Maybe an arrest warrant, too. Or maybe they just said, "To hell with procedure, we're going to nail this guy." Either way was bad news for Stokes, and probably meant there had been a big change in the case. What the hell could it have been? Why the hell was Millett so focused on Stokes, for God's sake?

"So," Stokes said, "anybody watching my trailer now?"

"Probably. Not that I can see, but if I could see them, then so could you, and they know that if you saw them, you'd go running off. So maybe they're watching your place and maybe they aren't. I have no idea. I just can't see anyone. And I keep a pretty good watch on things generally around here."

He took a puff on his cigar. Stokes watched the end glow brightly for a moment. "I watch a lot of things in this park, you know? For example, I see that you seem to be pretty good friends with Bobby's wife a few trailers down. Kind of a pretty thing, though she looks like she has about ten years more wear on her than her birth certificate probably shows. What's her name again?"

"Joyce."

"Yeah, Joyce. You two seem to be pretty good friends."

Stokes shrugged. Daniels sipped his beer.

"See, Charlie," Stokes said, "Joyce and I, we just—"

"Hell, Bobby's a dipshit. I don't care what you and his wife do." Daniels took another puff of his cigar. "Cops say you knocked some guy's head in. Did you?"

"No, Charlie, I didn't. I swear to God."

"They're just picking on you for no reason then?"

"Not really. The guy got his head knocked in when he surprised someone robbing his house, and the cops have reason to believe I've robbed a house or two in my day, plus I was seen last night in a bar a few blocks away from the guy's house, so they put these things together and decided to try to pin this one on me. It's bullshit."

Daniels nodded. "I see. But you weren't the one who robbed that house last night. You weren't the one who brained that guy, right?"

"Swear to God, Charlie. On my mother's grave. I was in that bar last night, sure, but shit, so were a lot of guys who could have pulled that job. The problem is, this cop on the case, he questioned me a couple of weeks ago about another burglary, a different one, and—"

Daniels interrupted. "You do that one?"

Stokes shrugged. "It's possible that I might have."

"But not this one."

"Nope. Not my style, assaulting people. Never did it, never will."

"Not your style."

"That's right."

Daniels seemed to be sizing Stokes up, judging his character and veracity. That was still never a good thing for him, in Stokes's experience.

"He died, you know," Daniels said. "The guy who got his head busted. He died a little while ago."

Oh, man, Stokes thought. Now Millett was going to go crazy to try to pin this on him, to try to bring his godfather's killer to justice. Well, screw Millett and screw his godfather. Stokes had no plans to take the fall for this one. He was *not* going down for murder. Plenty of other guys in this town knew how to break into a house. Any one of them could be a legitimate suspect in that job last night.

This changed things for Stokes, though. Maybe it was time to cut and run. He'd done his best for the girl, he truly had, but sticking around now was suicide. How long could he evade the cops? If he saw this through now, tried to save Amanda, even if he was successful, did he have any hope of slipping safely out of town when it was all over?

Daniels was watching him.

"I didn't do it, Charlie. I didn't kill that guy. My hand to God."

Daniels nodded, raised the beer can to his lips, tipped his head back, and drained the last of his Budweiser. He looked hard at Stokes.

"The thing is," Daniels said, "I heard a couple of the cops talking outside my trailer—I guess they didn't think anyone could hear them—but I heard them saying that the guy with the busted head woke up from a coma or something long enough for them to show him a bunch of pictures. Before he died, he picked you out."

"Jesus Christ," Stokes said. "Are you kidding me?"

"Nope."

Daniels took a puff on his cigar.

Goddamn it. This was very bad. "Look at my face, Charlie," Stokes said. "Looks just like everybody else's, doesn't it?"

Daniels looked at him a moment before making a gesture with his shoulders and head that was somewhere between a shrug and a nod.

Stokes normally wouldn't have given a rat's ass whether Daniels believed him, but he couldn't afford to have his neighbor calling the cops, telling them he was just talking to the man they were all looking for, so he really needed Daniels to believe him.

"Look," Stokes continued, "the guy wasn't even in his right mind probably, seeing as somebody had recently cracked his skull, but they still believe him when he picks me out of a photo lineup? Hell, the cops already thought I did it. They probably showed the guy my picture along with a dozen black guys, maybe threw in a couple of women and a one-eyed albino midget."

Daniels looked skeptical again. Goddamn it. Stokes knew his face really was a pretty common type. He would have bet his life savings, if he had a life savings, that a solid dozen of the guys in town capable of breaking into that house last night were dark-haired white guys in their thirties with little or no facial hair. Guys who looked a lot like him. Goddamn it.

"Shit," Stokes said, "I'm just saying that my face is a common one and it'd be easy for some half-conscious guy to pick it by accident. But I swear to God, Charlie, I didn't do this. I swear to God."

Daniels took a big puff on his cigar, held it for a moment, then let loose a cloud of smoke. Finally, he nodded to himself, as if coming to a decision.

"All right," he said.

"You believe me?" Stokes said. "That I didn't kill that guy?"

Daniels did that shrug-nod thing again, which Stokes took to mean that he mostly believed what Stokes had said. Stokes mentally sighed with relief. Maybe he'd be able to skip town after all.

Amanda's scared, brave face popped into his head.

No, no, no. Sticking around town would be insane. I tried my best, but things are different now . . .

But the little girl . . .

Stokes could call the cops anonymously, let them worry about it. Why was it *his* problem now?

But he couldn't call the cops. The kidnappers would know if he did. They'd made that clear. And they'd probably kill Amanda.

She had no one to save her. No one but him.

Goddamn it.

Daniels watched with casual curiosity as Stokes played mental ping-pong.

"Listen, Charlie," Stokes finally said, "not only didn't I kill anyone last night, but tonight I'm trying to do something good."

Daniels showed his doubt by chuckling. "Yeah, like what?'"

"Like trying to save somebody's life, maybe."

The older man knitted his bushy eyebrows together in a skeptical look. "Whose life?"

"A little girl's. She's just a kid. Six years old, I think."

"Who's she to you?"

"Nobody, really."

"Nobody?"

"Never even met her. But I'm gonna save her."

"How?"

"With this," Stokes said, tapping his backpack with his foot.

"What's in there?" Daniels asked.

Stokes hesitated. "A flashlight, a picture of the kid I'm gonna save, and a lot of money."

"A lot?"

"Yeah."

"How much?"

"A lot."

"You steal it?" Daniels asked.

"I found it."

"What are you gonna do with it?"

"Save the kid, like I said."

"Why does she need saving?"

"Look, I don't really have time to go into it. If I'm gonna save her, I gotta get moving. The only reason I even bring it up is 'cause I need a car."

"Wasn't that you driving off in Bobby's truck a couple of hours ago?"

Man, this guy didn't miss a thing that went on around here.

"Yeah, well, I left that in the woods near here. But I obviously can't go back to it now. After talking to Bobby and Joyce, the cops will be looking for it."

Daniels nodded, seeing the sense in that. "And you need a car to save some little girl's life tonight, some little girl you never even met."

"Right."

"So you want to borrow mine."

"That about covers it."

"What happened to your motorcycle?"

"Wrecked it."

Daniels took a long puff on his cigar. "OK."

"OK, what? I can take your car?"

Daniels nodded and Stokes almost let out an audible sigh.

"I'm a nice guy, Stokes," Daniels said.

"I can see that."

"No, I mean, I'm a really nice guy. Ask anyone around here, they'll tell you. They'll say, 'That Charlie Daniels, he'd do just about anything to help just about anyone.' Ask anybody in the park here, Stokes. They'll tell you."

"I hear you," Stokes replied. "And I believe you."

"Well, hold on, I'm making a point here."

Stokes waited while Daniels took another long puff on his cigar.

"You remember last year," he finally said, "when my Gloria had pneumonia."

"Uh . . . " Stokes wasn't sure. He thought he might have remembered something about that. Or maybe not. But he'd take Daniels's word for it.

"Yeah, I thought you might not remember. So you probably don't remember that because you weren't employed at the time—like most times, I guess—and you were hanging around your trailer a lot, and I was still working down at the glass factory, well, I asked you to look in on the missus once or twice a day. You know, just to see if she needed anything. Nothing too big, really. Maybe a glass of water if she was thirsty. Maybe ask her if she'd been taking her meds. Anyway, I asked you to do that. You remember?"

Stokes was starting to remember. He nodded.

"It's coming back to you, I guess. So maybe you remember what you told me."

Stokes said nothing.

"No?" Daniels said. "You don't remember?"

Stokes did, but he shook his head.

"If I recall correctly—and I do, believe me—you said that if you wanted to play nurse to some old lady, you'd find yourself a rich old widow so that at least maybe she'd leave you something in her will. You said, at least then maybe there'd be something in it for you. Any of this ringing a bell?"

Stokes blew out a breath.

"Gloria died a few months later," Daniels said. "Remember that part?"

Stokes nodded. Daniels was just jerking him around. "So you were just stringing me along? I can't take your car?"

"No, no. You can still take it."

"Huh?"

"You can't borrow it, though. I can't loan a car to someone the cops are looking for. You're not worth going to jail for. You have to steal the car. Fortunately, everybody around here knows that I leave my keys, along with my spares, on hooks just inside my trailer. And I never lock my door."

"So I can take the car."

Daniels nodded.

"But what about all that with your wife," Stokes said. "You know, last year?"

"Water under the bridge, Stokes. You can take the car. Just give me a thousand dollars."

"What?" Stokes had said it too loudly. He lowered his voice and said it again.

"You heard me. You said yourself you got a lot of money in that bag. I want a thousand of it."

Stokes sputtered inarticulately for a moment before saying, "But I thought you said you were such a great guy."

Daniels took a swig of beer. "It's true, Stokes. I am. I'm a real sweetheart. Like I said, ask anyone. The fact is, if anyone else in this park needed my help like this—even that dipshit Bobby, I suppose—I'd do whatever I could, and gladly. I swear to God. Wouldn't charge a dime. I can't tell you the number of people around here who come to me when they need something. In August I loaned half my monthly social security check to Ben Woodland so he could get his truck running again. He still owes me most of what he borrowed. And just last week I fixed a hole in the roof of Mrs. Bertrand's trailer. I'm always willing to help."

"So then why—"

"Because you're different, Stokes. For you, it'll cost a thousand dollars."

Goddamn it. He should have just looked in on the old lady last year. Would it have killed him?

"But Jesus, Charlie, a *thousand*? Bobby only asked for a hundred."

"Well, that was before the cops were looking for you, wasn't it? Besides, you're only banging Bobby's wife. Mine, you treated like garbage. So it's a thousand. And for that, I promise not to call the cops on you."

Stokes gritted his teeth in frustration.

"And bring it back in one piece," Daniels said. "Don't smash it up and don't make me have to go fetch it from the woods somewhere."

Stokes didn't know for sure that he'd be in any shape to come back himself, much less make sure he brought the car back, but he agreed to do as asked.

Daniels sucked the last of the life from his cigar, dropped it in the dirt at his feet, and ground it beneath the heel of his shoe.

"I'll get you the key. Be right back." He stood. "Why don't you get my thousand dollars out of your big old bag of money there?"

As soon as Daniels stepped into his trailer, Stokes walked over and peeked in a window to make sure the son of a bitch wasn't calling the cops. He watched Daniels grab a key off a hook next to a mustard-yellow refrigerator, then open the fridge and grab a beer. When Daniels stepped outside, Stokes was standing right in front of his door.

"Didn't trust me, huh?" Daniels asked.

Stokes shrugged. Daniels held out his hand, and Stokes, shaking his head, gave him a $1,000 in hundreds. Daniels pocketed the money and handed the car key to Stokes, who stuffed it into his pocket.

"Thanks," Stokes said. *You bastard.*

Daniels nodded and popped the top on his cold Bud.

Stokes walked away, past Daniels's decade-old silver Toyota Camry. Daniels used that grating whisper again to stop him.

"Where you going? My car's right there."

"Yeah, I know," Stokes said, "but there's something I gotta do before I leave."

He hurried off into the shadows between the trailers again, praying that Daniels didn't hold enough of a grudge against him to call the cops—now that he had his money—despite his promise not to.

Stokes wound his way through a few small yards, past trailers, keeping to the shadows again and watching for cops, until he came to a heavy metal drainage grate set flush in the dirt in a dark corner of the grounds. He knelt and let the backpack slip from his shoulder. He reached down and hooked his fingers through the openings in the grate, got a firm grip, and leaned back. The grate came up like a trapdoor, though it wasn't hinged in place, just heavy so he couldn't lift it right up. He tipped it all the way over and gently lowered it to the ground. Lying down next to it, he reached into the darkness below. He could have taken the flashlight from the backpack and shone it into the storm drain, but he knew right where the plastic bag would be. His hand closed on it, in the corner of the small space, right where he'd left it, hanging from a rung of the metal ladder that descended into the deep drain. He reached his other hand down, untied the bag, and hauled it up.

He looked around, made sure no one was watching, and opened the bag. Inside was a collection of diverse items. He shook the bag gently until he spotted what he wanted from it, then reached in and removed a leather case about the size of an address book. Next, he took out a pair of black leather gloves and slid his hands into them. Then he removed the rest of the things, one by one, from the bag. First came a gold watch. Not a Rolex, but nice. No need to wipe it down. He'd worn the gloves the only time he'd touched it. He dropped the watch into the drain. After a moment of silence, he heard it splash into shallow water in the darkness below. Next from the bag came a silver monogrammed money clip—without the money, which Stokes had spent that morning on gas for his bike. He dropped the clip into the dark, and followed it with an expensive-looking gold pen, a notebook computer, miscellaneous women's jewelry, and a crystal figurine that was supposed to look like a bird maybe, which he'd wrapped in a dishcloth. He held on to the cloth. He dumped several more items down the storm drain before, finally, he took from the bag a solid-brass bookend in the shape of a column, the kind you'd see in ancient Rome. Dark-brown blood had dried and crusted on the top of it. He spit on the dishcloth and tried to rub away the dried blood. He wasn't having a lot of success, so he dropped the bookend into the drain, listened for the splash, and hoped that the water down there would do what his saliva couldn't do up here. After he dropped the towel and the plastic bag into the darkness, he gently lowered the grate back into place.

After being questioned about last night's break-in, he'd planned to come back here for this stuff, remove the gloves he was now wearing and the little leather case he'd set aside, then take the bag with the rest of the items in it to Lake Rushton and toss it all in. But things had changed and now he needed the things he'd kept aside. And with Sergeant Millett's godfather dying tonight, Stokes didn't want the rest of the things hanging a mere two feet below the surface of the grate beside the road, just in case the cops searched the park and someone decided to shine a flashlight down there. With the stuff lying in a pool of water ten or so feet down, maybe nobody would ever find what he'd dumped there. And maybe he'd get really lucky and a big rain would come soon and wash it all away.

Stokes stuck the gloves and the leather case into a pocket of the backpack, slung the bag on his shoulder again, and hurried through the shadows back to Daniels's Camry, where he was relieved to find Daniels, still alone, sitting in his lawn chair, sipping his beer, puffing on a new cigar. He looked too relaxed to have called the cops. He watched as Stokes dug the key out of his pocket and opened the car door.

A minute later, he was driving down the dirt road toward the exit of the trailer park, wondering if maybe there'd be a cop waiting there for him. It turned out that there was, but Stokes figured he was probably paying more attention to the way into the park than the way out. And he was undoubtedly looking for Bobby's pickup coming in, not Daniels's Camry going out.

As Stokes neared the police car, which was tucked into the shadow of a tree near the park's entrance, he snatched up a grimy red baseball cap Daniels had left on the passenger seat and put it on, pulling the visor low. He drove right past the cop and out of the park. When he was well past the cruiser and hadn't heard a whoop of a siren, he let out a deep breath he hadn't realized he'd been holding.

He hadn't meant to kill the guy last night. He hadn't even meant to hit him. After he did, though, he really hadn't thought much of it. Hadn't spent the day wondering how the guy was, whether he'd survive the blow, except to think now and then that if Stokes were ever caught, it would be far, far better for him if the guy wasn't too badly hurt. Now that he knew for a fact the guy had died, he was angry with himself. It had been stupid. If they ever did find a way to link him to the crime, his life might as well be over, too. He didn't want to spend a couple of decades behind bars. In the dozens of home break-ins he'd committed over the years, he'd never had to hurt anybody before. And it bugged him. He was screwed now. He was feeling angry, frustrated, a little scared, and, he realized, a bit guilty. He had to admit it. Not so guilty that he planned to walk into the police station, march up to Sergeant Millett's desk, and confess to the killing, but guilty nonetheless. He'd never wanted to kill anyone. Damn.

He still had no intention of going to jail for murder, though. Besides, he had more work to do tonight. He looked at his watch: 10:41 p.m. Less than three hours until he had to be at Laund-R-Rama to answer the kidnapper's call. Which didn't leave him a lot of time to come up with another $102,000—no, wait . . . after Charlie Daniels extorted another grand out of him, it was $103,000. Terrific.

He had no idea how to save the girl. No idea how this was all going to end. Equally troubling to him, he had no idea if there was any way it could end with the girl and him both going free—maybe one of them, but probably not both. That would take a miracle, and he'd never believed in miracles.

NINETEEN

WIGGINS & MARTZ WAS A big antiques store in the highest-rent section of downtown. It was the kind of place you couldn't just walk into and browse; you needed to make an appointment in advance, and when your time came, you rang a doorbell and they buzzed you in. Stokes had never been inside the place, though he'd looked in the windows plenty of times, wondering if it was worth the risk to try to break in one night. In the end, he'd always decided against it, because if he broke in he'd find two things: a lot of old stuff and an empty cash box. The "old stuff" was an assortment of antiques, of course, but Stokes didn't have the faintest idea which ones were truly worth taking, nor did he have the first clue where to fence the kind of junk he'd find in there anyway. Besides, assuming he even got past the place's security system, which he didn't really think was all that likely, he couldn't just carry a hundred-year-old piano or a roll-top desk out on his back. Just as importantly, however, Stokes had heard a reliable rumor that the store's owners never left any money on site after closing.

Everyone in town knew who Hugh Wiggins and Arthur Martz were. They were respected gentlemen, good and honest businessmen, supporters of numerous local charities and other institutions requiring assistance, such as the public libraries and homeless shelters. Word had it they'd met almost forty years ago, when they were each in their early twenties. They became fast friends and business partners for life and, somewhere along the line, life partners.

Stokes didn't care about any of that, though. What interested him about the men was something he'd heard during a poker game a while back. The old guys didn't trust banks. Though their business was robust and they took in good money each day, for some reason they refused to deposit all of their day's intake into their chosen institution. They typically held out a large percentage and took it home with them, to the house they'd shared for most of their adult lives. Stokes heard this from a guy he knew—Lenny Something-or-Other—who had driven a delivery truck for a while and had delivered some furniture to the antiques store. The owners were friendly and chatty as hell. Once Lenny realized that, he started asking questions and the old guys volunteered all kinds of information they shouldn't have been sharing. Not long after, about three years ago now, Lenny donned a mask and broke into their house. When he couldn't find the money, he simply threatened one of the gents with physical harm and the other fell over himself to get it for him out of a secret hidey-hole under an area rug in their den. Lenny got away clean with almost sixty thousand bucks. The thing was, according to one of the tellers at Wiggins and Martz's bank—a teller who was happy to answer a few questions in exchange for one of Lenny's twenties—after the robbery their bank deposits hadn't increased. So Lenny had planned on breaking into the antique dealers' house again and making another withdrawal. Before he got the chance, though, he was arrested for carjacking and was now serving a dime in prison. Which left Stokes with some useful—hopefully accurate—information.

Over the past few weeks, as the deadline for paying Nickerson ten grand of the hundred Stokes had owed him was approaching,

Stokes had pulled a few jobs, broken into a few houses and a couple of small stores, trying to come up with enough for the payment. He'd have gone right to Wiggins and Martz's house first, but a sign in their shop window said they had been on vacation in Italy for six weeks. Stokes figured they wouldn't have left a ton of money in their house while they were gone, so he'd had to wait until they returned. The men had been back in town and back in business for three weeks now, and Stokes's deadline for payment was two weeks away. He had planned to pull the job next week, which would have given him a week's cushion before he had to turn around and give the money to Nickerson, but today's events had forced him to speed up his plans.

Stokes had left Charlie Daniels's car around the corner. He stood now in the shadow of a huge oak tree or elm tree or some other huge old tree, across the street from the house that Wiggins and Martz shared. The place was a big, rambling Victorian, old—as true Victorians must be—but extraordinarily well kept.

Stokes looked at the houses on either side of the Wiggins-Martz residence. They were colonials, and not nearly as well kept. But like Wiggins and Martz's house, their windows were dark. Stokes looked at his watch: 10:58 p.m. He put the picture of Amanda Jenkins and her father, which he'd been looking at moments earlier, into a pocket of the backpack at his feet, then took the cell phone from inside his jacket and watched the house until the phone rang two minutes later. He answered it quickly.

"Hello," he said.

"In a few hours you'll see your daughter again," the kidnapper said. "You ready?"

Stokes still couldn't tell whether it was Iron Mike on the line or Danny DeMarco. It didn't matter, so he stopped thinking about it.

"Just about."

"Good. She's sleeping. Want me to wake her again?"

Stokes wanted to talk to Amanda, to make sure she was OK—as inconvenient as the hourly calls from the kidnappers had been, Stokes now definitely understood Paul's need to talk to her every hour—but he'd already woken her once. He didn't want to wake her again into the nightmare she'd find when she opened her eyes.

"Nah, just put the phone up to her face. I wanna hear her breathing."

"Whatever."

A moment later, Stokes heard peaceful breaths coming over the phone line, a rhythmic breathing that took him back to the little breaths he'd felt on his neck thirteen years ago. After a moment, the breathing was gone, replaced by the kidnapper's voice.

"Satisfied?"

"Yeah."

"Talk to you in an hour."

The line went dead. Stokes pocketed the phone, then left the security of the moon shadow beneath the big tree and hurried across Wiggins and Martz's beautifully tended lawn, around the back of the house, across a small brick patio, to a back door. As usual, he carried the bag of money on his back. In his pocket were Officer Martinson's pepper spray and the last of his plastic ties. Crammed into the backpack with the money was the cop's baton. Stokes had chosen to leave the gun in the car. He really didn't want to kill anyone else today. Besides, the men inside were in their midsixties. He figured that if things went wrong, the threat of the baton should be enough. He took off his leather jacket and shrugged out of his western shirt, leaving him in his black T-shirt. He put the jacket back on, then wrapped the cowboy shirt tightly around his head, adjusting it so the eyeholes he'd cut a few minutes ago in the car lined up properly with his eyes before tying it tight in back. In the outer pocket of the backpack were the black gloves and the small leather case he'd taken from the storm drain at the trailer park.

He knelt by the back door, in the shadow of the house, and peered into the window in the door. He saw an alarm panel on the kitchen wall just inside. A little indicator light glowed red, telling him the alarm was activated. A green light would have been too much to hope for. Stokes looked at his watch. This could go relatively quickly or this could take a while, depending on whether the cops showed up. He hoped he'd finally get a break and it would go quickly. He knew *he* didn't have a guardian angel, but if Amanda Jenkins did, maybe it would start pulling its weight.

He removed the gloves from the backpack, slipped them on, and inspected the door. Maybe Amanda Jenkins had a guardian angel watching over her after all. He'd gotten lucky with the lock on the door. No dead bolt, just a key-in-lock knob, which meant that to lock it from the inside, you'd push a button or turn a little knob on the doorknob inside the house. To unlock it from the outside, you'd just insert a key into the knob and turn. Easiest lock to pick, and it told Stokes how he might get around the security system. Perhaps the old guys believed that their beefed-up system would deter any future prowlers from even attempting to break in. Or if a burglar did break in, the resulting shriek of the alarm would send him running into the night. Whatever their reasoning, it was Stokes's good fortune.

He examined the lock briefly before removing the leather case from the backpack. Inside were the gleaming tools of his part-time trade: his set of lock picks. It was a damn-fine set. Sixty-nine pieces, including single-ball and double-ball picks, large and small diamond picks, short-hook picks and long-hook picks, C- and S- and L- and W-rake picks, and eight different tension tools. He even had twenty-eight picks and tools for use specifically in Europe, though Stokes had never had occasion to use those and couldn't imagine he ever would. A beautiful lock pick set, worth close to two hundred bucks. It was far more than Stokes ever needed, and he'd never have bought it for himself. He'd won it from Lenny the delivery guy in the same poker game where he'd heard that Wiggins and Martz kept money under their floorboards. Stokes had been cleaned out of cash and had to toss his forty-buck lock pick snap gun into the pot. The snap gun was limited in its use, really only good for opening pin-and-tumbler locks, and when Lenny had raised his bet by tossing the gorgeous lock pick set into the pot, Stokes had been forced to call the bet with his brand new HJC motorcycle helmet. Three jacks had been enough to take the pot. Just four hands later, though, he lost his shiny new lock picks back to Lenny, when he'd held a king-high straight and Lenny had pulled a goddamn flush on the seventh and final goddamn card. So a week later, Stokes was pleased to find that the door to Lenny's apartment had a pin-and-tumbler lock, on which Stokes's trusty old snap gun was perfectly effective. He broke into the apartment and took nothing but the expensive lock pick set he'd won and lost. Lenny had a good idea who'd stolen it, but he wasn't about to call the cops or report the loss to his insurance company, and the poor bastard got himself pinched for carjacking not long after, before he'd had the chance to get his picks back. Perhaps he was sitting in prison at that very moment, dreaming of the day he'd be released and could get his hands on his beautiful lock picks again.

Stokes selected a torsion wrench and the lock pick he wanted and got to work. He tried extraordinarily hard not to leave marks on the knob. Normally, he wouldn't have cared. But tonight it was important not to leave visible traces of his efforts. After a few brief moments, less than a minute and a half, he stuck the lock pick and torsion wrench into his back pocket. The door was unlocked. If he pushed it inward, the alarm would sound.

He pushed it in and the alarm screamed.

Stokes quickly reached around the door and felt the little button on the doorknob. He pressed it in and pulled the door shut as quietly as he could, locking it again. He scooped up the backpack and sprinted across the yard toward the trees lining the back of the property.

The alarm wailed.

Stokes slipped behind a thick tree trunk in a deep, dark shadow and watched the house. A light snapped on in an upstairs room. He glanced at the windows of the neighbors' houses. They remained dark, despite the shrieking alarm. A light clicked on downstairs in the Wiggins-Martz house, apparently in the foyer by the front door—Stokes could see its glow through the dark kitchen at the back of the house. No doubt there was an alarm panel by the front door, too, its indicator lights flashing frantically at that moment, a robotic voice saying over and over, "Intruder alert," or, more likely, something like, "Fault, kitchen door." A moment later, the alarm stopped. Either Wiggins or Martz had turned it off.

Stokes watched. Depending on how they had arranged things with their alarm company, either the cops would arrive shortly, or the company, which had received the alarm signal, would call the house to see whether there was indeed a break-in or whether, perhaps, the alarm had been tripped accidentally. A second later, Stokes heard a phone ring inside the house. That was good. Either Wiggins or Martz was probably telling the alarm company that everything appeared to be all right. A light snapped on in the kitchen, and Stokes saw one of the men—it looked like Martz, who had a full head of gray hair, as opposed to Wiggins, who was bald—appear at the back door. He wore blue silk pajamas and had a portable phone at his ear. He bent down to look at the knob, must have seen that it was locked. Stokes could see he looked a little sleepy and very puzzled. A moment later, he stepped to the alarm panel, pressed some buttons, and walked away, turning off the light as he went. Stokes watched the lights in the house turn off in reverse order, marking Martz's progress back up to his bedroom. When the light turned off in that room, too, Stokes checked his watch.

Ten minutes later, he slipped from the shadows of the trees, leaving his backpack behind, and hurried back across the lawn to the shadow of the house. He knelt by the back door again, saw the red light on the alarm panel, and took the lock pick and tension tool from his back pocket. Barely a minute later, he pushed the door open, setting the alarm screaming again, locked the door from inside as before, and pulled it shut quickly but quietly, before racing back across the lawn to his hiding place. By the time he got there, the light was already on in the upstairs bedroom.

He waited.

The light came on in the upstairs hallway, followed by the light in the foyer downstairs. A moment later, the alarm fell silent. Stokes looked at the houses to either side of the Victorian. Still dark. Inside the Victorian, the phone rang. Light bloomed in the kitchen, and Stokes saw Martz stride across the room to the back door. He tested the knob again, saw it was still locked. He looked more puzzled than before, a little less sleepy, and quite a bit more frustrated. He ran his hand around the doorframe, as if that would tell him anything. He opened the door and inspected the outside knob. This was a critical moment. The man likely didn't have an eye trained to spot subtle marks left by a decent lock-picker, but Stokes sweated it out for a couple of seconds anyway. But he needn't have worried. His careful work had left nothing for an untrained eye to spot, and Martz closed the door, no doubt locking it again. He set the alarm yet again and left the kitchen in darkness behind him.

Stokes trotted back to the house, ran through the same routine, and was back behind his tree before the alarm had been shrieking for six seconds. Lights came on in the house again, in the now familiar pattern—bedroom, upstairs hallway, downstairs foyer. This time lights turned on upstairs in the colonial to the left of the Victorian. A silhouette appeared at the window. Stokes knew he couldn't be seen where he was hiding, especially not by someone standing in a room with the lights on, so he returned his attention to the Victorian. The alarm ceased. The phone rang. Light flooded the kitchen again, but this time both gray-haired Martz, in his blue pajamas, holding the telephone to his ear, and smooth-headed Wiggins, in paisley silk pajamas, crossed the room to the back door. They both tested the knob and found it to be locked. Martz reported that to the alarm company. They both inspected the door frame, and Martz reported those findings, too. Stokes shifted so he was fully behind the tree now, peering out through a tangle of low branches, all but invisible from the house. Both Martz and Wiggins opened the door and inspected the knob on the outside. Martz said something into the phone, then spoke to Wiggins again. Stokes couldn't hear what they were saying. They debated for a while before Martz lowered the phone and ended the call with a punch of a button.

Stokes watched closely.

The older men pulled the door shut. They left the kitchen, turning off lights as they made their way back upstairs.

They hadn't reactivated the alarm.

Stokes looked up at the neighbor's window. It was dark again.

He checked his watch: 11:36. He waited two more minutes before recrossing the lawn, backpack over his shoulder this time. He looked through the window of the back door and saw the light on the alarm panel glowing green. He took the tools from his back pocket and unlocked the door. He returned the tools to their leather case, returned the case to the backpack, and stepped into the quiet house. He doubted the old guys were asleep just yet. More likely they were debating just what to say tomorrow to the alarm company that had obviously installed a defective system.

Stokes moved through the house. Enough light spilled in through the various bay windows to guide him through the living room and into the den. Even in the dim light he could see that the place was beautifully furnished, probably with valuable antiques.

The rooms were a little emptier than he would have expected, his mind conjuring images of dusty old houses he'd seen in movies, crammed with solid, imposing pieces of furniture—armoires, secretaries, bookcases, whatever. Perhaps the old guys liked things a little less cramped. Perhaps that was better taste. Stokes had no idea.

He saw a rectangular area rug in the center of the floor of the den. He put his backpack down and very quietly moved two armchairs and a small, round table to the side of the room. Rolling back one end of the rug, he saw in the floor a little wooden trapdoor—maybe two feet square—with a small, recessed metal handle. He pulled on the handle and the trapdoor swung up.

In the space beneath it was a combination safe.

Lenny never mentioned a safe.

Damn it.

This complicated things. Stokes wasn't a safecracker. Now, he would have to—

A sound made him turn around. Martz was standing in the doorway pointing a big handgun at him. Wiggins stood beside him. The son of a bitch had a gun, too.

TWENTY

"PLEASE PUT YOUR HANDS UP," Wiggins said. His bald head looked shiny, like a sheen of perspiration had sprouted on it. Stokes figured he was probably nervous. He also figured that if *he* were bald, he'd probably have the same sheen on *his* head just then. Staring into two gun barrels was making him a little anxious, too. He raised his hands.

"Easy, fellas," he said. "Careful with those things."

"We know how to use them," Wiggins said. "It might surprise you to know that we both served in the military. It's where we met."

"I did two tours in Vietnam," Martz said. "I've killed people," he added, not proudly, just stating a fact.

"I haven't killed anyone," Wiggins said, "but I could in the right circumstances. I'm sure of it."

"The point is," Martz continued, "we know how to use these weapons and are willing to do so if we must. You understand?"

Stokes looked at the way they held their guns. They weren't just a couple of senior citizens who bought guns for protection, then stored them unloaded on the top shelf of a closet, behind a hatbox and a stack of moth-eaten cardigans, praying they'd never have to use them. No, the guns rested comfortably in their hands. They knew what they were doing.

"Yeah," Stokes said, "I understand."

"Good," Martz said. "Now, at first we thought something was wrong with our security system, with the sensor on our back door, just like you wanted us to think. We'd gotten back upstairs again when we got to thinking that we'd spent a heck of a lot of money on our system—"

"A *heck* of a lot," Wiggins interjected. "So we thought maybe the system was working just fine after all, and maybe somebody *wanted* us to think our system was faulty so we'd leave it turned off."

Martz nodded at his partner. "So we left it off, just like you wanted, only we came back downstairs—"

"In the dark this time."

"Right, in the dark, but this time we brought our guns with us."

Stokes waited for Martz to add something, to continue the little dance these two did, finishing each other's thoughts and sentences like an old married couple, which was essentially what they were. But he said nothing.

"Mind pointing those things somewhere else?" Stokes asked.

"I don't think so," Martz said. "Now please, take off your mask."

Stokes didn't see any way he could refuse, so he tugged the shirt from his face and let it fall to the floor.

Martz studied Stokes's face. He turned to Wiggins. "Do we know him?"

"We don't," Wiggins said. "Unless he's the one who broke in here a few years ago, threatened to hurt you until we gave him our money."

"Wasn't me," Stokes said.

Martz ignored that. He looked at Wiggins. "Is he the same one?"

"I'm not," Stokes insisted. They continued to scrutinize him, and Stokes realized that his fate might rest on whether he could convince them that he wasn't the guy who had previously trauma-tized them. "It wasn't me. That guy's name was Lenny, and he's in prison now and will be for another seven or eight years."

Wiggins and Martz seemed to think about that. "You came here to rob us," Wiggins said. It wasn't a question.

"That's right."

"Not a very good idea."

"I see that now."

"Are you armed?"

Staring at the two older gentlemen with the big guns, Stokes formed a radical plan. He'd try the truth on these guys, see where it got him. It was either that or rush them, and he wasn't eager to do that, not with a couple of Vietnam vets, at least one of whom had seen action and who claimed to have killed and wouldn't be afraid to do so again—a claim Stokes wasn't eager to put to the test.

"I've got a policeman's baton in my backpack here," he said.

"Where'd you get a policeman's baton?" Martz asked.

"From a policeman."

"Did you kill him?"

"No."

"Did you hurt him?"

"Just a little. But I talked to him after, and he was fine. He even offered to forget the whole thing." Which was technically true, though Stokes left out the part about having to let Martinson go free if he wanted that forgiveness.

Martz nodded, thinking. "That bag looks like it's got more than just a policeman's baton in it. What else do you have in there?"

Sticking with his truthfulness plan, Stokes started his answer by saying, "First, let me tell you why I'm here."

"You're here to try to rob us," Wiggins said.

"Well, yeah, I am. But let me tell you why." Before they could object, he continued. "A little girl has been kidnapped. She's six years old, I think. I've talked to her. She's scared. Both her parents are dead. And her stepmother, believe it or not, was actually in on it with the kidnappers. They want three hundred and fifty thousand dollars in cash, or they'll kill the girl."

Wiggins nodded as he listened. Martz frowned.

"Who is she to you?" Wiggins asked. "The little girl."

"Nobody. Never met her."

They considered that for a moment before Wiggins said, "If the stepmother is in on it—"

Martz finished for him, "That means the father must have been the one from whom they wanted the money." They looked at each other, seeming pleased with their deduction. It wasn't all that terrific a deduction, not too great a leap of logic to get there, but at least they were paying attention to the story, even enjoying it a little, which was kind of weird, but so long as they weren't telling him to shut up or, worse, shooting him, Stokes didn't care if they made something of a game of it.

"Right," he said. "They wanted the money from the father. And he got it."

"The money?" Martz asked. "He got it?"

Stokes nodded.

"And he didn't call the authorities?" Wiggins asked.

"The kidnappers said they have people with the police and the FBI secretly working for them. The father ignored that, called them, and the kidnappers cut off one of the girl's fingers."

Wiggins's eyes widened. "They really have someone inside the police department then?"

"Yeah," Stokes said. "Maybe the FBI, too. So the father got the money and was planning to pay them later tonight."

He paused.

"But?" Martz said.

Stokes sighed. "He had a car accident. I found him."

"Dead?"

"Dead."

"And you found the money," Wiggins said.

"I found the money. And I'm planning to use it to ransom the girl."

Martz frowned at him, the picture of skepticism. "And you never thought about keeping it?"

Stokes snorted. "Shit, yeah, I thought about it. Of course I did. I thought hard about it. But then I made the mistake of answering the guy's cell phone when the kidnappers called. I talked to the girl."

They said nothing for a moment. The men were scrutinizing him again. He was fed up with people doing that today.

"I have to say," Martz said, "you seem the sort who would be more likely to keep the money in these circumstances."

"Yeah, I probably am more that sort of guy."

"But this is different somehow."

"Guess so," Stokes said.

Wiggins shook his head. "That's a lot of money."

"I know."

"So why help the girl instead of keeping it?"

Stokes shrugged. "It's complicated. But I have my reasons. I think."

Martz nodded slowly. He seemed willing to accept that. "Your bag then," he said. "If you're telling the truth, the money's in there."

"It is. All but a hundred and three thousand dollars of it."

"What happened to the hundred three thousand dollars?" Wiggins asked.

"I had to give it to someone. Well, a few people."

Stokes expected them to ask who he gave it to, but they didn't. They were thinking. They regarded him for a long moment. Then they looked at each other. They seemed to be communicating through pure thought. They swung their gaze his way again. They appeared to be sizing him up yet again, goddamn it, taking his measure.

Finally, Wiggins spoke. "And you came here, hoping to steal at least a hundred three thousand dollars to make up for the money you *had* to give away."

"Yeah, that's about it."

"So you're using your criminal powers for good now instead of evil," Martz said.

"Guess so. For tonight anyway."

"Ironic."

"Guess so."

"So you're saying you've got almost two hundred fifty thousand dollars in that bag," Wiggins said, "money you intend to simply give away, out of the goodness of your heart, to save a little girl you've never met."

"That's right."

"You can understand if we're a bit dubious," Martz said.

Stokes didn't know what *dubious* meant. "I'm telling you the truth." He nodded toward the bag at his feet. "May I?"

They considered for a moment. "Slowly," Martz said.

Stokes bent down and, moving very slowly, unfastened the flap on the backpack and opened it. The men looked at the bundles of money inside.

"You see," Stokes said as he closed the bag again, "you send me to jail, that little girl probably dies. But," he ventured, inspiration coming to him in a flash, "if you were to, say, loan me a hundred three thousand dollars, we might save her life together."

They looked at him in silence.

Stokes trudged on. "This really isn't so different from the money you've been giving away for years, money you give away to help people. Haven't you guys donated a bunch of cash to the library, the hospital, schools, places like that?"

They nodded in unison.

"Well, this is no different. You'd be giving money to help get a little girl away from some very bad men. Men who have already hurt her, who might even kill her if we don't help her."

They looked at Stokes a moment longer, then at the bag of money, then at each other. They seemed to exchange a few more telepathic thoughts before apparently coming to a decision. They turned to Stokes again.

"You made a mistake coming here," Martz said.

"I realize that."

"No," Wiggins cut in, "he means we don't have any money in the house."

"What?" Stokes frowned. "But I thought you guys didn't like banks. You used to keep most of your cash hidden here."

"That's right. We used to."

"But if you don't have any money here," Stokes said, "what's in the floor safe?"

"Nothing. It's empty," Wiggins said.

"So you put all your money into banks now?"

Stokes sighed. He'd counted on them having a more deeply rooted distrust and fear of banks.

"You don't understand," Martz said. "We're not putting money into banks, either. The fact is, we just don't have any money anymore."

"What? Wait a second, guys," Stokes said. "What about all the money you give away?"

"We gave it all away," Wiggins said.

Stokes didn't understand. "All of it?"

"Well no, we didn't give all of our money away. We spent some of it on living expenses, some on back taxes—"

"And we paid off a few creditors," Martz added.

"Right," Wiggins said. "The point is, our store stopped being profitable quite a while back."

"This economy has not been kind," Martz said.

Wiggins added, "We've been in the red for a long time now. We'll be closing our doors very soon."

Stokes shook his head. "But your donations—"

"Stopped two years ago. We're nearly bankrupt."

Now it was Stokes's turn to be skeptical. "Hold on, you say you're broke, but you somehow found enough money to spend, what was it, a month and a half in Italy?"

"We needed to get away. We hung a sign on the door of our store saying we were going to Italy. For the sake of appearances, of course."

Martz looked sheepish. "Actually, we spent six weeks at Hugh's brother's house in New Jersey. We went there to get away for a while—from our business, from our creditors. We took with us photographs of many of our fine antiques. Some from our shop, though there aren't many good pieces left there, and many from our house here."

"My brother is a man of means," Wiggins said. "And he has exquisite taste. He kindly offered to give us very fair prices for many of our pieces to help us manage our debt, to pay back more of our creditors. He's buying from us some of the pieces you see in this very room, in fact."

"You're so poor you have to sell your furniture?" Stokes asked. This was a big waste of time. He sighed.

Wiggins nodded sadly. "We've already sold many of our favorite pieces to dealers in other cities."

Stokes looked around, again noticing that the house seemed to be furnished more sparsely than he'd expected.

Martz said, "Eventually, we'll have to sell the house, too."

"But everyone in town thinks you're still rich."

"A charade we've managed, until now, to maintain. Our creditors know, naturally, but they also know we're trying to pay. Most of them aren't interested in slandering the good names of a couple of old, local businessmen like us."

"If you're broke, why the hell did you spend so much on a security system and a floor safe, especially if there's less and less in here to protect?"

"Those were the last significant purchases we made, I'm afraid," Martz said, "shortly after your friend stole sixty thousand dollars from us, but right before business took a sharp downturn."

Stokes blew out a breath. "So you can't give me the hundred thousand dollars?"

"No. As you put it, we're broke."

"Which is why," Wiggins added, "I'm sorry to say, we're going to have to keep that money you've got there."

Stokes wasn't sure he'd heard right. He looked at the two older men. Looked at their eyes. Then at their guns.

"You gotta be shitting me."

TWENTY-ONE

"WE DON'T WANT TO SHOOT you," Wiggins said, "but we will if we have to."

"And we'd get away with it," Martz added. "You broke into our home, engaged in those shenanigans with our alarm system. I think a couple of old men like us, pillars in this community, wouldn't have a problem convincing the authorities that we had no choice but to defend ourselves using, unfortunately, lethal force. Don't you?"

Sadly, Stokes did. The guns looked kind of heavy in the guys' hands. Their arms looked kind of skinny. Stokes was worried the strain of keeping them pointed at him might cause one of them to pull a trigger accidentally.

"Look, fellas," Stokes said, "we can talk this thing out. For now, why don't you give your arms a break? Let the guns hang in your hands, pointed at the floor."

They eyed him with suspicion. But it also looked to Stokes like there was hope on their faces, like they really did want to relax their scrawny arms for a while.

"I'm twelve feet away, guys," Stokes added. "I couldn't get three steps toward you before you shot me dead if you wanted to."

Wiggins and Martz looked at each other, then lowered their guns. Stokes thought about rushing them, but they looked a little jumpy and were liable to kill him even if they didn't mean to. Plus, again, as war veterans with combat experience, they might still have decent reflexes.

"Now what's this about keeping my money?" he asked.

"Well, it's not really yours, is it?" Martz responded. "You stole it yourself, didn't you? From a dead man?"

"Hell, fellas, it's more mine than yours."

"I'm not sure we agree," Wiggins said. "But we don't have to. The facts are these: You broke into our house intending to steal from us, so we don't really feel a great deal of affection for you. And we have found ourselves in dire financial straits—"

Martz cut in. "In no small part due to our lengthy history of philanthropy over the years."

"Right. And finally, you have a great deal of money in your bag there."

"Money that we need very badly."

"Money that, under the circumstances, you could never go to the police to complain about having been stolen from you."

"So you see," Martz said, "this truly could not have worked out better for us."

Wiggins shook his head, indicating his agreement that things couldn't have worked out better for them.

Stokes shook his head in disbelief. "You're robbing me," he said. He wasn't asking, merely summing up the situation.

"Ironic, we know," Wiggins said. "Now please step away from that bag." He raised his gun. Martz did the same.

Stokes shook his head but didn't move his feet. "I'm having a little trouble here, fellas. This isn't the way guys like you are supposed to act."

"Guys like us?" Martz asked.

"Relax, I don't mean *guys like you*. I mean guys who everyone respects, guys who donate money all over the place, stuff like that. So what gives?"

"Well," Wiggins began, "as we told you, we're nearly bankrupt."

"And we've been forced to sell many of our most treasured possessions," Martz added, "which pains us more than you can imagine."

Wiggins nodded. "And, well, we don't want to do that any longer."

Stokes blew out an exasperated breath. "But stealing? With an innocent kid's life at stake?"

Martz sighed. "We'd rather not steal, but we'd *much* rather not lose our precious antiques. It took us nearly a lifetime to collect them. We chose nearly every item in this house with great care, after much searching for just the right piece. Nearly everything of value in this house, everything we own, comes with a story, a story special to Hugh and me."

"That's right," Wiggins said. "Do you see that end table? It's nineteenth-century Italian neoclassic. We picked it up during a wine-tasting trip to Napa Valley ten years ago. A wonderful vacation."

"And that late Regency mahogany *secretaire* bookcase behind you?" Martz asked.

Stokes turned and saw a bookcase.

"It was crafted in 1829. Notice the cavetto cornice, the turned *rondle* decoration, the astral glazed doors—with the original glass, mind you, as well as the original brass beading and knobs. Even the lock and key are original. Extraordinary, isn't it?"

Stokes still saw a bookcase.

"It's one of our favorite pieces. Not because it's worth close to twelve thousand dollars, but because it was a fiftieth-birthday gift to me from Hugh."

"Do you see now?" Wiggins asked Stokes. "Maybe a little? Far beyond the fact that the items here have considerable monetary value, everything here has special meaning to us."

Stokes said, "Yeah, but—"

Martz interrupted. "Hugh and I have ingratiated ourselves to the members of this community through our charitable works and, with very few exceptions, we have been treated with nothing but respect. Still, we have always been outsiders. We've had only each other, really, for so many years. Only each other and this house."

"And all the wonderful things in it," Wiggins said. "And every item we've had to sell so far, and there have been quite a few, has been painful to part with."

"So maybe you can understand," Martz said, "why we need to do this. The money isn't yours anyway. And with it, we can keep from selling the rest of our treasures, maybe even buy back some of what we've been forced to sell off."

"If it's any consolation," Wiggins said, "we really are very sorry."

"But we are also quite desperate," Martz said, "and will do anything to keep our home together, and by that I mean the precious items in it."

"And what about the little girl?" Stokes finally asked.

Martz frowned. "That's regrettable, of course. We don't want to see her hurt. But in the end, it isn't our business, is it?"

"It really isn't our problem," Wiggins added.

"Besides," Martz continued, "she won't be hurt. Kidnapping is a serious crime, but murder is much more serious. When the kidnappers realize they won't be getting their money, they'll let the little girl go."

"You really believe that?" Stokes asked.

Martz hesitated just long enough for Stokes to see that he didn't believe it, not for certain. "I do believe it," Martz said. "We both do." He looked at Wiggins, who nodded. Stokes could tell that Wiggins didn't believe it, either.

"So here's how this will work," Martz said. "We'll escort you to the kitchen door, the one through which you entered our house, and we'll see you out. You will walk six feet in front of us. If you stop, we'll shoot you in the back. If you run, we'll do the same. If you turn around, we'll shoot you in the chest. When we get to the door, you will step outside and walk ten feet into the backyard. We'll have our guns trained on you the entire time. When you are outside, ten feet from the door, we'll lock the door, activate the alarm, and assume we'll never see you again, because in the morning the money will be in one of our bank accounts."

"And as for breaking in here ever again," Wiggins said, "I think you can see it would be a bad idea. Our security system truly is top notch, we're armed, and we no longer keep large amounts of cash in the house."

Stokes simply could not believe this was happening. After all he'd gone through so far today, that he could lose the money to people that *he'd* been trying to rob in the first place was unbelievable.

Martz motioned with his gun, indicating the direction he wanted Stokes to walk. Stokes didn't move. Martz motioned with his gun again. "Let's go now."

Stokes had had enough. "No."

Martz blinked at him. "What?"

"I said no. I'm not leaving. Not without the money anyway."

"We have guns," Wiggins reminded him.

"I know," Stokes said, "and you know how to use them. I get it. But I've had a really long day. It started out at the police station, which is never any fun. Then I flipped my motorcycle over a guardrail, which wasn't a lot of fun, either. But then I found all this money, and I could have skipped town with it, but I decided to do the right thing, get a little girl out of the hands of kidnappers, probably saving her life. And when this is all over, for all my effort, I'll probably go to jail for the rest of my life. So I'll be damned if I'm gonna let you keep this money. Not when I could have just kept it myself in the first place. And not when a little kid could die for it. So fuck you, I'm not leaving without the money."

Wiggins looked at Martz uncertainly. Martz returned a similar look before turning to Stokes. "Remember, we could shoot you dead and almost certainly get away with it, especially given your history and reputation."

"I know," Stokes said.

"And the police would never know a thing about the money. We could hide it long before they got here."

"I see that."

"And we've told you how desperate we are to have that money." Stokes nodded.

"And still, you won't leave without it?"

Stokes shook his head. "Guess you're gonna have to shoot me." He held his arms out in front of him, his palms up, and made an exaggerated shrug that said, *It's out of my hands now. Your move.*

Martz and Wiggins exchanged another long look. Finally, they seemed to come to some silent agreement. Wiggins lowered his head and Stokes knew he'd successfully called their bluff. So when Martz shot him, he was surprised—so surprised that someone could have knocked him over with a feather if the bullet hadn't already done the job.

TWENTY-TWO

AFTER MARTZ PULLED THE TRIGGER, things happened fast. Stokes's arms were still slightly away from his body and the bullet ripped along the inside of his left biceps, between his arm and his chest, ten inches away from his heart. Shock and the searing sting of the bullet creasing his skin made him spin and fall to the floor. As he dropped, he heard glass shattering and wood splintering and someone shouting. He thought he'd cried out in pain and surprise, but unless he was able to do so in stereo, the cries he heard hadn't come from him. He looked up and saw Wiggins and Martz—Martz with his gun still up in firing position—staring with horror. But they weren't staring at him, the man they'd just shot. They were staring over his head.

"The Regency bookcase," Wiggins cried. "Arthur, you shot it."

And he had. After burning a trench across the inside of Stokes's arm, Martz's bullet had shattered the glass in the door of the $12,000 bookcase behind him, then blown a hole in the back of the thing. From the looks on the faces of the antique dealers, you'd have thought they shot one of their mothers.

Taking advantage of the momentary distraction, Stokes ignored the blazing pain in his left arm and with his right hand grabbed the backpack, heavy with money, off the floor. In one fluid motion, he sprang to his feet and used the momentum of his rising to increase the power of his throw as he spun and hurled the bag at Martz. The throw didn't catch the guy in the face and knock him to the floor or anything, but the backpack sailed at his midsection. Instinct made him drop his gun and protect himself from the impact. The bag bounced harmlessly off him, eliciting a little "Oof," but the gun fell from his hands, which is what Stokes had hoped for. So Stokes, who had followed the backpack across the room, headed straight for the still-armed Wiggins, prayed the old guy was too shocked by both Martz shooting the antique and Stokes's flinging the backpack at his partner to squeeze off a shot, because if he did, and if the bullet hit Stokes anywhere important from only a few feet away, it would all be over.

But Wiggins didn't shoot. Stokes reached him in three steps, shoved his gun hand to the side, and punched him in his wrinkled, senior citizen face. Wiggins dropped his gun and staggered back against a wall, knocking a mirror to the floor, shattering it. Stokes turned, kicked Wiggins's gun away, and lunged for Martz's just as the older man shook off his stupor and reached down for the weapon. Stokes got there first and Martz straightened up. Stokes stepped over to the other gun. He picked it up and tucked it into his jeans at the small of his back. Martz saw the gun in Stokes's hand, and the look in Stokes's eye, then moved to his fallen friend and knelt beside him.

"You punched him," Martz said to Stokes, though he was looking at Wiggins.

"You *shot me*," Stokes said.

"You don't seem badly hurt, Hugh," Martz said to Wiggins. "Our mistake, you realize, was in standing too close together. Stupid."

"Your mistake was shooting me, you assholes," Stokes said. "I can't believe you shot me. You tried to kill me."

He was shaking with anger. Or maybe fear. Or maybe it was just the adrenaline raging through his system. Felt like anger, though, as he seriously considered just popping the two old men. But that moment passed quickly. He wasn't a killer. Well, he'd actually killed two people in the last twenty-four hours, one with his motorcycle and the other with a bookend, but he hadn't meant to kill either. But, Jesus, he was pissed.

"I just cannot fucking believe you tried to kill me."

Martz looked sheepish. "I suppose an apology wouldn't do much to calm the waters, would it?" he asked.

"Shit no."

"Are you going to kill us?"

Stokes blew out a breath. He sighed. "Not unless I have to. Goddamn it, though, I really should. Shit."

Martz was holding his partner's hand.

"He OK?" Stokes asked. The question had just slipped out. He didn't actually give a shit.

"I'm fine," Wiggins said. He started to rise and Martz helped him to his feet. Wiggins swooned a little and grabbed Martz's arm for support. Stokes watched and felt his own arm throb. He tried to keep from shooting someone. He was tense and angry, so when the cell phone in his pocket shrilled he nearly fired a shot at the old guys by accident. He forgot he'd left the ringer on. Normally if he was breaking into a house, he wouldn't even be carrying a phone, but if he happened to have one on him, he'd set it not to ring but to vibrate only. But in this case, he just didn't bother, thinking that by the time the top of the hour rolled around again, he'd already have the house's occupants under his control.

"Don't move," he said, nodding down at the gun in his hand for emphasis, "and don't make a sound."

The phone rang again and Stokes answered his midnight call. Wiggins and Martz watched him as he spoke.

"I'm here."

"Good," the kidnapper said. "Still got the money, right?"

"Sure."

"And your evidence, I assume."

"Of course."

"Good. Things go smoothly, this will all be over soon. Things *are* going to go smoothly, right, Paul?"

"They will on my end," Stokes said.

"And no heroics, right?"

"Me?" Stokes said.

"Yeah, you. You decide maybe you can save Amanda and bring some kidnappers to justice, maybe even keep your money to boot. Nothing like that, right?"

"I'm not the heroic type."

"I didn't think so, but I wanted to hear you say it. And you're not gonna cheap out on us either, right?"

"Cheap out?"

"Yeah, like maybe show up with only a hundred grand and figure we'll be satisfied with that. We won't be. We know you have our three hundred and fifty thousand, so don't try to cut a last-minute deal. Got it?"

"I got it."

"Good. We're getting close now, so I really need to make sure you understand. If things don't go *exactly* like we discussed, things aren't gonna turn out good. Answer the phone at Laund-R-Rama at one thirty, be there alone with exactly three hundred and fifty thousand and the evidence you say you have. If it doesn't go just like that, we'll kill your daughter. We won't make her suffer, don't worry about that. We're not animals. But we'll put a bullet in her head."

"Don't worry," Stokes said. "Things will go exactly like you said. I just want Amanda back."

Wiggins and Martz, who were still watching him, dropped their eyes a little. The kidnapper was silent for a moment, perhaps gauging Stokes's sincerity, perhaps just scratching himself somewhere. Finally, he said, "The kid's still asleep. Want me to wake her?"

"No. Let me hear her breathing again, like last time."

A moment later, Stokes heard the soft, peaceful sleep sounds of a little girl breathing. A moment later, the gentle breathing was gone and the kidnapper was back.

"Good enough?"

"Yeah," Stokes said.

"Got another car yet?"

"Huh? Oh, yeah, I borrowed one. I'm all set there."

"OK then. I'll call you in an hour, to keep our end of the bargain. After that, I'll call you at the Laundromat a half hour later and tell you what to do next. And an hour after that, at two thirty, we get the money and the evidence, you get the kid, and this is all over."

The line went dead. Stokes put the phone into his pocket.

"That was the kidnappers?" Wiggins asked.

"Yeah."

"Are you really not going to kill us?" Martz asked.

Stokes sighed. "I want to, but I shouldn't. You're right. If you'd killed me, the cops would have pinned medals on your bony chests. If I kill you, it's different."

Besides, he just wasn't a stone-cold murderer, despite the fact that one of the men in front of him had just tried to kill him.

"So what happens now?" Martz asked.

Stokes shrugged. "I take my money and leave. Try to find another hundred and three grand before I have to be somewhere at one thirty. Then I try to save the kid."

"And what about us?"

"You? I don't give a shit what you do. Just don't call the cops on me, at least not tonight. If you have to do that, for insurance reasons or something, do the right thing and wait until tomorrow. Give me a chance to save the girl. Other than that, I don't care what you do. So good-bye, good night, and fuck you for trying to kill me."

Stokes snatched the backpack off the floor, along with his cowboy shirt with the eyeholes cut in the back, and started for the back door.

"You're bleeding," Wiggins said.

"On our Persian rug," Martz added.

Stokes kept walking. "Screw your rug and screw you guys."

"Wait," Wiggins said. "We have a first aid kit. I still remember enough of my training to be able to do a field dressing."

"Let him go, Hugh," Martz said.

"The least we can do is repair the damage we did, Arthur."

Stokes heard Martz sigh behind him. His arm hurt. Blood ran down it. If he didn't let them patch him up, he'd have to find a way to do it himself before long. He stopped and turned. He noticed the shattered mirror on the floor, the one that broke when he'd knocked Wiggins into it. Crazily, he wondered which of them would be cursed with the seven years of bad luck. The person who knocked it off the wall, or the person who shoved that guy into it. Who was Stokes kidding? If he lived long enough, the curse was certainly going to be his.

"Where's the first aid kit?" he asked the older men.

"Under the sink in the kitchen."

He jerked his head. "Come on."

⸻

Stokes sat at the kitchen table with Martz's gun in his right hand and Wiggins's tucked into the back of his jeans while Wiggins dressed the wound on his left arm. Martz watched from a seat across the table, where Stokes had put him. While Wiggins cleaned and disinfected the wound, Stokes grimaced and called him vile names. When the man finished his work, he handed Stokes some extra gauze and tape. Stokes thanked him, then said "Fuck you" to them both one last time before walking out the door. At least he had a couple more guns, in case he needed them, which he hoped he wouldn't. He also had his very own bullet wound. What he didn't have was the rest of money he needed to get Amanda back alive.

TWENTY-THREE

THERE WAS SOMETHING ABOUT AMANDA Jenkins's eyes. She really wasn't a very cute kid, but her eyes sparkled in a way that most people's didn't.

Stokes was sitting in Charlie Daniels's Camry looking at the wrinkled picture he'd taken from the pocket of the backpack. He still wasn't sure she was worth everything he'd given up for her, or all the shit he'd been through today, but there was no doubt she looked like a decent kid.

Stokes's own daughter, Ellie, she was a cute one. He hadn't seen the girl in thirteen years, so he didn't know if she still was, and sure, she was only two years old when he'd left, but at the time, she had a face that could have sold anything—toys, diapers, baby food, anything. She was a little knockout. Even when she was being a pain in the ass—which all kids could be, he knew, especially two-year-olds—she was still cute as hell. She'd be screaming about some ridiculous little thing, like him giving her the blue cup with the fish on it, even though Mommy always gave her the yellow cup with the clown on it, and still he'd think, "Man, that's a cute kid." Of course, that only went so far. In the end, it didn't go far enough to keep Stokes from waking before dawn one morning and sneaking out of her life.

He took one last look at the picture of Amanda Jenkins with her father before zipping it back up in the pocket of his bag. He looked out the car window at the big house across the street. And it *was* a big house. All brick, with tall windows and tall white columns in front. It sat on at least three acres of land surrounded by a high wrought iron fence. At the top of the long driveway squatted a big fountain, which wasn't spouting any water at the moment. Scattered here and there on the lawn were statues and topiary, or whatever the hell you called bushes that gardeners trimmed to look like animals or whatever. An imposing gate spanned the bottom of the driveway. Beside the gate was a call box. If Stokes wanted to talk to Leo Grote about borrowing money, he was going to have to push the button on that call box, which would buzz somewhere in the house, maybe waking up Leo Grote. And Leo Grote was not a man to wake at twelve fifteen in the morning. Especially not if you were someone who had pissed him off the last time you were in front of him, pissed him off enough for him to have his guys kick the crap out of you.

But hell, Stokes was never as scared of Grote as he probably should have been. He had his reasons.

He popped the trunk of the car, then walked back there and stowed the two guns he'd taken from the antique dealers, the cop's gun and belt, and the bag of money. He closed the trunk and strode across the street. When he reached Grote's gate, he pushed the button on the call box and waited. A few seconds later, he pushed the button again. He was about to push it a third time when some guy's voice came through the box. "Get out of here."

"I want to see Mr. Grote," Stokes said.

"It's the middle of the night. Mr. Grote's asleep. Get the fuck out of here."

"I used to work for him."

"I know who you are. Get the fuck out of here."

Stokes looked up and noticed a security camera mounted on top of the fence beside the gate.

"Tell Mr. Grote I'm here," Stokes said.

"Fuck you."

The connection ended. Stokes pushed the button again.

"Am I gonna have to come out there and kick your ass?" the guy asked.

"You can come out and try. After you do, I'll step over you, trying to avoid the big puddle of blood, and walk inside and find Mr. Grote myself."

"You weren't so tough when we tossed you out of Mr. Grote's office two years ago. You ever find all your teeth?"

"That you, McCutchen?"

"It's Brower."

"Well, unless you've got McCutchen with you again, I like my chances."

"Fuck you, Stokes."

"Just let me in, will you?"

"Mr. Grote's asleep, I said. He'll kill me if I let you in."

"I can see the lights on in his bedroom. Don't forget, I worked for the man, too. I've been inside the house."

"Well, I ain't gonna disturb Mr. Grote for you, Stokes," Brower said. "Besides, didn't he tell you to stay the fuck out of his sight?"

"I don't remember."

"Do yourself a favor and get out of here."

"Goddamn it, just tell Grote I'm here, will you? I need to see him. It's important."

"He won't give a shit."

"So it finally happened then? You've had your head up Grote's ass for so long you finally made it all the way up into his head? You can read his mind now? Just go tell him I need to see him and see what he says, OK?" The call box was quiet for a moment. "He'll see me, Brower. Just tell him I'm here."

After another few seconds, during which Brower was probably thinking, or doing something closely approximating it, he said, "I'll tell him. But if he chews my head off because of you, I'll find you, and I'll make that little beating I gave you two years ago seem like a Swedish massage, you got me?"

"I think I just pissed myself in fear," Stokes replied.

"Fuck you, Stokes."

"Yeah, you said that."

The box went dead. Stokes raised his eyes to the distant house. He focused on the second-floor windows at the front right corner of the house. He'd figured Grote would still be awake. He was a night owl. Used to roll into his office around noon. Despite being an ugly son of a bitch, he got a lot of action. He had a hot wife thirty years younger than him, and hot mistresses who came and went as he pleased, whether or not the hot wife was home. Stokes wondered at first why she put up with it, then realized that any night some other woman was having sex with her fat husband was a night that *she* didn't have to do it. Knowing that Grote rarely passed a night without grunting and sweating on top of some poor young thing, Stokes was worried that the man might be in the middle of such activities at that very moment, which wouldn't be good for Stokes. But he had to take the chance. Besides, it wasn't like Grote would cuddle with whatever unfortunate gal he'd just rutted with, so unless Stokes had happened to call right in the middle of a sex act, or just before it, he figured he'd be OK.

In the window, an indistinct silhouette drifted behind the sheer curtain, passed to the next window, and disappeared from sight. Stokes waited. He let his eyes roam over the house. Was Amanda Jenkins somewhere in there right now?

Stokes didn't think so. Something as serious as kidnapping, Grote would want as few people to know about it as possible, so Amanda probably wasn't in the house. She was likely being kept somewhere with no connection to Leo Grote, just in case the whole thing went sideways.

Stokes couldn't believe he was there to try to get into debt with Leo Grote for more than $100,000, just so he could turn around and hand the money back to the asshole's toadies, along with the rest of the ransom money. And this, after finally climbing out of debt with Frank Nickerson after a year of being into the guy. Damn, this was nuts. And ironic. That's what this was, ironic. He couldn't believe it. In fact, he still couldn't believe that he hadn't just taken the money and run like hell hours ago, right after Paul Jenkins and his car became one with a tree.

Brower's voice crackled from the box. "It's your lucky night, Stokes. He'll see you. Then again, maybe it really ain't that lucky for you."

Stokes heard a chuckle before the box went dead again. A moment later, a buzz sounded and the gate swung slowly open with a faint electric hum. Stokes stepped through and heard the gate hum closed behind him. It shut with a soft but solid clang.

TWENTY-FOUR

STOKES COULD HAVE DRIVEN HIS borrowed Camry up to Grote's imposing mansion, but he felt better with as much distance as possible between his quarter of a million dollars and Grote and his men. So he hoofed it up the long driveway, toward the grand fountain. Even without spouting water illuminated by underwater lights, the fountain was impressive. Stokes remembered seeing it when it was working, and that was *really* something. He wondered whether Brower would turn it on for him when he left later, if Stokes asked nicely.

As he reached the front door, it opened. Brower stood in the doorway, just as Stokes remembered him. He was big and solid and round with muscle, an oil drum with limbs and a head. Stokes didn't really think he'd have fared too well if Brower had accepted his invitation to come out and fight, but he'd spoken that way because that kind of talk, up to a point, was expected and even respected in Brower's world. Again, up to a point. Stokes could push it sometimes, and had done so in the past, with unfortunate results. He told himself to try not to do so tonight.

He expected Brower to back out of his way and let him into the house, but Brower took his time about it, playing the tough guy, and

Stokes waited patiently for the one-sided bigger-balls competition to end. A moment later, with a smug look, Brower stepped aside and Stokes walked into a foyer six times the size of his whole trailer. He'd been in the house before but had forgotten how grand the place was. Yellow marble on the floor, marble columns giving support to split staircases curving gracefully up to the second floor. The foyer's ceiling was so high a helicopter would have room to lift off and hover, provided Grote could get a chopper in here somehow. Hell, he probably had one out in the garage, so maybe he'd given it a try.

"You're a fucking idiot," Brower said as he began patting Stokes down.

"Coming from a true genius like yourself, that hurts."

"Fuck you. And I meant you're an idiot to get Mr. Grote out of bed like this."

He ran his hands up Stokes's right side, into his armpit, before moving over to the left side. When he reached Stokes's left armpit, his hand bumped against the bandage covering the bullet wound on Stokes's biceps. Stokes sucked in breath with a sharp hiss.

"Did that hurt?" Brower smiled and gave the area an extra squeeze.

"Did what hurt?"

"This." Brower squeezed again. Stokes winced and hissed again.

"Nah."

Brower smirked as he continued his pat-down. "I really hope Mr. Grote turns me loose on you, Stokes. I'll kick every tooth out of that wiseass mouth of yours. Hey, what's this?"

He pulled Officer Martinson's pepper spray from the front pocket of Stokes's jeans. Stokes had forgotten about it.

"Pepper spray," Stokes said.

"I'll keep it."

"You think I came here, got Mr. Grote out of bed, just so I could shoot him in the face with pepper spray?"

"I'll just hold it for you anyway. Wait in the living room over there."

He nodded toward a huge arched doorway to Stokes's right. An elephant could have walked through it with ease, though a giraffe might have had to stoop a little. Stokes headed through it, his booted footsteps echoing in the cavernous foyer. He could hear the heels of Brower's Italian loafers clacking behind him.

"How about fetching me a beer, Brower?" Stokes said over his shoulder.

"Tell you what. After Mr. Grote tells me to throw your ass out, I'll get you one. Shove the whole bottle down your throat."

The living room was enormous and, Stokes thought, tastefully furnished, though he honestly had no idea if that were truly the case. The furniture and paintings and knickknacks and whatever else he could see looked nice, though. And expensive. A lot of leather and carved woodwork, brass and stained glass. Either Mrs. Grote had taste to match her looks, or she spent a bundle on a decorator's "vision." Either way, the room looked like it was ripped from a magazine. Maybe *Better Mansions and Topiary*, or whatever the hell those bushes outside were called.

Stokes took a seat in a comfortable wing chair before Brower could tell him to do so, which Stokes knew would piss off Brower. The bruiser glared at him and took up a position in the archway. He leaned against the wall and crossed his brawny arms, something Stokes was surprised he could do over his barrel chest.

Five minutes crawled silently by, with Brower trying to make Stokes uncomfortable with his tough-guy glare, and Stokes trying to piss Brower off by looking completely at ease. Finally, a soft slapping-sliding sound came from the foyer, getting closer by the second. A moment later, Leo Grote walked into the room in his pajamas and slippers.

The man was just as Stokes remembered him. Bigger than Stokes but smaller than Brower. Thick arms that used to be strong and probably still were under the little layer of fat covering them. Hair too dark to be natural on his sixty-year-old head. And goddamn ugly. Dark eyes too close together, a bulbous nose far too big for his pitted face, the awful craters left long after his adolescent acne had cleared up. And it wasn't just his features that were ugly, but the way he kept them arranged. A look like he was perpetually smelling fish that had gone bad. He just never looked happy, which Stokes had a hard time understanding, seeing as he was rich as hell, had people around him to do anything he asked, and slept with a different woman decades younger than he every night. Stokes couldn't figure it out, unless all of that simply didn't make up for being butt ugly.

Grote was standing in the room now, looking down at Stokes with half-lidded, impassive eyes. Stokes realized he should have gotten to his feet the instant he heard Grote's slippers slapping their way across the foyer. Belatedly, he stood. He knew Grote wouldn't want to shake his hand, so he nodded in what he hoped passed for a submissive gesture. Doing that rubbed him raw, but he wasn't stupid. Well, at least he was going to try not to be stupid in Grote's presence.

Grote sat on a sofa. Stokes remained standing. Grote let him.

"It's late," Grote said.

"Sorry about that," Stokes replied.

Grote nodded to himself. He pulled a nail clipper out of the breast pocket of his pajama shirt and started carefully clipping away. Stokes expected him to ask why he was there, but he didn't.

"The reason I'm here is—"

Grote looked up from his nails. Something in his eyes made Stokes stop talking.

"Last time I saw you," Grote said, "you wised off to me. Said some smart-ass things. Things I had a hard time overlooking."

Stokes nodded. "We both said things. I've decided to forgive and forget."

Grote looked like he might have been trying to decide whether to tell Brower just to start beating the hell out of him right then.

"You always had a smart mouth, Stokes. It's gonna get you killed."

"Tonight?"

Stokes thought Grote might have chuckled to himself at that one. Probably not, though. "We'll see. Your father had a mouth like that. Only he was funny sometimes."

"He was also an asshole."

Grote nodded. "Yeah, but that asshole kept me from having Brower and McCutchen put you in a wheelchair for the rest of your life two years ago. He was my friend, before he split town. When was that, Stokes? When did he walk out on you and your mother?"

Stokes smiled. This ugly bastard wasn't going to get to him. "Thirty years ago, I guess. I stopped counting a long time ago."

"Amazing that he could be gone so long, have left you when you were so young, yet you could be so much like him now. A loser with a smart mouth. Well, you know what they say about the apple falling from the tree."

I hope it lands on your head, splits your goddamn skull open, Stokes wanted to say. Instead, he just nodded respectfully. If he wanted the bastard to loan him over $100,000 so he could ransom little Amanda back from the son of a bitch, he was going to have to eat some shit.

"Sorry about those things I said back then, Mr. Grote. I really am. And I'm sorry to be bothering you tonight. I wouldn't have come if it wasn't important."

Grote regarded Stokes for a moment. "Important to who?"

"To me."

"Why should I give a shit about you?" He was back to clipping his nails. Three snips per nail, the little pieces flying everywhere.

"Because of my father."

Grote nodded and went to work on the nail of his ring finger. "Your father saved my life. That was a long, long time ago. I did something stupid, almost got killed, and your father saved me."

"Well, everybody makes mistakes."

"True, and I was young at the time, but too careless that night."

Stokes meant that his father was the one who made the mistake by saving Grote's ass. He was actually surprised he'd been able to stop himself from saying so out loud. It was exactly the kind of thing he might have said nearly any other time, the kind of thing he'd said two years ago to make Grote almost kill him.

Grote stared hard at him and Stokes wondered if the wiseass comments in his head showed on his face. Grote turned his attention to the nail on his pinky. "You have someplace else to be?"

"Huh?"

"That's the third time you looked at your watch. Usually, I see that one time, I have my guys take your watch. I see it again, I think about having your hand broken. I cut you slack here because of your father, but be careful."

Stokes nodded.

"So why'd you get me out of bed?"

Stokes drew a breath. "I need some money."

Grote stopped snipping. He seemed to stop breathing for a moment. It felt like the air had been sucked from the room. If Stokes thought he could look at his watch without pissing off Grote, he wouldn't have been surprised if it had stopped ticking.

"You got me out of bed for a fucking loan?"

Brower snickered.

"I figured maybe you thought you had some bright idea for me, something you thought I'd be interested in investing in. Some heist or shady land deal or something. There's no way I would have even considered whatever the hell you were talking about, of course, but I thought there would have at least been something in it for me. But no, you came here, got me out of bed, to ask for a loan?"

"Well," Stokes said, "I'm under a time pressure here. I need the money fast. I can't wait until the banks open tomorrow."

"Yeah, and I'm sure they'd be dying to open their vaults for a guy like you. What's this about? The money you owe Frank Nickerson? What was that? Seventy, eighty grand, right? Plus interest."

Stokes shouldn't have been surprised to hear that Grote knew about that loan.

"Nah, I paid Nickerson off."

"Really? All of it?"

"A hundred thousand."

"When?"

"Today."

"And you need money again already?"

Stokes shrugged.

"How much?"

"A hundred and three thousand."

"Why the fuck did you pay Nickerson off if you still needed the money?"

"His sons didn't seem like they were in the mood to negotiate."

Grote chuckled. "Yeah, those two are crazy."

"So how about it?"

"What? A loan?"

"Yeah."

"A hundred and three thousand bucks?"

Stokes nodded.

"What was it you called me last time you saw me? I can't quite remember."

Stokes sighed. "I can't remember, either."

"Try." It wasn't a request.

Stokes sighed again. "An ugly fuck." Grote nodded, like he was just now remembering. Stokes quickly added, "It was in the heat of the moment, Mr. Grote. I didn't mean it and I'd never say anything like that again."

"No? You called me something else, too, I think. What was it?"

Stokes hesitated before saying, "Don Corleone wannabe."

Grote nodded again. "Right again. I remember now. But I think it was 'Piece of shit Don Corleone wannabe.'"

Stokes lowered his head.

Grote asked, "You have any idea how many people have ever talked to me like that and lived?"

"Two dozen?"

"Goddamn smart-ass."

Stokes thought he heard Brower crack his knuckles. He knew if he looked at the bruiser, the guy would be grinning savagely from ear to ear.

"And what was it I said to you?" Grote asked. "Before my guys pushed you out the door."

"You mean pushed me *through* the door. It was closed at the time."

"Yeah, I remember. So what was it I said as you were leaving?"

"I don't think it was 'Have a nice day.'"

"What did I say?"

"You said not to let you see my face ever again."

"And what am I looking at right now."

"Your thumbnail."

"How about now?"

"My face."

And he was. He was looking at Stokes with a predator's cold eyes . . . the way a snake looks at you, without emotion, like he doesn't care you're there, you don't piss him off, you aren't even worth consideration, until he swallows you whole. Stokes dropped his eyes, which turned out to be a bad idea.

"Jesus Christ, Stokes, what'd I say about looking at your watch?"

"I'm sorry, Mr. Grote."

"What did I say?"

Stokes sucked in a breath. "First time, you take the watch."

"Then?"

Stokes sighed. "Something about breaking a hand."

Grote nodded, only he was nodding to Brower, who was suddenly striding across the room. Stokes backed up a step, bumped against a chair, and Brower shoved him down into it. Before Stokes could react, Brower pinned his left hand to a table, picked up an iron statue of a guy on a horse, and slammed the base on Stokes's fingers. Stokes howled. Brower smiled. Broken fingers throbbed. At least three of them. Grote clipped another fingernail.

Stokes rested his battered hand in his lap. His thumb and index finger seemed unharmed. The other fingers screamed in pain.

Grote gave Stokes a moment to collect himself. As long as his head was down, he stole a peek at his watch: 12:35. Holy shit, his hand hurt.

Stokes sucked in a breath, then another. He tried to speak without letting them hear the agony in his voice. "So what about the loan, Mr. Grote? I really need the money."

Grote looked surprised for a split second, as if he thought the finger-breaking incident would sour Stokes on the whole loan idea. He started in on the nails on his other hand, letting Stokes twist in silence for half a minute or so.

"What do you need it for?"

To pay to your goddamn thugs, you ugly bastard, to get a scared, inno-cent little girl out of your goddamn custody and back into her own life.

"I'd rather not say what the money's for, Mr. Grote."

Grote shook his head. "Your balls are way too fucking big, Stokes. They're gonna get you killed."

"I thought you said my mouth was gonna get me killed."

"Your mouth or your balls. One of them will get you killed."

"Tonight?"

This time Grote definitely didn't chuckle.

"So how about the money?" Stokes asked again.

"You came here thinking I'd give you a hundred thousand dol-lars because your father saved my life decades ago."

Stokes nodded. His broken fingers pulsed with the blood flow-ing through them, and each beat of his heart intensified the pain.

"Even though you don't have a dime to your name," Grote said, "and no collateral but that shitty trailer you live in, and no obvious means of repaying the loan."

"When you put it like that . . ."

"And you think I'll do this just because your dad saved my ass a lifetime ago."

"That was my plan anyway. So how about it? For good old, piece-of-shit, walk-out-on-his-family dad."

Grote fixed Stokes in the sights of his eyes. "Your father was a buddy of mine. He saved my life a long time ago. That's why I gave you a job a few years ago when you came knocking. That's why, when you pussied out and couldn't follow orders and only broke one knee when I told you to break two, and when you mouthed off with your smart-guy wisecracks, saying things no one without a death wish would say to me, thinking you were bulletproof because your old man saved my bacon one time, well, your father was the reason I only had my guys rough you up a little. It was why I didn't have them break every bone in your body, turn you into a vegetable, and leave you in a gutter, or maybe just put a bullet through your face. All that, I did for your father. Debt repaid, as far as I'm concerned. He saved me, I spared you. A life for a life. So I don't owe you a loan now. In fact, I ought to let Brower here loose on you again. He looks like he enjoyed smashing your fingers. I can only imagine how much he'd like to do whatever the hell he'd like to do to you."

Stokes looked over at Brower, who was smiling wide.

"But I'm not going to do that, Stokes. Out of respect for your father, asshole that he truly was. Not out of some sense of debt, but just respect. But seeing as I've already repaid my debt to your old man, it seems I'm granting you a favor here."

"Yeah?" Stokes asked. "What favor is that?"

"Not having you beaten to a pulp or killed."

"Oh, that one."

"Seeing as I'm granting you this favor," Grote said, "I guess you'll be in debt to me now. You owe me one now, right?"

Stokes wasn't sure he saw it quite that way, but Grote seemed insistent, so he nodded as noncommittally as he could.

"Good," Grote said. "So one of these days, I'll send one of my guys around to collect. Maybe you'll do a job for me to repay my kindness."

"Whatever."

Despite everything that happened two years ago, and despite Grote having Stokes's fingers broken just now, Stokes figured that somewhere behind that ugly face, up in what was certainly a mal-formed, abnormal brain, Grote held a grudging respect for Stokes's balls. And despite what the man had said, Stokes knew that he still felt indebted to Stokes's father for pulling him out of a bad situation a long time ago, making this life of decadence and crime possible. Stokes first discovered that deep-rooted sense of gratitude after he'd been in Grote's employ for only three months. He'd skimmed five hundred bucks off the top of a payment he'd collected for Grote, mistakenly thinking his boss wouldn't find out about it. But Grote did and, to his surprise, Stokes didn't permanently lose the ability to use one of his hands—something Stokes later saw happen to at least two others who skimmed half of what Stokes did. Stokes, whom Grote had told about his debt to his father when he hired him, realized why he'd been spared that day. Stokes never really took advantage of that deeply instilled sense of gratitude, probably because he wasn't sure how far he could push things. But he knew, he'd been aware of it, even subconsciously relied on it, when he hadn't been able to stop himself from mouthing off to Grote two years ago. It was why he'd had the balls to come here in the first place tonight and tell Brower to get Grote out of bed. And it was why he had the guts, or maybe the stupidity, to ask one more time. "So no loan, huh?"

Grote ignored him as he clipped yet another fingernail. Stokes looked at his watch again—the hell with it—and saw that it was 12:39 p.m.

"Well, if you're not gonna give me the money, I guess I'll be going. Want me to just throw myself out?"

"Unless you want help," Grote said without looking up from his nails.

"No thanks," Stokes replied as he stood and headed toward the foyer. As he passed Brower, the goon held up Stokes's canister of pepper spray, which Stokes took and shoved into his jeans pocket.

"No hard feelings, Stokes?" Brower said, smirking and holding out his left hand. "Let's shake on it."

Stokes's own left hand was sporting three purple, swollen, misshapen fingers now, so he had to use his right to give Brower the finger as he walked away.

Stokes's crossing of the huge foyer seemed to take several minutes, but when he looked at his watch outside, he saw that it was 12:41.

Shit, his fingers throbbed.

Nineteen minutes until the next phone call. Forty-nine until he had to be at the Laundromat. And he still needed to come up with $103,000.

He had only one option left. He knew who would have almost exactly what he needed. He really had no other choice. He just wasn't looking forward to it. At all.

TWENTY-FIVE

12:45 A.M.

FRANK NICKERSON AND LEO GROTE may have been professional rivals for most of the illegal action in and around Shady Cross, and they may have maintained their personal offices on opposite sides of town, but—fortunately for Stokes—they lived in the same upper-class neighborhood. Stokes made the drive from Grote's to Nickerson's in under two minutes, which was good, as time was growing terribly short for him.

Stokes pulled the Camry to a stop in the moon shadow of a big tree, half a block from Nickerson's house. The place wasn't quite as grand as Grote's, but it wasn't far off. No fence around the property, which was helpful, and a little less acreage to cover before he reached the house, which was also helpful, but the house itself, while maybe not as big as Grote's, wasn't a hell of a lot smaller, which wasn't helpful at all.

He had driven there with the intention of asking Nickerson for a loan, hoping for better luck than he'd had with Leo Grote. He knew the odds were against him, considering that he'd taken nearly a year to pay back the last loan, which he'd repaid that very day, and also given the fact that it had looked to Nickerson's crazy sons like he'd been about to skip town without paying off his debt to their father. That it was nearly one in the morning didn't make Stokes feel any more confident about Nickerson flipping open his wallet and handing Stokes a hundred grand. So during the two-minute drive to Nickerson's house, Stokes had come up with a different plan, one that was risky, stupid, suicidal even, but at least seemed possible now that he saw both of the Nickerson boys' silver Escalades parked in front of the house, right where he hoped they would be.

Stokes glanced at his watch: 12:46. He had fourteen minutes until the next call from the kidnappers. If he were smart, he'd wait for the call before going into the house. But he couldn't. Every second counted now. In their last conversation, they had been clearer than ever that Amanda's life depended on everything going as planned. And that meant Stokes needed another $103,000, and he needed to be at Laund-R-Rama in forty-five minutes. So he didn't have fifteen minutes to kill by sitting in the car, waiting for the phone to ring.

He popped the Camry's trunk with his right hand—he did everything now with his right hand—and went around to the back of the car. He took his lock pick set from the backpack, and he took the two guns he'd taken from the antique dealers. One he put in the pocket of his jacket; the other he stuffed into his belt at the small of his back. Except in the Wild West fantasies of his youth, he'd never fired a gun in his life. But he knew how they worked.

He left the money in the trunk and turned toward Nickerson's house. It was dark but for a light on by the massive front door. Nickerson's property had plenty of big trees on it, and Stokes trotted toward the first clump of them. He moved quickly across the lawn, slipping from shadow to shadow. Finally, he was at the house. Everything was quiet. He slid over to a window and cautiously peered in. It was dark inside but enough moonlight drifted through the windows to outline the features of a kitchen. A nice one. Gourmet, with marble countertops and big, shiny appliances. He looked for evidence of alarm sensors on the window and saw none.

Despite the chill in the October night, Stokes was sweating like a kid on his first date, or a guy about to break into the house of a criminal with ties to the Mafia and two violent, batshit-crazy sons.

He slipped his cowboy-shirt mask over his face and tied it behind his head. Then he sneaked along the side of the house, pausing at each window as he did. He saw an exercise room stocked with expensive, professional equipment that he doubted had ever been used by Frank Nickerson, but which he was fairly certain saw regular use from the iron-pumping Nickerson boys. Next came a spacious bathroom. He stopped at the corner of the house and peeked into the backyard. No signs of a dog, which didn't surprise him as he hadn't heard any barking. Still, that was a break. One of his few today.

There were no lights on back here. He moved through the shadows along the back of the house. Through another window he saw a desk. Books on the wall. Looked like an office or study. That was the kind of room where they'd stash money. At least it felt that way to Stokes. He'd start his search there.

He sneaked along two-thirds of the length of the house before he came to a back door. He blinked sweat from his eyes and set about inspecting the door for signs of an alarm system. He found none. He looked through the door, into what appeared to be a TV room, and saw no alarm panel. Though he hadn't counted on this, he'd been hoping for it—hoping that Nickerson was arrogant enough to think that no sane person would break into his house to steal from him. Of course, he was probably right; no sane person *would* steal from him. But Stokes was too desperate at the moment to be in his right mind, so there he was, on the verge of the stupidest breaking and entering of his life. But the lack of an alarm system was another small break. He'd been prepared to try the same trick he used on Wiggins and Martz. If that didn't work, he would have rung the doorbell, stuck a gun in the face of whoever answered it, and asked for the money he knew they had because he'd given it to them just a few hours earlier.

But there was no alarm and Stokes silently thanked God—in whom he didn't truly believe—that he had the ability to pick locks. In the next breath he cursed God, if he existed, for giving him this ability, because without it this crazy operation wouldn't even have been a possibility, and Stokes could have given up with a marginally clear conscience.

What the hell was he doing? He couldn't bring himself to punch a clock for his own daughter, yet he'd thrown away a shot at a great new life—and was now risking his shitty old one—for a kid he'd never met? This was insanity. This was suicide.

He looked at his watch: 12:49. He really should wait, he knew. But with luck, he'd be in and out quickly. Unlike when he broke into the antique dealers' home, though, this time he took out the cell phone, flipped it open, and figured out how to engage the silent ring mode. He slipped the phone back into the inner breast pocket of his leather jacket and pulled out his set of lock picks. He examined the dead bolt and lock-in-knob on the door, selected his tools, and got to work. It was tough with broken fingers on one hand, so it took longer than it should have, but he managed it. Too bad he wasn't this good at something legitimate.

He slipped a black leather glove on his right hand, looked at the ugly, twisted fingers on his left hand, then put the second glove back into his pocket. He took a deep breath, grasped the doorknob, and opened the door a few inches, tensing for the scream of an alarm in case he'd been wrong about that.

The house remained silent. He let out his breath in a shaky rush. He'd broken into homes before. Dozens of them over the years. He'd long ago learned not to be too nervous about it. But this was different. If your typical home owners caught you, they'd just start screaming and you'd either run or you'd take the offensive, as Stokes had unthinkingly done last night. There was always the risk they'd have a gun, but most people didn't want to shoot anyone. They'd rather yell down through the darkness, from the safety of the top of the stairs, that they were armed and you'd better leave because they'd already called the cops, which was probably a lie, but it usually wasn't worth sticking around to find out, so you'd get the hell out and try your luck somewhere else some other night. But this was different. If Stokes were caught tonight, he wouldn't have to worry about the cops. Actually, he'd be praying for a cop to come along and save him from Frank Nickerson and his psycho sons, who would be pretty miffed about his being there, and who would probably do awful things to most parts of his body while he prayed for death, which would certainly arrive eventually, but which would take its own sweet, cruel time getting there.

After listening for another moment at the door and hearing nothing, Stokes slipped into the house. He left the door open an inch or two in case he had to make a fast getaway.

Though not necessarily easy to accomplish, his plan was simple. Find the money Stokes had paid the Nickersons earlier, then get the hell out. It was nearly five o'clock when he gave them the money, and, because all the banks in town close at four on Fridays, they couldn't have deposited it. So, seeing the Escalades out front, which was what Stokes was hoping he'd find as he knew the Nickerson boys still lived with their father, he figured the money was almost certain to be somewhere in the house right now, hopefully in the study, which was where he planned to start looking. All he had to do was find it and sneak out. The sooner the better. And if the money was locked in a safe, what then? Well, he'd have no choice but to do something completely insane. He'd slip upstairs, jam a gun barrel into a sleeping Nickerson's ear—whichever one he came across first—and get the combination. He'd have to tie and gag the Nickerson after, which could be dangerous work—he might even have to coldcock the bastard with the butt of a gun, but he'd have no choice. That whole scenario was a truly frightening prospect, so Stokes kept his unbroken fingers crossed that the Nickersons hadn't bothered to put the money in a safe.

He looked around. He was in a family room of sorts. A huge flat-screen TV hung on one wall with a big, soft couch facing it. He left the room, passed a bathroom bigger than his whole trailer, then walked through the kitchen. His stomach rumbled loudly enough that he worried the sound could have carried upstairs. He hadn't eaten since he'd taken a few bites of meat loaf at Tootie's Diner, back when all this started many hours ago. But seeing as this wasn't the time or place to fix himself a sandwich, he walked on, moving as quietly as he could toward the end of the house, where the study was, listening hard for sounds that anyone was awake.

He glanced at his watch: 12:54. He'd never make it. He wasn't going to be able to find the money and get out in the next six minutes. But he'd gotten inside without alerting anyone to his presence, and the place was huge, so he was confident he'd be able to find someplace where he could answer the phone, which would ring silently, and carry on a quick conversation before finishing what he came for. Maybe the bathroom he just passed. Slip in, shut the door, talk quietly, and get back to work. The kidnappers had been punctual all night, calling right at the top of every hour as they'd promised Jenkins they would do. All Stokes had to do was shut himself away at 12:59 and wait for the call. For now, he'd keep searching. Again, every second was precious.

Stokes walked through a huge, formal dining room, then a huge living room. As he moved through the house, his eyes scanned each room for drawers and cabinets, places they might be likely to stash the money for a few days, just in case it wasn't in the study as he hoped. He passed through a smaller living room—they probably called it a sitting room or something like that—and saw a pair of open wooden doors in the far wall. As he neared them, the corner of a desk became visible and Stokes's heartbeat quickened. For some reason, he felt confident the money would be in that study—hopefully in a desk drawer, but maybe in a safe in the wall or floor. It was possible that Nickerson didn't bother with a safe, though. After all, if he wasn't worried about anyone breaking into his house, why should he worry about someone searching his house for money?

Stokes slipped into the study. Two walls were lined with books, none of which Stokes believed a single Nickerson had read. The wall behind the big desk was covered with floor-to-ceiling windows. Two leather chairs faced the desk. On the wall behind the chairs hung another big flat-screen TV. Through an open door on the other side of the room, Stokes saw a sink. Another bathroom. He checked his watch: 12:57. He decided to take a minute to search for the money before slipping into that bathroom to take the kidnappers' call. After he hung up, he'd find the money, if he hadn't before then. And if he didn't find it fast, he'd fall back on his monumentally stupid backup plan to drag a Nickerson out of bed with a gun in his face and have the bastard find the money for him. He figured that if he could leave the house by one fifteen, he could be at the Laundromat in time for the kidnappers' call.

He had rifled quickly but quietly through the three drawers on the left side of the desk and was about to duck into the bathroom for his hourly call when something flashed faintly in the corner of his eye. He looked back through the sitting room, into the dining room, where light now spilled in from the hallway. Someone had turned on a light in the hall.

Oh, shit.

Stokes's heart began to beat so hard and so loudly that he almost expected whoever was in the kitchen to come rushing into the office to find the source of the pounding. He listened for approaching footsteps but had trouble hearing over the roar of blood in his ears.

He stepped closer to the double door, where he could listen better. Someone was moving around in the kitchen. He heard a plate placed onto the marble countertop. He heard the refrigerator door swing shut. He heard a cabinet close. He heard the refrigerator door open and close again. Finally, he heard footsteps and prayed they'd move away from him. They didn't.

He unconsciously patted his jacket pocket, feeling the weight of the gun there, as he moved quickly across the room toward the bathroom. As the footsteps got closer, probably entering the sitting room now, Stokes slipped into the bathroom. He considered closing the door behind him, but Nickerson or whoever was approaching might have remembered that it had been left open. He looked around for a window and saw a big one near the toilet, big enough for him to crawl through if he had the time, which he didn't think he did, but he didn't want to do that anyway if he could avoid it. He'd have much preferred that whoever was coming would grab a book or something from the office, something to read in bed, but Stokes realized this was unlikely given that the Nickersons weren't known for their intellectual curiosity. But the footsteps were almost there already and going out the window was no longer an option anyway.

Stokes stuck his right hand into his pocket and curled his fingers around the gun he desperately hoped he wouldn't have to use, but which he fully intended to use if he had to. He squeezed behind the door, which was wide open, and pressed his body against the wall separating him from the office. From where he was he could just see Nickerson's desk through the crack between the door and the doorjamb.

He held his breath. His heart slammed. The blood pounded through his aching fingers. If he was really, really unlucky, whoever was out there had to use the toilet and had some strange preference for this particular bathroom out of the ten or so that could likely be found in the house.

As Stokes watched, one of Nickerson's identical twin sons, either Chet or Carl—he had no clue which—walked into Stokes's limited view. The man was wearing pajama bottoms and no shirt and carrying a glass of milk and a plate with a few cookies on it, which, at any other time, Stokes might have found amusing. Nickerson set them down on the desk and took a seat in the chair behind it. He stuffed a cookie into his mouth whole, washed it down with a big gulp of milk, and pulled a cell phone out of the pocket of his pajama bottoms. He pushed a few numbers and waited.

A moment later, something really bad happened. The cell phone in Stokes's pocket began to vibrate. He'd remembered to set it to silent mode but hadn't really considered what that might mean, other than that it wouldn't audibly ring. Well, it didn't. But it vibrated. And with Stokes leaning face-first against the wall separating the bathroom from the office, the phone, pressed between his body and the wall, vibrated in short little bursts, the volume of the vibrations amplified by its contact with the wall. The phone kept buzzing and the buzzing carried into the wall and, too late— far too late—Stokes leaned away from the wall. He saw Nickerson look toward the bathroom before pressing a button on the phone, putting an end to the vibrating in Stokes's pocket. He reached for a desk drawer.

Stokes knew he was going for a gun. He'd reacted quickly for a guy Stokes had never considered too bright. He had called a man who was supposedly somewhere across town, the phone had buzzed in the bathroom of his home, eight feet away from where he was sitting, and he immediately reached for a gun. No stupid look of puzzlement, no look of dumb shock that would have given Stokes time to come up with a good way to react in this situation. No, Nickerson went right for a gun. Of course it was possible, Stokes thought, that reaching for a gun was his default reaction to anything. Chef overcooked his steak? Reach for a gun. Flat tire? Grab a pistol. Ran out of potato chips? Start shooting. Anyway, Nickerson going for a gun left Stokes no choice. He elbowed the door out of his way and spun past it, into the office, yanking his own gun from his pocket as he moved. He raised the weapon, pointed it at Nickerson's face, and waited for Nickerson's hands to rise.

They didn't.

The man's eyes, the eyes that held that wild, dangerous light, looked back at Stokes's masked face as he felt around in the drawer, heedless of the unspoken command to stop reaching for the gun and to raise his hands. He looked down into the drawer now and kept digging around, moving papers aside, searching the back of the drawer.

Finally, Stokes said, "Stop that. Put your hands up."

Nickerson closed the drawer and opened another one.

"I said put your hands up."

"Fuck you," Nickerson said. "I know my dad keeps a gun in this desk somewhere. I'm gonna find it and shoot you in your balls, then ask what you're doing here."

Jesus, the guy was crazy.

"And then," Nickerson continued, "I'm gonna really start hurting you."

He closed the second drawer and opened a third.

"Goddamn it," Stokes said, "close that drawer right now or I'll blow your head off."

Nickerson laughed. The crazy son of a bitch laughed and kept searching for that gun.

Stokes didn't want to shoot Nickerson. It would wake other Nickersons. Nickersons with weapons. Nickersons as nuts as this one. Which would ruin any chance there was for this whole thing to turn out all right. But there was more going on here, he was starting to realize. Things had changed with that phone call he'd just missed, the one Nickerson had placed, but Stokes hadn't had time yet to think it through. All he knew was that he really didn't want to have to shoot this idiot if he could help it.

But then Nickerson smiled and brought a gun up from behind the desk.

"Drop that," Stokes warned.

Nickerson ejected the magazine, checked to see that it was loaded, and slammed it back into place.

Stokes took a step toward the desk.

"Put that thing down right now," he said. "Last warning."

Nickerson laughed, clicked off the safety, and raised the gun.

TWENTY-SIX

1:02 A.M.

AS THE GUN ROSE, ITS muzzle turning toward Stokes's crotch, thoughts ricocheted chaotically around inside his head. Though he didn't know the reason, the adrenaline coursing through his system caused a surreal slowdown of events and, in the heat of the moment, with only a split second to act, he was able to make sense of some of the thoughts careening through his mind.

He had no doubt that the crazy son of a bitch would shoot him. Still, Stokes didn't want to have to shoot Nickerson if he could avoid it. And he obviously couldn't let himself get shot. So he charged toward the desk. As he did, he threw his gun at Nickerson, whose wild eyes grew wilder as the weapon bounced off his forehead, snapping his head back on his neck. Thankfully, the gun didn't discharge. Nickerson's gun was pointing off to Stokes's left now as Stokes kept coming. Another step and he launched himself across the desk, crashing into Nickerson, setting the wheeled chair spinning and rolling.

Stokes wasn't a small guy, and when his 190 pounds slammed into Nickerson, he was gratified to hear the other guy's breath explode out of him. The chair snagged on the area rug and over it went. Nickerson tumbled out of it with Stokes on top of him.

Stokes concentrated first on Nickerson's gun. While Nickerson fought to regain his breath, Stokes punched him hard in the face with his gloved right hand, then knelt on the wrist just below the hand that held the gun. The hand opened and Stokes knocked the weapon a few feet away. He punched Nickerson a second time. Without thinking, he punched the asshole yet again, this time with his left hand, slamming his broken fingers into Nickerson's cheekbone. He stifled a scream and saw white spots blooming on the edges of his vision.

Nickerson was big and strong, and even though Stokes had surprised him and initially got the better of him, he was capable of putting up a good fight. And he did. A real good one. Lying on his back, he swung up at Stokes again and again, and Stokes, regaining his senses and kneeling over Nickerson, swung back. A jab knocked off Stokes's mask, and Nickerson looked surprised to see Stokes's face, but that didn't slow down even one of the bastard's punches.

Both men's fists were covered with the other's blood. Stokes's good right hand began to throb as badly as his damaged left one. Still, he kept throwing punches at Nickerson's eyes, his nose, his throat, all the while trying to dodge the blows from two fists flying at his face. He was surprised at the force Nickerson was able to generate while lying on his back. He was even more surprised when a sudden surge of movement and twist of body bucked him to the side and Nickerson was able to scramble out from under him and lurch to his feet. Stokes did the same.

They were just three feet apart, breathing hard, staring at each other. Nickerson's homicidal eyes, always scary, were wide and white and staring from that mask of slick blood, which made them even more frightening than usual.

In a flash Stokes understood something terrible: one of them would die tonight. If, incredibly, Stokes somehow won without killing Nickerson, he'd have to kill the guy anyway before he left, now that his mask had come off. There was no way someone like him would take a beating like this and forget about it. He was too arrogant, too violent, too crazy for that. No matter where Stokes went, no matter how many miles he put between them, Nickerson would hunt for him. It would never end until one of them was dead. He sighed. He wasn't looking forward to killing Nickerson, if he could. He'd never wanted to kill anyone intentionally. But he had no choice. He knew that. And he could bring himself to do it, if he got the chance. Maybe he couldn't have before, but he could tonight. He knew that, too. He was even more certain that if Nickerson prevailed, he'd kill Stokes, probably slowly, certainly painfully . . . and he'd enjoy it. And with Stokes having only one truly useful hand, the smart money wasn't on him to be the one to survive.

But he was going to go down fighting. He still couldn't have Nickerson yelling for reinforcements. Though their battle had been noisy, the house was huge and there was a chance that no one had heard the commotion. But they'd certainly hear Nickerson yelling, if he chose to call out. Stokes could still feel the second gun he'd taken from the antique dealers pressing against the small of his back, but he didn't bother pulling it because Nickerson had already shown no fear of guns and Stokes had no intention of shooting him, at least not yet. So Stokes quickly attacked again before Nickerson had the chance to call out if he wanted to do so.

They punched and gouged, clawed and choked, doing anything they could to get the better of the other. Stokes was so past caring about pain that he was even landing blows with his damaged hand. It was brutal and ugly, and, after a few moments, Stokes knew he was losing. It was the pepper spray that finally ended it. Stokes was able to sneak his good hand into the front right pocket of his jeans and close his fingers around the canister he'd taken from the cop. He twisted his broken fingers into Nickerson's hair, yanked the asshole's head back, and shot him right in the eyes with the chemical. Nickerson cried out and pulled his head away and Stokes drove his forehead straight into Nickerson's nose. Something caved in with a sickening crunch and Nickerson dropped like someone had blown out both his knees with a shotgun.

Well, maybe it was the head butt more than the pepper spray that finally ended it, but the spray sure came in handy.

Stokes fell back against the desk, breathing hard. He hurt everywhere. And he was bleeding everywhere. Mostly from his nose, it seemed, but other places, too. His broken fingers made him want to scream. He wiped his nose with his sleeve, grimacing at the pain he felt from the pressure. He looked down at Chet or Carl Nickerson, who was stunned but conscious. The guy coughed and blood spurted from his mouth. Stokes wondered briefly if he'd damaged some vital organ, but figured the blood was more likely from Nickerson's ruined nose. And it was *ruined*. Stokes winced looking at it.

As he watched Nickerson wheezing, spitting out blood every few seconds, his crazy eyes dull now as they rolled stupidly in their sockets, Stokes listened for voices or footsteps. He heard nothing, just Nickerson's wet wheezes. But he still had to make sure Nickerson didn't cry out, which he was far more likely to do now that he realized he wasn't invincible—that he had actually lost the fight. So Stokes knelt down, ignoring a pain in his knee where Nickerson must have kicked him, and yanked off one of Nickerson's socks. He leaned over and stuffed it into the asshole's mouth. He was a little worried that, with nowhere else to go, all the blood would back up in there and Nickerson would drown in it. He wasn't all that concerned about the guy dying, seeing as he'd already figured that Nickerson would have to die anyway tonight, but he didn't want him dying before Stokes got some answers, so he watched the man for signs of true distress, and for signs that he was coming back to his senses, as he searched for something with which to tie him up.

He found fancy ropes of some kind, braided red and gold with fringed tassels at both ends, tying back the heavy drapes on the windows. With one hand he worked them free. He rolled Nickerson around as he used one of the ropes to tie his hands behind his back, which was hard as hell with one good hand and only his thumb and index finger on the other. After that, he tied Nickerson's feet. Nickerson coughed a little, then more violently, and Stokes pulled the sock from his mouth. Nickerson coughed again and blood erupted from between his swelling lips. He gasped for breath. When no more blood came, Stokes shoved the bloody sock back in. Nickerson's eyes were clearing as he started to recover whatever senses he normally had. He struggled against his bonds.

"Cut that out," Stokes said.

Nickerson kept struggling, so Stokes leaned over, put his thumb against Nickerson's wrecked nose, and gave a little push. Nickerson grunted savagely into the sock in his mouth and stopped struggling. The look in his eyes was the stuff of nightmares.

Stokes listened to the house again but heard nothing to alarm him. He pulled the wooden doors quietly closed and dragged Nickerson over in front of a leather wing chair—one facing the doors—and sat down. He took a deep breath. It hurt when he did. Bruises on his chest, maybe his ribs. He looked down at Nickerson, and blood dripped from his nose as he did. He wiped it on his sleeve.

He looked at his watch: 1:07. Holy shit. The entire fight had lasted only five minutes. Felt like twenty to Stokes.

He looked down at Nickerson, who glared up at Stokes with cold, hard fury. Stokes thought for a moment. He didn't get it. Nancy Filoso said she'd borrowed the money from Leo Grote. She'd even accurately identified Iron Mike and Danny DeMarco as the guys she'd cut her deal with, the ones she'd hatched her kidnapping plan with. Was she lying? If so, how would she know what those guys looked like?

"Gotta ask you some questions," he said to Nickerson. His words sounded a little strange to him. His lips felt funny. He realized they were swollen.

Nickerson said something that sounded a lot like "Fuck you," only Stokes couldn't be sure with the sock stuffed in his mouth.

"This isn't a good time to play tough guy. Which are you, by the way, Carl or Chet?"

Nickerson replied the same way again and Stokes leaned down, put his thumb against Nickerson's nose again, but before he could apply any pressure Nickerson shook his head urgently and grunted something that didn't sound like "Fuck you."

"What was that?" Stokes asked. "Did you say you're Carl?"

Nickerson nodded.

"OK, Carl, I gotta ask you some questions. You know Iron Mike, don't you? I don't know what his last name is. And Danny DeMarco? They work for Leo Grote. You know them, right?"

Carl hesitated. Stokes shook his head sadly and reached for the mess that used to be the bastard's nose. Carl thrashed his head violently back and forth.

"You saying you don't know them?"

Another shake of his head.

"Oh, you were telling me not to push on your nose. Gotcha. So, you know them?"

After a brief hesitation, Carl nodded.

"They work for your father?"

Carl shook his head.

"Are you sure?"

Carl nodded.

"They still work for Grote, right?"

Carl nodded again. This didn't make sense.

"You lying to me?"

He reached down toward Carl's face and Carl shook his head emphatically. Stokes believed him.

He just didn't get it. If Grote was behind the kidnapping, which clearly seemed to be the case, why was Carl Nickerson, the son of Grote's biggest professional rival, making the phone calls?

He needed more thorough answers than he could get from a mouth with a sock in it.

"Listen, Carl," he began, "you're not gonna kill me, at least not tonight. I think you can see that. But I'm not gonna kill you, either. I don't want the heat from that, not from the cops, and even more, not from your family."

He was telling the truth about not wanting the heat, but he was lying about not killing Carl. With any luck—which nothing in his experience led him to believe he'd have, but he still had to hope for it—no one would ever know it was Stokes who'd broken in tonight, who had killed Carl.

"So you see," he continued, still lying, "you can come out of this OK, except for a few bumps and bruises. Maybe you need a nose job, I don't know. Either that or you gotta break Chet's nose, too, so you guys can keep up that identical twin alibi bullshit. But all in all, you wouldn't be too bad off. But you have to answer my questions. Otherwise I might just say 'Screw it' and let you choke to death on your own blood the next time you start coughing. Or if you don't, I could step on your throat until you choke to death that way. Whatever it takes. You hear me?"

Carl nodded. He looked confused. Maybe he was confused about how Stokes could have beaten him in a fight. He was probably more confused, though, about why Stokes was in his house and what the hell he was doing with the phone that Paul Jenkins was supposed to have. In other words, while Stokes was baffled about Carl's involvement in all this, Carl was probably equally puzzled about Stokes's. Fortunately for Stokes, *he* was the one asking the questions.

"So," he said, "you can come out of this all right if you want to. All you have to do is answer my questions. I'll take that sock out of your mouth and ask you what I want to know. You yell for help and I stomp on your face, you got it? It'll hurt like crazy, maybe even kill you. And if it doesn't kill you, I'll kill you some other way before I run like hell. And if I don't have time to run like hell, I'll start shooting the second that door opens. Who knows? Maybe I'll end up killing all of you fucking Nickersons, get a medal from the mayor, maybe the key to the city. So do we understand each other?"

Carl looked up, burning with rage, and nodded. Stokes reached down and pulled the sock from his mouth. It was bloody and it stuck to his lips as it came free. Stokes was ready to jam it back in if Carl started yelling, but he didn't have to. Carl glared at him silently for a moment. "You're gonna die, Stokes."

"Yeah, I know. But not by you. At least not tonight." *Actually, not ever by you, because you're gonna die in the next few minutes.*

Stokes looked at his watch: 1:10. Twenty minutes until he was supposed to be at the Laundromat, though that didn't matter now, he realized, seeing as the guy who was probably supposed to call him then was now bleeding on the floor in front of him. What did matter, though, was that Amanda was out there somewhere, and Stokes had no idea how these recent developments would impact his chances of saving her.

"I don't want to screw around here, Carl, trying to figure out the right questions to ask, listening to you jerk me around with evasive answers, having to stuff the sock back into your mouth and lean on your nose again. And I don't think you want that either, so why don't you just tell me what the hell is going on, OK?"

Carl spit some blood out through his swollen lips. "What do you mean?"

Stokes sighed. "I'll get you started. Stop me when it starts to sound familiar. Leo Grote's guys kidnapped a little girl named Amanda Jenkins. The stepmother owed Grote some money, so she sold out her own kid, got Iron Mike and Danny DeMarco to kidnap the girl to extort money from the father, Paul Jenkins—who you thought you were talking to all day, I guess. Any of this ringing a bell? And don't make me step on your nose."

"Where's Jenkins?" Carl asked.

"He's out of the game. I'm pinch-hitting for him. But believe me, I intend to pay. All I want is to get the kid back. Now tell me, what the hell do you have to do with all this?"

Carl spit more blood, only this time he spit it up at Stokes. The bloody spittle sprayed the legs of Stokes's jeans. Stokes almost kicked Carl in the side of the head. Instead, he took a breath to calm himself down.

What the hell was going on here? If Carl Nickerson was involved in the kidnapping, the whole family probably was, too, Father Frank included. But why would Leo Grote and Frank Nickerson be working together, especially on something like the kidnapping of a six-year-old girl. Couldn't be for a mere $350,000. Grote and Nickerson were rich. They didn't need the risk this entailed. Stokes couldn't get his head around this.

"I'll ask you one more time before I start hurting you, Carl. What's your family's part in all this? What the hell's going on here?"

"My question exactly."

That hadn't come from Carl. Stokes turned. He'd been so focused on questioning the guy that he hadn't heard Frank Nickerson open the door to the study. Yet there he was, Frank himself, looking down at his bound and bloody son on the floor . . . and pointing a gun at Stokes.

Stokes reached behind him for the gun he'd kept tucked back there. It was gone.

TWENTY-SEVEN

1:13 A.M.

STOKES'S BACKUP GUN MUST HAVE slipped out of his waist-band toward the end of the fight. It was probably lying on the floor behind the desk. He saw his other gun, the one he'd bounced off Carl's forehead, lying under the window ten feet away. His first instinct was to bolt for it, but he knew he'd never make it.

"Good choice," Frank Nickerson said, as if reading Stokes's mind.

Frank looked like he had a year ago, the last time Stokes had seen him, only now he was wearing pajamas. He was fat and lumpy, like a Hefty bag stuffed with cottage cheese. He wasn't really round, but he was too thick, too fat all over. His torso was fleshy and soft, his arms flabby, his legs chunky. He probably hadn't had a moment of exercise in twenty years. That was one of the drawbacks, Stokes guessed, of having people around who did whatever you told them to do. You never had to do anything for yourself. Never had to move a muscle, if you didn't want to, unless you had to go to the can—and you could probably find ways around that, too, if you really felt like it.

Frank raised the gun an inch. "I've killed twenty-one people in my life," he said, "and left a lot of others in far worse shape than I first found them in. I tell you this not to brag but as a warning: I won't hesitate to kill you."

"So why haven't you yet?" Stokes asked.

Frank nodded. "I thought about it, to tell you the truth. As soon as I saw my son lying there like that, I thought about killing you. And I probably will, don't get me wrong. But not just yet."

"What are you waiting for?"

Frank looked at him appraisingly. "You're a brave one. Or you're monumentally stupid."

"Probably a little of both," Stokes admitted.

Frank was far better spoken than his sons were, though Stokes knew he wasn't the best judge of something like that.

"Come on, Dad," Carl said from the floor, "make him untie me."

Frank looked down at his son. "Untie him," he said to Stokes.

Stokes looked at the gun in Frank's hand, then at the one on the floor across the room.

"You'd never make it," Frank warned.

Stokes considered his chances. A moment later, he bent down and untied Carl. Again, his broken fingers made it tough and excruciatingly painful to do, but he managed it. Carl labored to his feet, shaking the loose rope from his wrists, and slugged Stokes in the face hard enough loosen a few teeth. Flashes popped in the air before Stokes's eyes, as if he were suddenly a celebrity on TV and the paparazzi were snapping shots of him walking up a red carpet. Just when his vision cleared, Carl hit him again and the room got a little wavy.

"That's enough," Frank said, and though Stokes could see that Carl wanted to hit him again, and again, and not stop until Stokes was a quivering pile of bloody pulp, he obeyed his father. Frank might have been fat and getting old, but he still commanded respect and obedience from his crazy-violent son.

"Help me out here, son," Frank said.

"It's Carl."

Frank nodded.

Stokes's ears were ringing from Carl's last two blows, and his vision was still a little fuzzy. If he'd ever had a chance to go for one of his guns, it was gone now. It would be a few minutes before he'd even be able to stand without getting dizzy, much less dive for a gun, twirl around, and fire accurately at not just one, but two people, one of whom was armed, the other of whom was nuts.

Frank was studying him. "Do I know you?" he asked.

"His name is Stokes," Carl said. He sounded really nasal, like he had a terrible head cold, or like someone had recently obliterated his nose in a fistfight. "Maybe you remember, Dad, he's the one paid his loan in full today. A hundred thousand."

"A hundred and two," Stokes said.

"Shut the fuck up," Carl said.

"I was asking him, not you, Carl," Frank said. Carl lowered his head in a show of subservience. Man, if Carl-Fucking-Nickerson was afraid of his father, how worried should Stokes have been at the moment? It was a moot question actually, because Stokes couldn't have been any more worried than he already was.

"So," Frank said, "I loaned you money some time ago and you paid it back today. With interest, I assume."

"A shitload of it," Stokes replied.

"Well, that's business, isn't it? So what is all this then? You decided to break into my home to steal the money back? Very, very unwise, Mr. Stokes."

Stokes shook his head but remained silent.

"Nothing to say?" Frank asked.

"What *can* he say, Dad?" Carl said. "I caught him in the act. He broke in. He was here in your office."

Frank Nickerson fixed cold eyes on his son, and Carl stopped talking. "Sit down, Carl," he said. Carl did, in the wing chair opposite Stokes.

"Mr. Stokes," Frank said, "you obviously know who I am, so you must know that this is a very stupid thing you've done. I know how money troubles can make one desperate, but what would possess you to take this risk? Surely there are other, far less dangerous ways you could have gotten your hands on money, if you need it that badly."

Still, Stokes was silent.

"It's time for you to open your mouth," Frank said, "or I'll open it for you."

"Not gonna have Carl do it for you?"

Frank shook his head. "No, I'll give this gun to Carl and I'll work on you myself. And I should tell you, when I was a few years younger, I did some truly, truly awful things to some people. And now, knowing that you broke into my home, and seeing what you did to my son, I'm thinking about doing some of those things again if you don't start talking."

Stokes believed him. Nickerson was different from Grote, who, earlier that night, had threatened to have Brower work Stokes over while he sat on his ass and watched. Nickerson liked to do his own dirty work.

"Now," Frank continued, "let's hear it, or things get very unpleasant for you."

"They aren't all that pleasant at the moment," Stokes said.

Frank said nothing.

Stokes took a deep breath, let it out, and said, "I'm here because of Amanda Jenkins."

Still, Frank said nothing. He stared blankly at Stokes. Finally he said, "Who's Amanda Jenkins?"

"The girl you kidnapped."

Frank just stared.

"The kidnapping you're working on with Grote."

Frank frowned and said, "Maybe I need to clarify my instructions. I don't just want you to speak, I also want you to make sense."

"Goddamn it, I'm talking about the little girl you and Grote kidnapped. The one you guys said you'd kill tonight if I don't show up in time with the money you asked for."

"Grote?" Frank asked.

"Yeah, Grote."

"*Leo* Grote?"

"Jesus Christ," Stokes said, "why the hell are you playing dumb with *me*? You've got the gun and your psycho son right next to you, and you're obviously gonna kill me, so why pretend you don't know what I'm talking about?"

"Shut the fuck up, Stokes," Carl said from his chair.

"What's the matter with you guys?" Stokes asked. "Look, I don't have a goddamn clue why you and Grote are working together on something like this, but it's obvious you are, so let's cut the bullshit and get on with whatever we're gonna do to end this."

Frank regarded him curiously for a moment before sliding his eyes over to Carl, who was looking down. Frank looked back at Stokes.

"Let's pretend for a moment, Mr. Stokes, that I truly don't have any idea what you're talking about. Please fill me in."

Though it didn't seem to matter any longer, Stokes looked down at his watch: 1:22 a.m.

"Someplace you have to be?" Frank asked.

"Not anymore, I guess."

He wasn't sure why he had to tell the whole story, seeing as Frank Nickerson had to be in on this, but Frank was the one holding the gun. Or *was* he in on it? Could Carl have been acting on his own? With Grote and his men? But that didn't make—

"I'm waiting," Frank reminded him, and his look said that he wasn't used to waiting and that he didn't enjoy it on those rare occasions when he had to.

Stokes shrugged. "I came across a car accident today. A single-car accident. The driver was dead. In the car was a bag with three hundred and fifty grand in it."

Stokes recounted much of what had transpired that day, talking about how he gave Carl and Chet some of the intended ransom money to pay off his debt to Frank before realizing just how serious the kidnappers were about receiving every cent they asked for, and that he therefore needed to get the ransom money back up to $350,000. He described going to Amanda's stepmother's house and learning of her involvement, about stashing her and the cop in a vacant house. He told Frank about the hourly phone calls Paul Jenkins had insisted on, and about how he'd posed as Jenkins, apparently fooling Carl and Chet all day, which earned Carl a mildly disgusted look from his father. He mentioned that he'd gone to Leo Grote's house, hoping to borrow money that he intended to simply turn around and give back to him, via his underlings, to ransom Amanda.

"And Grote turned down your request for a loan, I assume?" Frank said.

"Just like you would have," Stokes said.

Frank nodded. "Which was why you decided to break into my house and steal the money back."

Stokes said nothing.

"And you're such a Good Samaritan, Mr. Stokes, that you have a quarter of a million dollars in your hands right now, and you were looking for another hundred grand from me, and rather than keep all that money, you were going to use it to get this little girl back? Is that what you're saying?"

Stokes shrugged.

"Why?" Frank asked. "Why help the girl?"

"I'm not sure. Not really."

Frank appraised him for a moment. "So you still have the money then? What is it, almost a quarter mil? Where is it now?"

"In the trunk of the Camry on the street out front."

Keeping his gun trained on Stokes, Frank stepped over to his desk and picked up Carl's cell phone. He flipped it open, studied it for a moment, and pressed a single button—Redial, apparently, because a moment later the phone in Stokes's pocket began to vibrate and buzz.

"You want me to answer it?" Stokes asked.

Frank ignored him. He ended the call and turned to Carl.

"Well?" he asked.

Carl played dumb, which probably wasn't a big stretch for him. "What?"

"You know you don't want to make me ask you again, son. I'm waiting."

Stokes watched Carl. He'd known the Nickersons since their school days. He was shocked to see, for the first time in his life, a Nickerson showing fear. Frank sat on a corner of his desk, facing his son, keeping one eye—and his gun—on Stokes.

"Dad, let's just kill this guy and—"

"Are you going to make me ask you again?" Frank asked.

Carl lowered his head. "No, sir."

"OK then."

Carl started in a somewhat shaky voice, which surprised Stokes as much as the fear that flickered across his battered face a moment earlier.

"See, Dad, it's like this . . . Chet and I got to thinking about you."

"Me?"

"Yeah, about you. And Leo Grote."

"What about Leo Grote and me?"

"Well, about how he has a bigger business than you."

"And?" Frank said.

"And, uh, we thought maybe you should have more of a take, that's all. That maybe you should be getting a little more and Grote should be getting a little less." Carl paused. Frank remained silent, so Carl continued. "I mean, we probably take in, what? Seventy percent of what he does, maybe seventy-five? Why? Why should he have more than us? Why should he be bigger than us? Bigger than you, Dad?"

Frank finally spoke. "What did you do, Carl?"

Carl used his pajama sleeve to blot some blood gingerly from what remained of his nose. "We ran into a couple of Grote's guys in a club, guys we knew. We all had a lot to drink and they started talking, bragging about a big score they were gonna make. Told us about this lady who owed Grote some money and instead of paying it back, she was helping them set up a kidnapping. Her stepdaughter."

Frank's eyebrows rose.

"Yeah, her own stepdaughter," Carl said. "Crazy, right?"

When Frank didn't respond, Carl continued. "Anyway, the father and stepmom are divorced. He's got over a third of a million in cash he's saving for the kid. Guess where he got it from." When Frank didn't guess, he continued. "Stole it from Leo Grote. The stupid bastard did some accounting or something for Grote and skimmed over the years. How stupid can you be, right?" Frank said nothing and Carl plowed ahead. "So the stepmother tells Grote's guys that if they grab the kid, the father will give up all the money in a heartbeat. She offers to split it with them. They were gonna screw her over on that, of course, keep the whole thing, except for what she owed Grote. I mean, what was she gonna do? Call the cops?" Still, Frank remained silent. "Anyway, we could see that these guys, Grote's guys, were doing this on their own, you know?

Without Grote signing off on it. They were gonna give him the money the lady owed him and pocket the rest. So we ask why they weren't bringing the deal to Grote. Turns out they don't have a lot of loyalty for their boss. They were gonna give him his money, stash the rest of the ransom for a little while—which he wouldn't even know about—then skip town in a few months. When Chet and me heard how they talked about Grote, an idea came to us, a way to do something we'd been kicking around for a while."

"And that was?" Frank asked.

Carl cleared his throat. "Uh, getting Grote out of the picture."

"Out of the picture?" Frank repeated.

"Yeah, out of the picture. We figure that with him gone, his business comes our way. Your way, Dad. Even if someone else takes over his operation, they aren't gonna be able to hold it together like Grote did. They'd fall apart over there before long. More people would turn to you. And you'd be the biggest fish around, instead of the second-biggest fish."

Frank processed this for a while. So did Stokes. This was big stuff Carl was talking about now. For the moment, as he listened, Stokes almost forgot his own situation, the fact that he was probably going to be killed by gangsters any minute.

Frank was composed, but his face betrayed hints of anger and confusion.

"And how would kidnapping a little girl get Leo Grote out of the picture?" he asked.

Stokes listened to the plan. Carl and Chet had convinced Iron Mike and Danny DeMarco that if they worked together on this, once Grote was out of the way, Frank Nickerson would take them in and make them wealthy, important men in his operation. They were going to set Grote up. It was a little complicated, and Stokes had some trouble following, but he thought he got most of it. He wasn't sure what their original plan had been, but it was clear to

Stokes that once Paul Jenkins told them he had evidence against Grote, the four thugs improvised and decided they could split the entire $350,000 that Jenkins had stolen from Grote and stuck in an account for the kid and make it look like the kidnapping had been about nothing but the evidence all along—that Grote had ordered the girl to be kidnapped so he could obtain the incriminating evidence as ransom. When the cops found the evidence, whatever it was, they'd have a solid link between Grote and the kidnapping, which he wasn't actually a part of, and they'd also have hard evidence of other crimes Grote actually *was* responsible for.

Frank asked, "How did Grote's men plan to avoid being implicated?"

"Well, they figured none of Jenkins's evidence would incriminate them specifically in anything," Carl said, "and Grote didn't know anything about the kidnapping, so he couldn't point fingers their way about it."

As Stokes listened, he realized that a thought had been nibbling on part of his brain like a pesky rodent. Something one of the Nickerson twins had said. Something from earlier that day.

"You were gonna kill Jenkins," he said abruptly, interrupting Carl's narrative. "You were gonna frame Grote and his guys for it. And you're gonna kill the girl, too."

Carl looked at him.

"Jesus Christ," Stokes said. "None of this mattered. Nothing I did today mattered. Not trying to collect all the ransom money you guys demanded, not trying to figure out where to meet you. I had no chance of saving that girl. You were gonna kill her no matter what. Because kidnapping's a sucker's crime, right? You never get away with it because you always leave a witness . . . unless you kill the hostage. Isn't that what you told me today?"

Carl didn't respond.

"I'm right, aren't I?" Stokes asked.

Carl ignored him. Stokes knew he was right. Goddamn it.

"Well?" Frank asked.

Carl looked up at his father. "Yeah. The original plan was to wait till the father drops the money and the evidence, then kill him. But he . . . I mean Stokes here . . . changed things up on us, insisted on seeing the girl first, so we figured, no big deal, we'd let them see each other, then kill them. But Iron Mike doesn't know that. He thinks it's just a kidnapping and we've got a plan to pin it on Grote somehow. What he doesn't know is that we have a side deal with DeMarco, who has already planted evidence at both Grote's house and Iron Mike's, fake evidence showing that Grote ordered the kidnapping and told Iron Mike to do it. But Chet was going to kill both Iron Mike *and* DeMarco tonight, after they got the money, making it look like they panicked, killed the kid and the father, then killed each other over something . . . probably the money. We were gonna leave fifty K behind to give the cops something to think they fought over. No one would ever know we were involved."

Frank stood up. "*Chet* was going to kill them? He's not upstairs?"

Carl shook his head.

"Goddamn it, Carl," Frank said, and Stokes could see in the father's face a little of what kept his son—*both* his sons, no doubt—in line.

"See, Dad," Carl said quickly, "it's a good plan. DeMarco thinks he's fucking over Iron Mike, but the truth is, Chet and I are fucking them both over. Pinning everything on the both of them. And on Grote, too. When the cops look at this mess, they'll see a kidnapping gone bad, one that Grote ordered, one that ended up with the victim and her father dead, and the two kidnappers, too. And Grote, who supposedly ordered it all, goes to prison on conspiracy charges, felony murder, whatever. He'll be wrecked."

Stokes thought he'd probably taken it all in, though he'd been only half listening. He was mostly thinking about the chubby little girl in the picture, the one whose life would end tonight.

He let his head fall into his hands. All for nothing. Everything he did today, everything he'd tried to do, everything he gave up. None of it mattered. And the poor kid. Amanda. She never had a chance. He never had a hope of saving her.

"So what do you think, Dad?" Carl asked Frank. "What's next?"

Stokes looked up. This part interested him.

"Next," Frank said, his eyes sliding over to Stokes before drifting back to Carl, "it's time for a little punishment."

Carl nodded. Stokes closed his eyes.

TWENTY-EIGHT

1:33 A.M.

STOKES WAITED TO FEEL AGONY, a gun butt to the teeth, maybe a bullet shattering one of his knees. But when the pain didn't come right away, he opened his eyes in time to see Frank Nickerson launch a solid punch into his son's already savaged face.

"Jesus, Dad, what was that for?" Carl said, the words sputtering out of his mouth along with flecks of blood.

Frank threw a second punch, and Carl cried out in confused pain. A third blow snapped his head back.

"God, Dad, please, stop it, just stop. I can't take it."

But Frank didn't stop. He hit Carl a fourth time, then a fifth, and the wet sound his fist made on contact with his son's face made Stokes's stomach twist. Stokes was surprised the big, fleshy guy could throw punches like that. Finally, Frank stepped back, breathing heavily. That was probably more exercise than he'd gotten in decades. And though short in duration, it had been quite a workout. Stokes was glad—and surprised as hell—that Carl had been the punching bag instead of him.

And on this night of surprises, perhaps the biggest one of all came when Carl Nickerson started to cry, very softly.

"Stop that, son," Frank said, "or I'll give you something to really cry about."

How many times had Stokes heard that himself before his father walked out of his life for good? Carl sniffed a couple of times. He stopped crying. He looked up at his father with genuine pain in his eyes, and Stokes wasn't sure the pain was entirely physical.

"Why, Dad?"

"That you even have to ask tells me how unbelievably stupid you are." He shook his head. He sat back on the desk and let loose a sad, heavy sigh. "What makes you think I wanted a bigger cut of the action, Carl? What makes you think I'm not perfectly happy with the way things are?"

Carl looked truly confused now. "But . . . Grote's operation is bigger than yours." He was having trouble speaking now through lips that were puffy and split in a couple of places. His face was covered in blood. Blood ran down his neck, trickled out one of his ears. It had even pooled in the white part of one of his eyes. The other eye was swollen nearly shut. At least one tooth was missing. It was hard to know for sure which damage Stokes had inflicted and which was the result of the beating Frank gave him. Either way, the guy was a mess.

Frank wiped his bloody knuckles on the leg of his pj's. "My God, Son, I don't want Grote out of the picture. Without him around, the cops would have no one to concentrate on but me. As it is, I take in less than Grote, have my hand in fewer things, hurt fewer people, so the authorities spend more time on him than me. But if he's gone, I'm the only ship on their radar."

Understanding seemed to dawn on Carl's ruin of a face.

"Besides," Frank continued, "what do you think Leo Grote would do if the authorities fail to put him away? Let's say the evidence you planted isn't enough, or Grote gets out on bail. Hell, he can even still give orders from behind bars. So who do you think he'd suspect of trying to get him 'out of the picture,' as you say? Who do you think he'd retaliate against?"

"You?"

"That's right, me."

Carl looked like he might cry again.

"See, Carl, Leo Grote and I have had a certain arrangement for many years now," Frank said, "and it's worked fine for us all this time. He may be a professional rival, but the rivalry is an amicable one. And for the same reason I want him around, he wants me around. I take at least some of the heat off him. Neither one of us wants to have to manage the kind of operation it would take to oversee all the major crime in this area. Shady Cross may not be the biggest city in the state, but there's enough action here and in the outlying areas where we do business that Grote and I have both become as rich as we need to be, especially because we both use the profits from our less-than-legal enterprises to fund other profitable and completely aboveboard activities."

Frank sighed.

"Son," he said, "did you ever ask yourself why I've never tried to have him killed? Why he's never tried to take me out?"

Carl thought for a moment. He shook his head.

Frank shook his head, too, sadly.

"Carl, Carl, Carl," he said, "if you weren't my son, and if I didn't love you, you'd be dead by now. And within minutes of Chet walking through the front door, he'd be dead, too. That is, if he weren't my son and if I didn't love him. But you are my sons, so instead of killing you both, I'm going to instruct you to fix this. Fix this so it never touches Leo Grote, and it definitely never touches me. Call it off."

"What about the kid?" Carl asked.

"The kid?" Frank said, as if he hadn't given the little girl a moment's thought. He frowned, thinking. Stokes held his breath.

Finally, Frank turned to Stokes. "Mr. Stokes, have you told anyone about Leo Grote kidnapping the little girl?"

Stokes thought about it. "I told people about the kidnapping, but the cop I stashed in that vacant house is the only one who might have heard Grote's name. I can't remember for sure if I mentioned it. The stepmother knows, of course."

"But nobody knows our part in this, Dad."

Frank looked at his son with contempt.

"You mean *your* part in this. And no, you're right. Mr. Stokes here wasn't aware of your involvement until a few minutes ago, so he couldn't have told anyone. Still, things could get messy. I'm very angry, son."

Carl winced slightly, perhaps expecting another blow, or perhaps feeling the pain of parental disappointment. Or maybe the pain was merely from one of his numerous wounds, which could have included broken bones and ruptured organs.

"Did you two at least have the good sense to wear a mask around the girl?"

Carl hesitated before saying, "Yeah. Even though we were planning to kill her, we thought we should wear masks. It made it easier to . . . well . . . it just made it easier."

Frank pursed his flabby lips in concentration. Finally, he opened his eyes and said, "I don't want the girl killed, Carl. She'll be released. But you will tell Chet to kill Grote's men. They'll complain about us calling this off. They'll want the money they were promised. They might do or say something stupid tomorrow. So Chet has to kill them tonight, like you planned. But someplace where the girl can't see or hear. She can't know what happens to them."

"Why not kill the kid, Dad?"

"Because Chet's going to bury the bodies of Grote's men, someplace they hopefully won't be found anytime soon. If men like that disappear, no one will shed too many tears. Even if they're found, the police won't worry all that much about two of Grote's men being murdered. They'll think the men were involved in something illegal, something that went wrong and got them killed, which will be true, but that's beside the point. The point is, the police won't lose much sleep over their deaths, nor will they expend undue energy in trying to find their killers and bring them to justice."

"And the kid?"

"My God, son, are you listening?"

Stokes looked at the tiny ribbon of blood leaking out of one of Carl's ears and thought maybe his father should cut him some slack if he was having a little trouble hearing.

"Although the police won't care overly much about the murders of two men working for Leo Grote," Frank continued, "they would no doubt care a great deal about the disappearance of a six-year-old girl. And the public would care, too. As would the media. And soon everyone would be looking everywhere for her, and somebody would have seen or heard something that you or your idiot brother or those two imbeciles who work for Grote did or said, and then this would come back to me. To Grote and me. And as I told you already, this will *not* come back to me. Understand now?"

Carl nodded weakly. He was in rough shape.

"Now," Frank said as he handed Carl's cell phone to him, "I assume Chet has his phone with him. You will call him and tell him what I told you. That he is to make Grote's men disappear, and that he is not to harm the girl at all. In fact, he should leave her somewhere safe when his other work is done, someplace open all night, like a church or hospital or something.

Carl was nodding and dialing as Frank spoke. Now he had the phone to his ear. He waited for Chet to answer. Frank waited, too. So did Stokes. They all kept on waiting. Carl blinked a drop of bloody sweat from his nonswollen, blood-filled eye. They waited some more. Finally, Carl looked at the phone with despair further distorting his already badly distorted features.

"What time is it?" he asked.

Frank looked at Stokes. Stokes looked at his watch.

"One forty-nine," he said.

"Oh, shit," Carl said.

"What?" Stokes and Frank asked at the same time.

"He's probably already on his way up there."

"Up where?"

"Where we were gonna have Jenkins meet us. In the old ballroom up at Paradise Park."

Stokes knew Paradise Park well. The old amusement park had been closed for twenty-five years, but everyone who had ever been a teenager in or near Shady Cross knew every inch of the park's grounds as well as they knew their own backyards, if they had backyards. After the park's owners went bankrupt, they'd simply shut things down and moved on, leaving behind most of the structures on the land, which made the place a popular hangout with kids. The dozens of buildings left standing, the rides with their rails and tunnels and cars, were irresistible attractions for young people looking for a cool, remote place to drink, smoke pot, and just goof around. And predictably, guys had been bringing girls there since just after the amusement park closed up shop. The toll the years took on the place only added to its mystique. The cops made an occasional show of sweeping the grounds clean of restless kids, and now and then a politician looking to get elected would promise to find the funds to have Paradise Park well and truly closed, with the buildings and rides torn down and the debris removed and the land put to good use, but the promise was invariably forgotten as soon as the election was over.

The choice of the defunct amusement park as a place to meet Jenkins was a good one, Stokes thought. Like everyone else who grew up in this area, the Nickersons had spent many hours exploring the park. While the cops might know a dozen ways in and out of the park, the Nickersons would know three times that many. And they knew places to hide, if it came to that. And places from which to ambush.

"So try calling your brother again," Frank said. "Stop him."

"I don't think I can, Dad."

"It wasn't a request, Carl."

"I mean, I probably can't reach him. He's not answering. The cell reception is bad up there. That's why one of us had to stay back here and make the last calls to the kid's father."

Frank closed his eyes. It looked to Stokes like he was counting silently to himself. He'd probably read one of those stress management books advising people who are angry to count to ten to keep from losing control. If his reputation was deserved, Stokes doubted he'd used the technique many times over the years. He certainly hadn't used it a few minutes ago when he pummeled his son without mercy.

Carl was probably right, though. The old Paradise Park grounds were a few miles out of town, up toward the top of either a really big hill or a really small mountain, depending on how you looked at it. Stokes thought of it as a big hill; mountains were in short supply in Indiana. The old amusement park was set on land carved out of the deep woods that draped the entire hill. Stokes had driven the roads through those woods. Cell reception was never good up there.

"Wait a minute," Stokes said to Carl. "You were supposed to call me a few minutes ago on the pay phone at Laund-R-Rama. Shouldn't Chet and Grote's guys have waited to hear from you, to hear that things were still on track with Jenkins? Weren't you gonna use the last phone calls to move Jenkins around, see if he was being followed by the cops or something?"

Carl shifted in his seat. "Well, we wanted him to think that. The truth is, everything we heard about this guy, we figured he didn't have the balls to do anything but what we told him to do. And his ex-wife confirmed it, told us he wouldn't dare do anything that could put the kid in any more danger than she was already in. And after we cut off a couple of the girl's fingers, we thought there was no way—"

"You did what?" Frank said.

"He called the cops, Dad. Ken Haggerty told me." Stokes figured Haggerty must be their inside man with the police. "We had to stop him from doing it again," Carl said, "so we cut off a couple of fingers."

Frank nodded slowly. Stokes couldn't tell if he approved or disapproved of his sons' tactics in this regard.

"If you were so sure Jenkins would follow orders," Stokes said, "why'd you keep going on in our phone calls about following instructions to the letter and what would happen if I didn't?"

"Like I said before, just in case Jenkins grew some balls. But the ex-wife really didn't think he would and we didn't, either. So we figured there was no need for our guys to wait around for the one-thirty call. I mean, things had been going fine all day. Jenkins was answering the calls . . . well, we thought it was him, anyway . . . and you," he said, looking at Stokes, "you said you had the money. So everything looked fine. We only had a few more calls to make." He ticked them off on his fingers. "The one o'clock, which is when I heard your phone ring in the bathroom there, the one thirty I was gonna make to you at the Laundromat, and one more after that. We figured everything was going smoothly, so after Chet talked to you at midnight, he decided to get a head start up to the park."

"Wait a minute," Stokes said. "It was Chet who called me an hour ago?"

"Yeah. He made most of the calls today 'cause he's got the kid with him. I was supposed to make this call, send you to another pay phone in a pool hall across town, then call you there one last time at one forty-five and tell you to meet them at Paradise Park at two thirty, with the money and the evidence. That's when you were supposed to believe the exchange was gonna take place, giving you forty-five minutes to get up there, which should have been enough time. But meanwhile, they'd have had almost two hours to get up there and get into place."

"And what happens if nobody shows at two thirty?"

Carl hesitated. "Same thing that would have happened even if Jenkins did show, only they won't be able to kill him, too, like we planned. Well, we thought we were gonna kill Jenkins. Guess it would've been you. But Chet figured that even if the father didn't show for some reason, the big picture plan would still work. We wouldn't get the money or extra evidence on Grote, but Grote would still go down for the kidnapping."

"So Chet's definitely gonna kill the girl?" Stokes asked.

Carl nodded. "After Chet saw the money, he was gonna shoot the father, then Grote's guys, then the kid. Make it look like Grote's guys killed the father and the kid, then got into it with each other over the fifty K, leaving both of them dead."

"And if nobody shows," Frank said, "the shooting starts?"

"Jenkins was supposed to show at two thirty, but if he's not there by quarter to three, Chet kills the kid and the other guys. Either way, the cops will find the evidence DeMarco planted in Grote's house and Iron Mike's place. It'll still look like a kidnapping gone to shit, one ordered by Grote."

Jesus Christ. Stokes said, "And you had no plan for calling things off—the girl's murder or killing Grote's guys—after they get up there."

"We didn't think we needed one. Things had gone fine all day . . . well, we thought they had."

Neither Stokes nor Carl saw Frank's next blow coming, though it didn't much matter that Stokes didn't see it, given that it was Carl, not him, on the receiving end. Frank had pushed off the desk where he'd been leaning, and with his body's momentum behind it, his fat fist slammed squarely into his Carl's already-crushed nose. The wet, crunching sound was terrible. Carl's strangled cry of pain was nearly as bad. Frank stood back with his fist raised, apparently contemplating throwing yet another punch. Carl's bloody chin dropped to his chest. He was out. Maybe dead. But no, Stokes could hear low, liquid, ragged breathing.

"Idiot," Frank said.

He sat on the corner of the desk again. He looked at his son, slumped unconscious in the chair. A look of sadness touched his face. Stokes didn't know whether he was sorry for what he'd done to his son, or sorry that his sons were such morons. Maybe it was a little of both.

Nah, Stokes thought, it was probably just that his sons were morons.

They sat for a moment in silence—silence but for Carl's wet wheezing—until Stokes finally said, "What now?"

Frank looked over at him. He sighed. "I think I have to kill you," he said.

Well, that sure as hell wasn't what Stokes had been hoping to hear.

"Why?"

Frank shrugged. "Because you broke in here. Because you came to steal from me. Because you beat the hell out of my son," which sounded a little hypocritical to Stokes. "Because you know too much about what my stupid boys have done."

"Why don't we stop this? Killing the girl, I mean?"

"You heard Carl. Can't reach him on the phone."

"How about if we went up there?"

Frank frowned. "What do you mean?"

"I mean you and I drive up there. You tell Chet not to kill the girl."

Frank pursed his thick lips again. He shook his head.

"No, I can't get anywhere near this."

Stokes blew out an exasperated breath. "But you said you wanted to stop this. You said it could get messy if Chet goes through with it. You might be implicated somehow."

"True, but I will definitely be implicated if things go wrong and I'm found at the scene. Or stopped on the drive there with a wanted man, as you said you are. Or on the drive home with you and Chet after he's killed Grote's men, which I would still want him to do." He paused, thinking again. "No, I definitely cannot be a part of this."

"I'll go by myself then."

Frank laughed.

Stokes looked at his watch.

"It's two minutes before two. That gives me thirty-two minutes before Jenkins is supposed to show up, plus the extra fifteen minutes Chet's supposed to wait before the killing starts if Jenkins doesn't show. Forty-seven minutes. If I drive a little over the speed limit, but not fast enough to get pulled over, I can make it up there just in time. It'll be past two thirty, but I should get there before two forty-five, when Chet's gonna start shooting people. Maybe I can stop him."

Frank narrowed his eyes. "I'm supposed to let you go and simply believe that you'll go up to Paradise Park and try to stop my son?"

"That's right."

"Forget it. You'll just take off and leave town. We'll still have this mess on our hands while you're out there somewhere knowing way too much about it all."

Stokes stared hard at Frank. "I could have just walked away a rich man hours ago. Instead, I chose to save that kid. I've been through a *lot* of shit today trying to do that. The cops are already looking for me for breaking and entering and murder. Soon they're gonna want me on kidnapping charges—kidnapping a cop, no less. I've had plenty of chances to walk away from this since it all started, but I didn't. I stayed, risking everything, because I want to save that kid. And don't ask me why because it's none of your business. But that's what I'm gonna do. I'm gonna save her." He paused. "If you let me go, I mean."

Frank thought for a moment. "How will you stop him?"

"I'll tell him what you said. That you don't want him to kill the girl."

"You won't hurt him? I mean, I doubt you could, if he saw you coming—you probably surprised Carl here, that's how you beat him—but Chet's different from Carl. He's tougher. And while he's certainly no genius, he's smarter than his brother. He's also not a bad shot. No, if he knew you were there, he'd get you." Frank eyed Stokes. "But maybe you were thinking of sneaking around up there and shooting him in the back, something like that."

Stokes shook his head. "I'm not. I won't have to. I'll just tell him everything you said. He'll recognize your words, right?"

Frank considered this. "You could tell him I said he either listens to you or he goes into the lockbox."

"What's that mean?"

"That's none of *your* business. But Chet will know I sent you."

"OK, lockbox, got it."

"What about Grote's guys?" Frank asked.

"I don't give a shit what he does with Grote's guys. I'll take the girl and get the hell out of there. He can do whatever he wants after that. So what do you say?"

Frank rubbed his eyes. "I don't know . . ."

"The clock's ticking, Frank."

Frank opened his eyes and stared hard at Stokes. "I think you mean Mr. Nickerson."

"Yeah, of course, that's what I mean. But the clock's still ticking."

Frank scratched his neck.

"OK," he said. "I'll let you go. Do what you can to stop this. I don't want my son killing that girl. He may be smarter than his brother, but he's still not always the best thinker. He could make a mistake, leave evidence behind. Like I said, no one's gonna worry too much about a couple of thugs like Grote's men, but they'll work hard to find the killer of a little girl. I don't want Chet taking that chance." He nodded to himself. "You go, Mr. Stokes, and stop him from killing the girl. Just the girl. You understand?"

Stokes nodded.

"And when you drop her off somewhere safe, do so in such a way that neither my sons nor I will be implicated. Are we clear on this?"

Stokes nodded again.

"After this is over," Frank continued, "I think it would be best if you found another place to live."

"I'm not all that attached to the trailer I live in."

"I meant another city, preferably one very far away."

"I know what you meant. I agree. When this is over, you'll never see me again."

Frank nodded. Stokes stood up, wincing as he did. He'd forgotten how hard Carl had fought before the head butt took him down. He ached everywhere. He walked over and picked his guns up off the floor. He tucked one into his waistband at his back, the other into his front pocket. Frank watched. Despite Stokes's promise not to hurt his son, Frank watched him take the guns and said nothing.

Stokes was ready to go. He didn't need the $100,000 he'd tried so hard to collect, seeing as it was never actually about the money for Chet anyway. No, all Stokes needed was time, which he was rapidly losing. And as powerful as Frank Nickerson was, that was something even he couldn't provide.

Stokes nodded to Frank and walked out of the office. He wound his way through the mansion, finally reaching the front door. He'd originally planned to leave by the back door, through which he'd entered the house, but there was no need now. He opened the door and stepped out into the night.

As he trotted down the driveway toward Charlie Daniels's car on the street, it occurred to him for the first time—hit him with the force of one of Carl's punches to his face, actually—that he wasn't going to have to give up the money after all. It was right there, in the Camry's trunk, waiting for him. Frank hadn't demanded that he hand it over. And if Chet listened to Stokes and believed that Frank wanted the whole thing called off, Chet wouldn't be expecting any money. And if he *didn't* listen to Stokes and started shooting the moment he realized Stokes wasn't Paul Jenkins, then Stokes was going to have to try to kill him, despite his promise to Frank Nickerson. And Grote's guys, too, if Chet hadn't already done it. Either way, if Stokes survived, he kept the money. And he'd save Amanda, too. All he had to do was get to Paradise Park before Chet killed the girl.

Stokes was almost to the end of the drive, walking in the shadows of the big trees lining it, just thirty feet from his car, when a police cruiser pulled to a slow stop a few yards behind the Camry.

TWENTY-NINE

2:06 A.M.

AS SOON AS STOKES SAW the police car, he stepped off the driveway and ducked behind one of the huge trees beside it. He peered around and watched a cop step out of the cruiser, hand on his gun, while his partner stayed in the car and spoke into a radio mic. The first cop, a big blond bastard who looked to Stokes like he was probably named Randy or maybe Todd, approached the Camry slowly. Stokes saw him unsnap his holster and draw his gun.

"If there's anyone in the vehicle, show yourself," Officer Randy-Todd said. "Show your hands."

No one answered.

"This is your last warning."

The empty Camry was silent.

Randy-Todd touched his shoulder mic and said something too low for Stokes to hear. The cop in the car, who had dark hair and seemed to have a darker complexion, and who looked like maybe a Tony to Stokes, touched his own shoulder-mic and responded.

Stokes knew what must have happened. Good old Charlie Daniels, everyone's buddy at the trailer park, happy to help whoever was in need, had broken his promise to Stokes and called the cops. He no doubt told them that someone had stolen his car, but almost certainly left out that Stokes had given him a thousand bucks for the key. To top it off, he probably said that he'd gotten a look at the guy as he drove away and he looked a hell of a lot like Stokes. That son of a bitch.

Officer Randy-Todd took a wide arc around to the side of the car, where he could see in through the window. He inched closer, gun at the ready. Stokes took a last, longing look at the closed trunk of the car, where his money was, and hurried as quietly as he could back toward Nickerson's house. He kept to the shadows, finally breaking into a full run as he neared the mansion. He risked a glance over his shoulder and saw that Officer Randy-Todd and Officer Tony were both by the Camry now. They were looking around for him. Any second they'd look his way, but before they did, he slipped around the side of Nickerson's house and out of their view. He sprinted to the back door, which he'd left unlocked and ajar earlier, and hurried inside.

He ran through the house, retracing his route to Frank's office. As he did, he stole a glance at his watch: 2:10. Only thirty-five minutes to get to Paradise Park before Chet killed Amanda.

I'm not going to make it.

He pushed that thought aside and ran faster down the hall, through the dining room, to the office, where he found Frank sitting in his leather desk chair, his slippered feet up on the desktop, his ankles crossed. He was watching CNN on the big TV on the wall opposite his desk, eating one of the cookies Carl had carried in on a plate earlier. Carl was still slumped unconscious in his chair, squeezing out ragged breaths. When Frank saw Stokes, mild surprise touched his jowly face. Stokes saw that he had a milk mustache.

"Shouldn't you be speeding toward Paradise Park right now? You're running out of time."

"We both are, remember? And yeah, I should be on my way up there, and I would be if it weren't for the cops standing by my car."

Frank frowned and dropped his feet to the floor. The chair beneath him groaned in protest—or perhaps exhaled with relief—as Frank heaved his bulk out of it and moved over to a window behind the desk. Without moving the drapes—which were hanging nearly closed since Stokes had used their ropes to tie up Carl—Frank peered through the crack between them. He nodded.

"They've probably called for backup," Frank said. "And if by some chance they found the police officer you kidnapped and hid somewhere, the backup will be here very soon."

"There's also a sergeant who's got a hard-on for me about this guy they think I killed last night during a break-in."

"They think?"

Stokes shrugged. "That's what they say."

"Are they right?"

"Do you really care?"

"You've been a busy man lately, Mr. Stokes."

"Yeah well, I need to get busy again, and real fast, or Chet's gonna kill that kid, which you said you don't want to happen any more than I do."

Frank shook his head. "No, I don't."

"So distract the cops for me."

"I've told you how reluctant I am to involve myself in this matter."

"You're already involved, like it or not. And you'll be a hell of a lot more involved, and in something a hell of a lot more serious, if Chet kills the girl and either leaves evidence behind, or gets nailed by something someone saw or overheard as he and Grote's idiots planned this thing."

Frank considered this.

"How would I help you?" Frank finally asked.

"Open the door, start yelling."

"What would I be yelling?"

"Whatever. Just get them away from my car. Hell, tell them I broke into your house looking for money. They'll believe that."

Frank pondered that. "They'll want to come in. They'll see Carl here."

Stokes looked over at Carl, unconscious and bloody, his arms and legs spilling out of the chair like those of a doll some kid had tossed there.

"Tell them you heard noises, came down, and found him like this," Stokes said. "They know I was driving the Camry out there. They'll think I broke in and beat him up for some reason."

"Which is true," Frank said.

"Yeah, whatever. Listen, I have to get going."

He looked through the curtains at the cops standing by their car, clearly waiting for their backup to arrive before beginning a more thorough search of the area.

"So you'll do it?" Stokes asked.

"Yes, but think about it. There are two ways events could unfold. When I open my front door and call to them, both officers might come up here, either on foot or in their car, or alternatively, one will come alone while the other stays with your car. If they both come, you're all set. But if only one does, the one who stays behind will be on high alert. He'll either shoot you or capture you. He's trained for this kind of thing. You're not."

Stokes nodded. He thought quickly. "OK then. Give me the keys to one of your cars. You must have half a dozen or so in the garage."

"Four."

"OK, give me the keys to one of them, the fastest one—"

"The Porsche," Frank interjected.

"—and I'll wait by the garage. If both cops come, I'll drop the keys and run through the shadows to my car and drive away, get a nice head start and lose them in the city streets. If only one comes, though, I'll 'steal' your car, which you'll realize at the same time the cops do, and I'll drive away, only a hell of a lot faster because I'll be in a Porsche instead of a Camry."

Which would mean leaving his money behind, Stokes knew, which would absolutely break his heart. He prayed both cops would come running.

Frank was thinking the plan through. Stokes looked at his watch: 2:13. Goddamn it.

I'm gonna be too late, he thought. *I'm still gonna try like hell, but I'm just not gonna make it.*

"Come on, Frank," Stokes said sharply, more sharply than Frank was likely accustomed to. But Frank just nodded.

"OK," he said. "Go down that hall, past the billiard room, to the garage on the other side of the house. There are keys hanging just inside the door, each clearly marked. There's a garage door opener in the Porsche."

"Got it. Give me a thirty-second head start."

Stokes started for the doorway.

"Mr. Stokes," Frank said, and Stokes stopped. "When this is all over, if you succeed and survive . . ."

"Yeah?" Stokes said impatiently.

"Before you leave town for that faraway city where I'll never see you again, leave my car somewhere I can find it. Lock the key inside. I have a spare."

Stokes merely waved a hand over his shoulder as he took off at a run. He flew down the hallway and opened the door at the end. It was fairly dark in the garage, but Stokes couldn't risk turning on a light and having it seen from the street. He could see the Porsche, looking sleek and fast, gleaming silver even in the faint light bleeding in through the windows in the garage doors. He squinted at the keys hanging on little hooks by the door and found one with a label on the wall above it reading, "Porsche." He grabbed the key just as he heard Frank start screaming bloody murder on the other side of the house, yelling that his house had been broken into, that his son was badly hurt.

Stokes hurried over to the window and saw one of the cops— just *one* of the goddamn cops—sprinting up the long drive. It was Randy-Todd. Down on the street, Tony rushed back to the cruiser and leaned inside. Stokes knew he was calling in to report this new development.

Shit. Stokes's goddamn money was in the Camry. He had no choice now. He had to leave it behind.

Forever.

Shit.

He hurried over to the Porsche, opened the door, and sank into a leather seat so smooth and comfortable and perfect for driving, and so unlike anything he'd ever experienced in a seat of any kind, that he almost wanted just to sit for a while and enjoy it. But he jammed the key into the ignition and brought the engine roaring to life as he stabbed at the button on the garage door opener clipped to the passenger-side sun visor. He didn't want to use his mangled hand, so he reached across his body with his right hand and pulled the car door shut. The garage door rose and Stokes was backing out even before it had risen all the way. He shot under it with mere inches of clearance and continued a few yards, cutting the wheel left as he did, before screeching to a stop, spinning the wheel right, and rocketing forward down the drive. He thought he was doing pretty well driving mostly one-handed. Out of the corner of his eye he saw Randy-Todd at the open front door with Nickerson. They both turned his way as he screeched off.

The Porsche's engine growled deep in its throat, and the car thrummed with power as Stokes sped down the drive, toward the road. Officer Tony was standing by the police cruiser, radio mic in hand, watching in openmouthed surprise. He scrambled into the car as Stokes shot out of the drive and banged a hard right, the high-performance tires gripping the road with confidence. He was lucky he needed to go in that direction anyway, as it forced Tony to have to turn his car around, costing him valuable time while Stokes raced off in a machine built for speed.

As Stokes poured on as much gas as he could without risking a violent wreck, he heard Tony's siren begin to wail behind him. Soon, a few more joined the chorus. Backup had arrived and entered the chase.

This was nuts, Stokes thought. This was reckless and stupid and had very little chance of succeeding, and everything he'd done that day had been leading toward this stupid, stupid end. It was over for him. He was going to spend the rest of his life in prison. All for a kid he'd never even met.

He was a goddamn idiot.

But still he drove. Not toward the highway out of town, toward a life somewhere far away, but toward the road leading up into the hills, where he hoped he'd find a little girl in a defunct amusement park.

He shook his head and asked himself why he'd done this, and he told himself to just shut up and drive.

The cops were back there but didn't seem to be gaining on him as he tore through the streets. They might even have been losing ground. He figured more cops would pull in front of him up ahead somewhere. Not a roadblock. They hadn't had enough time to set something like that up. But there was probably a cruiser or two patrolling the area he was driving through, especially because the route he had to take brought him through one of the rougher parts of town, and the cops inside those cruisers would be aware of what was happening and would have been instructed to cut him off. But they hadn't appeared yet, and the cops following him weren't in sight, so when Stokes saw a group of seedy-looking guys in muscle shirts and tattoos hanging around outside a dive bar—maybe gang members, maybe just gangbanger wannabes—gathered around a dark and dented SUV of some kind, a Ford Explorer maybe, Stokes jerked the wheel and screeched the Porsche into an alley just past the bar. He leaped from the car and ran the half block back toward the group. They watched him come, eight or nine of them, some impassively, some with open curiosity. As he neared them, he pulled one of his guns while at the same time speaking rapidly.

"I don't wanna hurt anyone, but I don't have time for bullshit." He imagined how he looked to them: covered in blood and bruises. "The cops are after me. I want your truck, but I'd rather not have to steal it from you. You can have my Porsche, though you'll probably wanna wait a while before taking it out of that alley. So who owns this truck?"

They were all a little too surprised to answer, though a few heads turned toward a wiry guy, maybe twenty-five years old, who must have been the truck's owner. Stokes could sense a few of the young men thinking about pulling weapons of their own. He looked at the wiry guy, raised his gun a little in as nonthreatening a threat as he could make, and held up the key to the Porsche.

"Like I said, I don't have time for bullshit. We have a deal?"

One of the tough guys said, "What'd you do, man?"

Stokes ignored him and focused on the owner of the truck. He could see the guy running through his options. Turn the deal down, maybe get shot, and lose the truck anyway. Accept the deal, lose his truck, but in return receive a Porsche, which he knew he wouldn't be able to keep but which he could no doubt sell to the right person or maybe a chop shop for a hefty profit. Of course, he had no idea the car belonged to Frank Nickerson. When he found that out, he'd be insane to do anything but leave the car the hell alone, or maybe even return it with a sincere apology. But he wouldn't find that out until he looked in the glove box and found the registration, which would be after Stokes was long gone with the truck.

A chorus of sirens wailed in the not-too-distant distance.

Stokes pointed the gun at the wiry guy and tossed his key at the guy's feet. Negotiations were closed. Done deal. The other guy nodded, dug a key ring out of his pocket, removed one key, and threw it to Stokes. Stokes couldn't catch it with his busted fingers so he let it hit the ground. With the gun still held firmly in his good hand, he carefully picked up the key with just the thumb and index finger of his injured hand.

"Thanks," Stokes said. "You don't owe me any favors, but try to keep this to yourselves for a while, OK guys? Maybe you should go back inside for one last beer."

He waved the gun a final time before hustling into the truck. The younger guys milled about for a moment, then did as he suggested.

Stokes started the truck and drove off as quickly as he dared, while keeping his speed low enough not to attract attention. He figured he could push it a bit, though, seeing as the cops would be occupied by looking for a silver Porsche tearing through town and wouldn't worry too much about a black Explorer exceeding the speed limit by a few miles per hour.

A minute later, Stokes heard a single siren getting closer and closer and a police car screamed around a corner a few blocks ahead of him. He tensed until it shot past and continued in the other direction. Soon, another cruiser blew past, siren shrieking, lights flashing, looking for the same silver Porsche.

Stokes was confident now that he'd make it out of the city proper. He gave the truck a little more gas and looked at the dashboard clock.

It was 2:25.

He had twenty minutes to reach Chet before the asshole was supposed to kill Amanda. If he drove a bit insanely, which he could probably afford to do now that he was nearly out of town and driving a vehicle the cops had no reason to be looking for, it would still almost certainly take more than twenty minutes just to reach Paradise Park, probably closer to twenty-five. Then figure another few minutes to ditch the car and find Chet and the others.

And he had only twenty minutes.

He gunned the truck through the city's outskirts and onto the two-lane road leading up to the old amusement park. He sneaked another look at the clock in the dash. His heart sank.

Shit, he thought. *I'm not gonna make it.*

THIRTY

IT WAS 2:39 A.M. WHEN Stokes brought the black Explorer to a crunching stop in the gravel on the shoulder of the road. He'd driven with suicidal recklessness, racing along the winding two-lane road at careless, stupid speeds, barely touching the brake pedal, several times narrowly avoiding the same fate Amanda's father suffered—sailing his vehicle off the road, into the woods, headlong into a tree. It was incredible that he'd survived. Thankfully, he'd passed no cops.

Stokes backed the truck into a small gap in the trees, far enough that it wouldn't be seen easily from the road. He reached up and turned off the dome light. Just around the next bend, he knew, was the entrance to a huge gravel lot now carpeted with weeds. Decades ago it would fill with cars every day, cars that carried happy families to Paradise Park for a day of wholesome fun, tasty though less-than-wholesome food, and lasting memories. But those days were long gone. After operating for sixty-eight years, the amusement park shut down twenty-five years ago. Stokes's parents had taken him once, when he was five. The image that stuck with him most from that day was his father—his hand never without a beer in it, his lips never without a cigarette between them—waiting impatiently for

Stokes and his mother to get off each ride. Stokes recalled his father smacking him on the side of the head when he'd asked for cotton candy.

As Stokes exited the truck, shutting the door quietly behind him, he tried to remember something else from that day, something pleasant. He remembered a lot of colors, the miasma of food smells, spinning on some ride with his mother, seeing other children with big, colorful balloons but being afraid to ask for one of his own. These memories fluttered in his mind for a moment before disappearing like scraps of paper in a strong wind. He was left again with the image of his father, a big cup full of beer in his hand, a cigarette dangling from one corner of his mouth, a look on his face as lacking in warmth as it was in patience.

Stokes ran across the road and entered the woods. He knew his way well, moving as quickly and quietly as he could, reassured by the weight of the antique dealers' two guns in his jacket pockets and the feeling of Officer Martinson's bigger gun pressing against the small of his back. He was confident he'd know his way around the grounds once he reached them, so he shouldn't have trouble finding the old ballroom at the park's center. He could have chosen to drive into the weed-and-gravel lot and walk through what used to serve as the park's main entrance, but he figured Chet Nickerson might have posted one of Grote's boys there to watch it. Though they were expecting someone, that someone wasn't Stokes. He knew he'd have to reveal himself eventually, but he'd rather be fairly close to them when he did . . . close enough to do whatever it was he was going to have to do.

Stokes trotted though the woods. Over the decades, the trees surrounding the park had encroached on the grounds, so it was only when Stokes started passing dilapidated shacks and booths and rusted pieces of machinery that he realized he'd crossed the perimeter of the old park itself. He pressed on and the trees gave way to thick overgrowth. He resisted the urge to look at his watch, but every moment he was afraid he'd hear gunshots.

I'm not gonna make it.

The moon was bright and the sky clear, so Stokes was able to get his bearings. He was beside the run-down fun house, its once-garish colors muted by time and weather. He walked through thigh-high weeds, as quietly as he could, farther into the park, keeping a watchful eye for movement and listening hard for any sound that didn't belong in this place at this time of night.

Stokes knew time was running out fast and he'd have to sacrifice a bit of stealth for a little more speed. As he quickened his already-quick pace, making a direct line for the old ballroom, he couldn't help but recall some of his many wasted hours there in the park. He'd smoked his first joint behind the Dunk the Clown stand. He remembered a few other hours spent in this place that weren't so wasted. He'd touched his first naked breast, sitting in a rusted bumper car, feeling the soft, warm flesh beneath his clumsy, groping fingers, ignoring the cramped space and the hard metal seat that had long before lost any padding it once had. And less than two months later, he'd lost his virginity to Lisa Genovese, the both of them lying half-naked on a scratchy blanket he'd spread out on the floor of the empty penny arcade.

As the hulking rectangular shape of the ballroom finally came into view, Stokes realized he'd be spotted soon. He was counting on the fact that it was night rather than bright day, and that he bore a passing similarity to Paul Jenkins—at least in that they were of similar height and neither was overweight—to get him close enough to do something to save Amanda Jenkins. Just what that something was, of course, he had no idea. It was time to figure that out. It was past time, actually. He checked his watch: 2:47. He was late. Chet was going to start killing people any second. If Carl had been telling the truth, and if things worked out as they planned, Chet would start with Grote's men, then move on to Amanda.

The absolute best time for Stokes to make his move would be after Chet had killed Iron Mike and Danny DeMarco, thereby removing two of Stokes's potential obstacles, but before he shot Amanda Jenkins. But there was no way Stokes could time it like that. He'd have to face all three of them. His only hope was that he'd get close enough before they realized he wasn't Amanda's father, because even though he wasn't afraid to use the guns he was carrying, he had no idea if he could shoot straight, seeing as he'd never pulled a trigger in his life.

Acutely aware that his time was completely gone, that shots might shatter the night quiet at any moment, Stokes paused for a brief moment in the shadow of a booth that used to house some kind of game of chance, and checked all three of his weapons, making certain their safeties were disengaged. They were.

He left the shadows and stepped into the light of the clearing that spanned the twenty yards between him and the ballroom. No time left for subtlety. He broke into a run through the tall grass and weeds, hoping his guns wouldn't fly out of his pockets or waistband as he ran. As he neared the building, he saw that it was as he remembered it. Maybe sixty feet wide and three times as long. Most of the glass in its windows had been broken by kids with rocks ages ago.

He was racing for a doorway at one end of the building—the door itself was long gone—wondering if he would be recognized the instant he stepped through it, recognized as *not* being Paul Jenkins, and would be shot without hesitation. But he kept going, running right into the building, skidding to a stop just inside the door. He threw up his hands and said to nobody in particular, "I'm here, I'm here. Please don't hurt her." He was out of breath.

Stokes kept his hands up but tried to keep his head down, his face in shadow, as he swept the room with his eyes. In the middle of the cavernous space he could make out three tall figures and a shorter one. That meant that all of them—Chet and both of Grote's men, as well as Amanda—were inside the building. He was surprised at first that Chet hadn't positioned the others in a place where they could watch for Jenkins's approach from outside, and watch for cops at the same time. But maybe he'd had watches posted earlier, and when two thirty had come and gone and Jenkins still hadn't shown, and when the extra fifteen minutes he'd planned to wait had ticked by, too, he'd called the others inside to kill them.

"I'm here," Stokes repeated, hoping that his build was indeed similar enough to Jenkins's, that his voice could still pass for the father's, that his face was deep enough in shadow.

"You're late," someone said. Sounded like Chet. He apparently still believed that Stokes was Jenkins. "I was beginning to think you weren't coming."

"I had trouble finding this building."

"Where's the money?"

Stokes took a breath. "You think I'd hand it over without seeing Amanda first?"

"Where's the fucking money?" Chet asked. "And the evidence?"

"I hid it in the park on the way here. After I know Amanda's all right, I'll take you to it."

"You asshole," Chet said. No doubt he was considering how this impacted his plan just to kill everyone right here in the next few minutes. "Fucking *asshole*." He sounded really pissed, maybe pissed enough to just start shooting right now, hoping he'd find the money and the evidence hidden in the park himself. Stokes wouldn't put it past him. The guy was a lunatic. Stokes was having serious doubts about his ability to use the *lockbox* code word Frank Nickerson had given him to stop Chet from killing anyone. Besides, as Stokes had already realized, this was never truly about the money, and it wasn't about the evidence, either. If their little kidnapping-gone-terribly-wrong scenario played out as he planned, they didn't really need any more evidence. Finally, Chet said, "OK, fine. Whatever. The kid's OK, as you can see. Other than a couple of fingers."

"That true, Amanda?" Stokes called.

And for the first time, Stokes heard that little voice in person. "I guess I'm OK. I just want to go home." Her voice made something twitch in Stokes's heart.

"It'll all be over soon," Stokes said.

"Come over here," Chet said.

Stokes started walking toward them. He raised his eyes a little as he did. He took a chance and lowered his hands, slipping his damaged left hand into his pocket as surreptitiously as he could. That hand needed a head start. He gambled on the fact that they thought they were dealing with Paul Jenkins, because everything they knew about Paul Jenkins told them that he wasn't going to give them any trouble.

But he wasn't Paul Jenkins.

And they were about to find that out.

THIRTY-ONE

STOKES STRODE ACROSS THE LONG, dark ballroom, through puddles of moonlight spilling in through the occasional hole in the ceiling. He kept his face as much in shadow as he could as he walked toward the figures in the center of the room, wanting to get as close as possible before they realized that he wasn't Jenkins . . . before things went to shit.

There he was, the lone gunslinger facing down the bad guys, his fingers twitching near his guns, just like he'd imagined as a kid. The possibility of other outcomes had teased him all day, made him think it didn't have to come down to something like this, but Stokes wondered if this was inevitable, if from the moment the Nickersons took him off the bus that afternoon, it was always going to end this way.

In the final moments of this hellish day Stokes still didn't understand exactly why he was doing this—why he'd thrown away his chance at a brand-new life for a little girl he'd never met. He knew for certain that he wasn't Paul Jenkins, but he was no longer sure exactly who he was.

He was just forty feet away when Chet said, "That's far enough."

Stokes kept going. He started walking faster. Loudly, he said, "Chet, your father doesn't want you killing anyone."

"What?"

"Lockbox," Stokes blurted as he marched forward, "lockbox."

"I told you to stop," Chet said, his voice rising.

Stokes looked up while at the same time reaching for the gun in the right pocket of his jacket. He also had the two good fingers of his left hand on the gun in his other pocket—the index finger hooked around the trigger, the thumb and three broken fingers providing as much support on the handgrip as they could. Even though he'd never fired a gun before, he got the general idea. Hell, idiots shot other idiots all the time. Stokes figured he was enough of an idiot to be able to do the same. He had no idea how many bullets were in the three guns he had, but he knew the weapons were loaded and he had a gun for each guy in front of him. And if the three guns weren't enough, hell, he probably didn't deserve to survive anyway.

When Chet saw Stokes's face he asked, "Who the hell are you?" Then Stokes saw confusion and recognition light Chet's eyes at the same time and the guy raised his gun.

Stokes kept coming. "Lockbox," he called one more time, just in case. Chet was to the left of the group. Amanda was sitting on a big, overturned wooden crate two feet away from him. Iron Mike and Danny DeMarco stood together a few feet away, to the right. Chet hadn't responded to the *lockbox* code word, so Stokes knew they'd be shooting this out. He broke into a trot. He wanted to take Chet down first, but Grote's men were already drawing their weapons. He had both guns out now and he yelled, "*Get down, Amanda!*" as he started pulling triggers. The guns recoiled in his hands, much harder than he'd anticipated, and his bullets sailed wide and high. He was a lot closer to the mark with his good hand. His other bucked wildly, his fingers causing him agony. But he held on to the gun and kept coming at them, correcting his aim as he did, and bullets kicked off the cement floor. Bullets flew his way, too. Amanda screamed from her position, crouched behind the wooden crate.

DeMarco screamed too as a ricochet caught him in the leg. Stokes kept firing, trying to keep from shooting too close to the girl, the muscles in his forearms begging for a break already. But he was getting the hang of it, improving even though he was running now as he fired, ignoring a bullet that hummed just to his left. DeMarco fell on his ass and Stokes caught him full in the chest with a round. He fell back. Stokes didn't know if he was dead but he was certainly out of the fight for a while, so Stokes turned his attention to Iron Mike, who was backing away and fumbling with his own gun.

Amanda kept screaming but Stokes barely heard her. His ears were ringing, and he was still firing away. He squeezed off a couple of rounds at Iron Mike, whizzing bullets all around the asshole but failing to hit him. But the fusillade caused Iron Mike to worry more about running for his life than standing his ground, and when he spun and sprinted for a side door, Stokes turned to look for Chet.

Stokes registered Amanda's terrified screams at some deep level of his hearing, in some remote part of his brain, but didn't pay attention to them. His thoughts had turned black. He was nothing but a man with guns now. He was just someone who shot people. It was all he cared about, all he focused on. Shooting people. Chet was moving sideways toward another side door. He had his gun out and was squeezing off shots of his own. Stokes dimly realized that Chet had been firing already when Stokes caught sight of him.

Stokes turned his gun on Chet and pulled the trigger once, then again, before that gun was empty. He dropped it, switched his second gun into his good hand, and fired immediately. He felt sure he would have nailed Chet dead center if the son of a bitch hadn't stumbled as he turned for the door.

Besides Chet, Amanda, and Stokes, there was nothing in the room but the wooden crate with a laptop on top of it, a pile of jackets the men must have taken off and tossed on the floor, and DeMarco's dead body. Other than that, nothing. So there was nowhere for either Chet or Stokes to hide, nothing behind which to take cover. Chet scrambled for the door and was only a few feet from it when Stokes drew a bead dead center on his back. No way he'd miss this shot. He pulled the trigger.

And heard a loud click. He'd emptied both of the antique dealers' guns.

Chet stopped and turned. He'd heard the click, too. He smiled, raised his piece, and fired as Stokes, in one surprisingly fluid movement that belied his inexperience with firearms, dropped into a crouch and pulled Officer Martinson's gun from behind his back. He and Chet fired at the same instant and Stokes felt something buzz uncomfortably close to his neck. Chet wasn't so lucky as Stokes's bullet caught him in the arm. Before Stokes could fire again, Chet scuttled through the open side door and into the night.

Stokes blew out a breath he felt like he'd been holding since entering the ballroom. In a firefight at close range, with bullets buzzing all around, Chet had run while Stokes had held his ground. Who was the crazy one here?

"Your father wants you to call this off," he yelled after Chet. "*Lockbox*, you crazy bastard," he added, though he knew it was far too late for that.

He wanted to sit down and rest, but he knew that Chet could lean around the doorway and start shooting again any second, so he hurried over to Amanda, who sat behind the crate with her knees up to her chin and her hands clamped over her ears. Tears streamed down her chubby little face. Stokes reached out and pulled one of her hands from her ear. The other fell a moment later, and Stokes saw that it was heavily bandaged.

"It's OK," Stokes said. "You're OK."

Amanda sniffed. The tears kept rolling.

"He's dead," she said, her eyes cutting over to DeMarco lying on his back in a pool of blood the size of a small area rug.

She was right.

"But you're OK," Stokes said.

"You're hurt."

"No I'm not," Stokes replied.

She sat up and nodded. He frowned and looked down. Blood was running freely down his chest from a wound on the side of his neck. Must not have hit a major artery or he'd be dead already, but it was bleeding pretty badly. He felt a throbbing in his leg now and noticed another wound there, in the meat of his thigh toward the inside of his leg. It was hurting, as was the wound in his neck.

"Come on," he said. "We have to get out of here."

He started to walk away, quickly, toward the side door through which Iron Mike had escaped.

"Where's my daddy?" Amanda asked.

Stokes turned. She had stood up but remained rooted in place.

"He couldn't get here. He asked me to come."

They really had to get going. Both Chet and Iron Mike had survived, and neither was likely to want them to leave the park alive. Stokes thought he might have heard low voices outside. The men out there might have found each other and were making plans. Stokes considered calling to Iron Mike, informing him that Chet had been planning all along to kill him, but he didn't think Iron Mike would believe him. Why should he, seeing as Stokes had been the one trying to kill him thirty seconds ago?

"We really have to move," Stokes said.

"Who are you?" Amanda asked.

"A friend."

"My daddy's friend?"

Stokes thought about that. "Your friend."

It was her turn to think. Stokes glanced nervously at the doors, then the windows. Finally, Amanda took a tentative step toward him.

"We have to hurry," Stokes said.

"Where are you taking me?"

I don't know.

"Away from here," he said. "Away from the men who brought you here."

That seemed to be good enough for her. When Stokes started off at a trot, limping a little and wincing a lot, she followed as closely as her little legs would allow.

He thought of something and realized that Chet and Iron Mike were no doubt thinking the same thing: all he had to do was survive long enough for the cops to come, which they were certain to do before too long. Someone would have heard the gunshots. They weren't so far out in the sticks that a couple of dozen rounds fired from semiautomatic handguns would go unnoticed. There were houses not far down the road. Someone in one of those houses would call 911. So all Stokes had to do was keep Amanda alive until the cavalry arrived . . . which might not be all that easy.

Stokes had hoped to save Amanda, drop her off safe somewhere, and ride off into the sunset—preferably with the quarter million dollars, though that part of the dream was now dead. But he'd still hoped to sneak out of town when this was all over, and it was starting to look like that wasn't going to happen, either . . . at least not if he was going to see this through. Sure, he could leave the girl now and probably have a fair chance to make it out alone, out of the park, out of the city, out of the goddamn state, but whatever strange force was behind his actions all day kept him from even considering that course of action now. No, he knew he'd go all the way with this. Which meant he had to stay alive, and keep Amanda alive, until the cops showed up. Of course, Chet and Iron Mike knew that, too. They knew the cops would come, and they sure as hell didn't want to be there when they did. They also couldn't allow Amanda or Stokes to be there waiting, alive and able to talk, when the police arrived. So Stokes knew they'd regroup out there in the dark, as quickly as they could, then come after the girl and him with everything they had. He felt like both Butch Cassidy *and* the Sundance Kid, holed up and surrounded by the Bolivian army at the climax of the movie—a movie that ended with the cowboys making one final, desperate dash for freedom, guns blazing, leaving the audience with no doubt that the heroes were about to be blown to bits by a hundred rifles.

Stokes shook that image from his mind. He had to get Amanda out of there now. They were almost to the door when he stopped. She stopped beside him and clutched his good leg. He'd heard something outside. They'd come around the building. Or, more likely, one of them had while the other stayed on the far side. No doubt, they planned to shoot Stokes and the girl if they tried to leave the ballroom. And if he and Amanda didn't try to get away soon, they'd probably rush in and shoot the two of them to pieces.

Stokes had no idea what to do. Whatever he decided, he'd have to do it really, really soon. But he was at a total loss. He looked down at Amanda. She looked up at him with fear in her eyes, though he sensed that it wasn't him she was afraid of. And there was something else in her eyes, too, something it took a moment for him to recognize because he hadn't seen it in the eyes of anyone looking at him in a long time. It was trust. She believed he'd save her. He wished he felt the same way.

They were trapped. There were four doors to the place, one in the middle of each side of the rectangle. If it were Stokes in charge out there, he'd position them so they could each watch two of the doors, thereby covering every exit.

Finally, Stokes heard what he'd been hoping to hear. Sirens. Not close, but not too far away, and getting closer. He just had to buy time. He looked around the room again. Wooden crate, coats, and a dead body. That was it. They couldn't stay here. They'd be like targets in one of the games of chance—a shooting game—that used to be so popular out on the midway. They had to run for it. But that meant running right into either Chet or Iron Mike. Alone, Stokes thought he might have had a chance. He might have been able to run fast enough to keep whichever bad guy was waiting outside the door he chose from getting a good bead on him before he disappeared into the darker recesses of the amusement park. But with Amanda in tow, he didn't think much of his chances. Or hers.

The sirens were getting closer, which was good because the cops were on their way, but bad because Chet and Iron Mike wouldn't be able to wait any longer. Any second they'd burst in through separate doors, emptying their guns as they came. So Stokes couldn't wait any longer, either. He had to do something, and he had to do it now.

———

Seconds later, stokes exploded through one of the doors and into the night, gun in hand. "Stay still," he said to the coat-wrapped bundle slung over his left shoulder.

The shot came from his right, and he could practically feel the heat from the bullet as it sizzled just in front of his face. He half turned as he ran and squeezed off two blind shots to buy time, then pumped his legs as hard as he could. The wound in his thigh hurt like a son of a bitch, and more than once he nearly collapsed, but he kept running, issuing a loud and steady stream of instructions over his shoulder as he did, things like "Don't cry," "Keep your head down," "You gotta stop squirming." He also said soothing things like "You'll be OK" and "We'll get out of this." He heard two more shots, but neither found its mark, and soon he was half running, half hobbling through the park, stumbling through the tall grass and weeds, fighting the growth that had taken over the grounds.

He heard shouts behind him and the sounds of pursuit. He never stopped speaking, never ceased his flow of comforting words. And he never stopped running. Still, they were gaining. But the sirens were getting closer, too, much closer. One way or another, this was going to be over soon.

Stokes was starting to feel light-headed as he loped past rusted rides and badly listing booths. To his left loomed a huge structure. The roller coaster, still standing after all these years. Trees and vines had grown up, through, and around its metal girders, like giant snakes twisting through the bones of a dinosaur skeleton.

Stokes's encouraging words had sunk to a whisper. His little burden, so light before, felt heavy now. As did his legs. He was getting dizzy. It was the blood loss, he knew, accelerated by his mad, shambling run across the park. Stokes looked down as he stumbled along. The front of his shirt was soaked with blood. His pant leg was dark crimson.

The dizziness grew worse. The moonlight-draped landscape of the park became ringed in deep black as he lost the edges of his vision to darkness.

The pursuit behind him was getting much closer. The sirens sounded as though they might have been in the old gravel lot in front of the park.

Stokes limped on. His head became lighter, his thoughts more jumbled. He no longer knew where he was running and had but a tenuous memory of who was chasing him. A shot rang out from behind, then another. Stokes thought he might have felt an impact.

Please, God, no.

"Amanda," he mumbled. "Are you hurt? Did they hit you?"

No answer.

Another shot.

"Amanda," he cried, "*answer me.*"

Silence.

Jesus Christ. Nothing to do but keep running. He was trying to buy time for them both, time for the cops to arrive and save them. Had Ellie been hit? Had she . . . ? No, not Ellie, that wasn't right. It was . . . Amanda. Yeah, that was it, Amanda. Stokes prayed she hadn't been struck by one of the bad guys' bullets. His dimming vision blurred, and he was surprised to realize that tears had come to his eyes. He couldn't think clearly. *Had* the girl been hit? She wasn't moving a muscle. If only he'd run faster. If only he'd carried her in front of him in both his arms instead of over his shoulder, leaving her more exposed.

Just hold on, Ellie. I've got you. The cops will be here soon. Just hold on.

He no longer knew whether he was speaking aloud or whether the words were in his head.

The darkness on the edges of his eyes was spreading inward, shrinking the tunnel of his vision with every step. Then, not far ahead, in the center of his sight, he saw the mouth of an artificial tunnel and the yawning darkness beyond it, a darkness that could provide cover, buy them the last bit of time they needed. He stumbled toward the ruins of Miner's Run, a broken-down thrill ride in which park patrons sat in old-fashioned mining cars and raced on tracks through nearly total darkness. Stokes sought that darkness now. The footsteps behind him were faster than his, and very close now. Another shot ripped the night.

"We're almost there," he whispered aloud.

I'm not gonna make it, he said in his head.

As he neared the mouth of the tunnel, he tripped on the rusted track that ran down into the blackness. He dropped to one knee. A gunshot cracked and a bullet tore into his right shoulder, spinning him around. Finally, Stokes dropped his burden.

Chet Nickerson and Iron Mike were walking toward him. They were short of breath, but not nearly as badly as he was.

Voices drifted through the park. Footsteps crashed through thick green growth. Radios crackled. Flashlight beams bounced through tree limbs and waist-high weeds.

As Stokes knelt in the dirt, Chet and Iron Mike stared at the ground in front of him. Stokes followed their gaze to the pile of empty coats spilled on the ground—their coats, the ones he'd taken from the ballroom. He'd wrapped Amanda's coat around theirs, thrown the bundle over his shoulder, and run like hell. For a moment, he was as surprised to see them as his pursuers were. Then he smiled. He remembered. He'd forgotten but now he remembered.

In their desperation to leave no witnesses alive, Chet and Iron Mike had gambled everything on being able to catch and kill Stokes and the girl, then disappear into the woods before the cops caught up with them. Now, staring at their coats lying open and empty on the ground, hearing the cops just behind them, they knew the girl would live. They might even have figured out that she was hiding under the overturned crate back in the ballroom, which Stokes himself, weak and confused from the blood loss, had remembered only a moment ago. Maybe they understood that Stokes had been hoping they'd hear him saying encouraging words as he ran. They certainly realized they'd been tricked and were now totally screwed, because the cops, who were bursting into the clearing at that very moment, would find the girl and the girl would tell them everything. Yeah, they realized that. Stokes could see it in their eyes. Especially Chet's. Stokes tried to raise his gun but couldn't. Chet had more success. He pointed his gun at Stokes and pulled the trigger. Stokes felt like someone hit him in the chest with a shovel, and he fell.

As he lay on his back, a coldness crawling through his body, he heard more shouts and more gunshots. A moment later—or was it an hour—he heard voices, urgent voices.

Time drifted lazily by as the cold inside him spread.

He thought he might have dozed off. He must have, because now he was lying on something, being carried through the night. He looked up at the stars. He thought he recognized a few constellations. Some were real, he knew, and some were the ones his father had made up a long time ago, but he could no longer remember the difference.

Faces looked down at him. Voices spoke—to him, to each other, to him again. They seemed to want a reply. He couldn't give them one.

He was poked and stuck and prodded.

More voices.

"Everyone dead back there?" someone asked.

"Yeah, two of them."

"Any of ours hurt?"

"No, Sergeant. They fired on our guys, our guys fired back and took them down."

"You checked the girl out?"

"Yeah. Looks like she'll be OK."

At that, Stokes smiled dreamily. The cold inside him started to feel less cold. Soon, it became a warmth, welcome and soothing.

"How about this one?" a voice asked.

"He's fading fast."

He'd done it. He'd saved the little girl. He lost everything, but he'd saved her. Strangely, it didn't seem like a bad deal to him. He was tired. He was halfway between the waking world and the world of dreams, and yet things looked clearer to him than they ever had. He realized that *this* was what she'd seen in him so long ago. *This* was what Jenny had seen. Jenny, the girl he should have married, the girl who gave him a daughter he should have raised. She'd seen something in him he never saw in himself. And this was it. This was what she had seen. The capacity to do . . . *this*.

Stokes knew that faces were still peering down at him, but he could no longer see them. His eyes were open, but he just couldn't see. The stars above were gone.

He'd done what he'd had to do to save the girl, and things had turned out how they had to turn out. He found he had no regrets about that. There was only one thing he wished. He wished he knew what would happen to her. That's all he really wanted. To know.

The activity continued around his body, he felt pressure in places, hands tending to him.

"We're losing him."

Miraculously, a life began to flash before his unseeing eyes, like he'd read about, like he'd seen on TV. Only this was different. Whether it was the product of a delirious mind or the answer to a prayer, the life that played like a home movie in his head was Amanda Jenkins's. He saw her as a young girl, older than she was that day, but still young, and smiling, standing between a man and a woman Stokes didn't recognize, people with kind eyes in gentle faces. Suddenly, she was a young woman, no longer chubby, pretty enough, but confident, full of life. Before Stokes knew it, she was older still, sitting in a living room somewhere with sunlight streaming in through a window behind her. A man sat beside her, holding her hand. Crawling across the floor at their feet was a pudgy baby in footed pajamas. The image shimmered, dissolving into a different one. Same room, same woman, only she was older now, quite a bit older, as was the man at her side. Three good-looking kids—teenagers—swept into the room and, one by one, kissed each of their parents before sweeping out. The scene shifted yet again, and the woman was much older now, gray haired, a lifetime of smile lines etched into her wrinkled face. The man was no longer at her side. The three teenagers had grown into adults and were sitting in the room around her, holding hands with their husbands or wives, the floor of the room alive with kids crawling and toddling back and forth. As Stokes watched this life flash through his mind, he realized the woman's face had sometimes been that of Amanda Jenkins, and sometimes that of his own daughter, Ellie. He hadn't seen Ellie since she was two years old, so there was no way he really could have recognized her, but somehow he did. And he smiled, watching Amanda or Ellie or maybe both of them, surrounded by loved ones, drifting gently, gracefully into old age.

A voice intruded on his thoughts, and the images faded from his mind. "Does he have a chance?"

"I don't think so," another voice said.

The warmth was all through him now, all around him. He felt both suffused with it and wrapped in it, hugged by it, like the warmth was cradling him in strong, loving arms.

"Is that it then?"

"Yeah, he's not gonna make it."

Stokes was replaying in his mind the images of the life—maybe the lives—he'd been permitted to see moments ago. *To hell with you*, he thought. *I did make it.*

He smiled, closed his eyes, and simply let go, let it all go, and let the warmth embrace him.

ACKNOWLEDGMENTS

I owe thanks to many people for helping to bring this book to life. First, I thank Colleen . . . my wife, my friend, my first reader, my biggest fan, and my partner in everything. Thank you for walking beside me, and sometimes holding my hand, through the writing of this book and through all things. I also thank my sons, who inspire me every day in so many ways. Much appreciation goes to early readers and good friends Daniel Suarez and Adam Winston. I owe a debt of gratitude to my agent, Michael Bourret of Dystel & Goderich Literary Management, for all that he does for me. I thank David Downing for his keen editorial eye and for asking the right questions. I am also grateful to Alison Dasho for giving *Shady Cross* a home at Thomas & Mercer, and to Jacque BenZekry, Tiffany Pokorny, Gracie Doyle, and the rest of the T&M team for taking such good care of my book and me. I would be remiss (and possibly in trouble) if I did not thank my family and friends for their constant and kind encouragement, with special thanks owed to my wonderful parents whom I miss every day. And words cannot adequately express how much I appreciate the support of my readers, who make it possible for me to do what I love to do. Finally, I should note that because I invented Shady Cross, Indiana, I likely got the facts right about the city, but if there are any errors in the book on any other topic, they are mine and mine alone.

ABOUT THE AUTHOR

Bestselling author James Hankins pursued writing at an early age. While attending NYU's Tisch School of the Arts, he received the Chris Columbus Screenwriting Award. After career detours into screenwriting, health administration, and the law, Hankins recommitted himself to writing fiction. Since then, he has written three popular thrillers, each of which spent time in the Kindle Top 100. Additionally, *Brothers and Bones* received a starred review from *Kirkus Reviews* and was named to their list of Best Books of 2013, while both *Jack of Spades* and *Drawn* were Amazon #1 bestsellers. He lives with his wife and twin sons just north of Boston.